PRAISE FOR THE NOVELS OF RUTH GLICK WRITING AS REBECCA YORK

"Filled with sexual tension . . . a gripping thriller."

—*The Best Reviews*

"A steamy paranormal . . . danger, shape-shifters, and hot romance. The best of everything. Brava."

—*Huntress Book Reviews*

"A compulsive read." —*Publishers Weekly*

"York delivers an exciting and suspenseful romance with paranormal themes that she gets just right. This is a howling good read." —*Booklist*

"Mesmerizing action and passions that leap from the pages with the power of a wolf's coiled spring." —*BookPage*

"Delightful . . . [with] two charming lead characters."

—*Midwest Book Review*

"Rebecca York delivers page-turning suspense."

—Nora Roberts

"[Her] prose is smooth, literate, and fast-moving; her love scenes are tender yet erotic; and there's always a happy ending." —*The Washington Post Book World*

continued . . .

"She writes a fast-paced, satisfying thriller." —UPI

"Clever and a great read. I can't wait to read the final book in this wonderful series." —*ParaNormal Romance Reviews*

Don't miss these other werewolf romantic suspense novels from Rebecca York

SHADOW OF THE MOON

A journalist investigates a sinister world of power and pleasure—alongside a woman who knows how to bring out the animal in him . . .

CRIMSON MOON

A young werewolf bent on protecting the environment ends up protecting a lumber baron's daughter— a woman who arouses his hunger as no other . . .

WITCHING MOON

A werewolf and a sexy botanist investigate a swamp steeped in superstition, legend, and death . . .

EDGE OF THE MOON

A police detective and a woman who files a missing persons report become the pawns of an unholy serial killer in a game of deadly attraction . . .

KILLING MOON

A PI with a preternatural talent for tracking finds his prey: a beautiful genetic researcher who may be his only hope for a future . . .

Books by Rebecca York

KILLING MOON
EDGE OF THE MOON
WITCHING MOON
CRIMSON MOON
SHADOW OF THE MOON
NEW MOON

NEW MOON

REBECCA YORK

BERKLEY SENSATION, NEW YORK

THE BERKLEY PUBLISHING GROUP
Published by the Penguin Group
Penguin Group (USA) Inc.
375 Hudson Street, New York, New York 10014, USA
Penguin Group (Canada), 90 Eglinton Avenue East, Suite 700, Toronto, Ontario M4P 2Y3, Canada
(a division of Pearson Penguin Canada Inc.)
Penguin Books Ltd., 80 Strand, London WC2R 0RL, England
Penguin Group Ireland, 25 St. Stephen's Green, Dublin 2, Ireland (a division of Penguin Books Ltd.)
Penguin Group (Australia), 250 Camberwell Road, Camberwell, Victoria 3124, Australia
(a division of Pearson Australia Group Pty. Ltd.)
Penguin Books India Pvt. Ltd., 11 Community Centre, Panchsheel Park, New Delhi—110 017, India
Penguin Group (NZ), 67 Apollo Drive, Mairangi Bay, Auckland 1311, New Zealand
(a division of Pearson New Zealand Ltd.)
Penguin Books (South Africa) (Pty.) Ltd., 24 Sturdee Avenue, Rosebank, Johannesburg 2196,
South Africa

Penguin Books Ltd., Registered Offices: 80 Strand, London WC2R 0RL, England

NEW MOON

A Berkley Sensation Book / published by arrangement with the author

PRINTING HISTORY
Berkley Sensation mass-market edition / March 2007

Cover design by Brad Springer.

For information, address: The Berkley Publishing Group,
a division of Penguin Group (USA) Inc.,
375 Hudson Street, New York, New York 10014.

ISBN: 978-0-425-21602-6

BERKLEY SENSATION®
Berkley Sensation Books are published by The Berkley Publishing Group,
a division of Penguin Group (USA) Inc.,
375 Hudson Street, New York, New York 10014.
BERKLEY SENSATION is a registered trademark of Penguin Group (USA) Inc.
The "B" design is a trademark belonging to Penguin Group (USA) Inc.

PRINTED IN THE UNITED STATES OF AMERICA

10 9 8 7 6 5 4 3 2 1

NEW MOON

CHAPTER ONE

THE FOREST AT night was his playground, his domain. And werewolf Logan Marshall ran for the sheer joy of taking in his kingdom. A lithe gray shape, he was one with the night, the wind ruffling his fur and the sounds and scents of the night tantalizing his senses.

Tomorrow he would go back to work, focusing on the project that had brought him to this patch of Maryland woods. Tonight he ran free. Or as free as a man could be who must try to fit into two very different worlds.

His campsite was a mile back, in a patch of woods scheduled to be demolished by developers in the next few months. It made him sick to think that next year this magnificent hardwood stand would disappear—driving the forest creatures who lived here from their homes.

But tonight he could enjoy the ripple of the wind in the trees and the moonlight dappling the leaves.

He was two miles from camp when a new sensation crept into the edge of his consciousness.

No ordinary human would have noticed the subtle

difference in the night air. But a werewolf was blessed with senses that no man, except his brothers and his cousins, possessed.

He stopped short, lifting his head and dragging in a deep draft of the humid air. Unfamiliar scents tickled his nose. It was as though a door had opened, letting in dank air that had come from some other time and place.

In this one patch of woods, he sensed a rip in the very fabric of the universe.

A rip in the fabric of the universe? *Yeah, right.*

Yet he knew it wasn't impossible. The Marshall clan had fought a monster from another world. A creature that had lurked in the underground reaches of a private club in Washington, D.C., where the rich and powerful came to indulge their sexual appetites—egged on by the monster who fed on their emotions.

They had killed the creature, although the werewolves had only been the assistants. It was the strong Marshall women who had joined their mental energy in battle.

He had left while they were still celebrating their victory, because watching the other men and their life mates had made his chest tighten.

In the distant past—some twenty or thirty years ago—the werewolves had ruled their families like despots. Things had changed with the new generation of Marshall women. They were the equal of their men. And Logan could easily imagine living out his life with a mate like that.

But he'd met no women who could be "the one." So he kept to his bachelor existence, carving out a name for himself as a landscape architect who specialized in native plants. Which was why he was camping out this weekend, harvesting ahead of the bulldozers.

Only tonight some outside force had disturbed this patch of Maryland woodland.

A man might have backed away from the danger. The werewolf knew he had to investigate. Or was the compulsion to rush toward danger coming from outside his own mind?

A command below the level of his wolf's hearing seemed to pull him toward the unknown. And he obeyed, taking one step forward and then another, when deep inside he knew that he should turn and run for his life—for his sanity.

Disaster struck like a sharp-toothed animal lurking in the underbrush. But no animal could have possessed the steel jaws that suddenly snapped around his ankle.

The pain was instantaneous—and excruciating. He went down, howling as he rolled to his side, leaves and debris clinging to his stiff fur. For long moments, he was unable to move, the agonizing bite of the claws in his flesh mirrored by savage claws in his brain.

He had to . . . He had to . . .

It was impossible to complete the sentence. He was caught in a snare, and the saw-toothed steel that dug into his flesh did more than hold him fast. It made coherent thought almost impossible.

As waves of pain radiated through him, he knew on some deep level that he must free himself or die. He lay panting, gathering his strength, struggling to focus on wrenching himself away. But when he tugged against the thing that held him fast, a burst of agony seared his nerve endings—then shot upward through his body.

All he could do was lie there in the leaves with his eyes closed and his breath shallow, feeling his consciousness slipping away. He would die here in this patch of woods. Or perhaps fate had something worse than death in store for him.

He was trying to remember something important. A prayer his mother had taught him long ago in his childhood?

Now I lay me down to sleep. I pray the Lord my soul to keep.

They had said that together at night as part of his bedtime ritual. It wasn't until later that he had known why she asked God to watch over him.

Still, when he had changed from child to man—and man to wolf—he had come to believe that he was no longer under the protection of the Almighty.

In the back of his mind he knew that it wasn't the prayer he was trying to remember. It was something else. Something vital to his life.

He had to remember . . . remember the words that would set him free. But he couldn't pull them into his mind.

Not with the horrible burning pain

A long time passed. Or perhaps it was only seconds. His eyelids fluttered closed, and he drifted on a sea of agony. A noise somewhere close by made his eyes snap open again. Blinking, he saw a shape coming toward him through the forest. For a moment, he was sure he was hallucinating.

He saw a wolf.

CHAPTER
TWO

LOGAN HEARD HIMSELF make a gasping sound as the wolf trotted toward him.

Thank God! One of his brothers, Lance or Grant, had figured out what had happened to him, and they were going to set him free from the terrible pain. Or maybe it was his cousin Ross. He was the one who had started the cooperation in the family.

Squinting, he tried to figure out who had come to his rescue. But the longer he looked at the wolf, the more he thought that it was none of them. The size seemed wrong. This wolf was too small, and the coloring was off, too—more whitish than gray. Or were his senses fading?

He stared at the animal. Could it be a real wolf? From where? The forest? A zoo? There were no wild wolves in the eastern part of the United States, as far as he knew. Only his own relatives.

The animal was pretty. And delicate. Definitely no match for Logan—freed from his trap, that is.

So who was this guy? Nobody he knew in the Marshall clan. And in the wide world, they were the only werewolves that existed.

Or was that wrong?

He tried to focus on the animal as it walked toward him—with purpose and also with caution, as though it knew he was in trouble and had come to help, yet it didn't want to suffer the same fate.

It stopped a few feet away, sniffing at him and sniffing at the trap, obviously afraid to get too near the thing.

"Don't worry," he wanted to say. "It's already got me. It can't grab you, too." Or could the mind-numbing power of the thing reach out beyond the physical contact?

He tried to puzzle that out. But his brain was too dull to hold any thought for more than a few seconds.

Cautiously, the wolf circled him. He saw the wary eyes, the tense body. Then it moved in, nuzzling and licking insistently against his face as though trying to get his full attention.

He nuzzled back because the contact was strangely comforting. But there was little more he could do.

The wolf made a frustrated sound and stepped back to look him in the eye. He answered with a gurgling noise low in his throat.

Again the wolf ducked in close, grabbing his neck in strong teeth and giving him a shake.

What the hell do you want me to do? He couldn't ask the question aloud, only hear it buzzing in his head, competing with the pain. There was no way for werewolves to talk unless they were in human form. He and the other Marshalls had worked out a few sign language signals that they could give each other. But his brain felt too numbed by pain for communication. And probably this wolf didn't know the Marshall code.

He kept his focus on the delicate creature. It paced back and forth, then moved a few yards away.

When it looked like it was going to leave him, he felt terror jolt through him.

No, he silently screamed. He had always thought of himself as strong. But the trap was sapping the will from him. Not just from his body. From his spirit as well.

Logan's gaze stayed focused on the white wolf, and what he saw made him doubt his own sanity. He watched the creature go through a transformation. Not from wolf to man but from wolf to a naked woman.

Impossible. He must have slipped into a fog of unreality. He had wanted a mate—and here she was. Five and a half feet tall, with nicely rounded breasts and gently curved hips. A wolf who was also a woman. Jesus, if that wasn't a fantasy—what was?

He made a sound that would have been a harsh laugh if he'd been in human form. Yet the image of the woman stayed solid and true.

From where she stood looking at him, he saw the uncertainty on her face and knew she was making a decision. She would try to free him, or she would leave him to his fate.

THROUGH long practice, Falcone had learned that controlling people had as much to do with showmanship as force.

This evening, he feigned an attitude of studied unconcern as he leaned back comfortably against the soft cushions and plucked a ripe strawberry from the bowl on the table in front of him. After eating the juicy fruit down to the nub, he tossed the hull onto a plate beside the serving dish. He was one of the most powerful men on the Sun Acres city council, and today he wanted to give the impression that he had nothing more pressing to do than enjoy the spring bounty that had been prepared for him.

In reality, his nerves were jumping as he waited for word that his plans had fallen into place.

He dipped his fingers into a bowl of water, then dried them on a soft towel before reaching to stroke the burnished hair of the woman who sat next to him on the couch.

She gave him a knowing smile. Later he would take her to his bed and enjoy her lovemaking talents. And later still she would go back to her quarters and talk about his supposed state of mind.

He could easily manipulate her reactions, but he couldn't be sure of the other occupant of the room, a wizened little man named Avery, who sat across the table.

Avery might secretly be working for someone else on the council, since you could never be sure of the quick, convenient alliances and shifting loyalties in the power structure of Sun Acres.

You had to stay alert and watch your ass—or you might end up in a back alley with a knife in your heart.

Falcone had seen too many murders, including the ones of his own parents. When he was only twelve, he had vowed to do what it took to keep from ending up the same way.

Of course, he could have opted for a safe, meaningless existence if he'd kept his head down and paid tribute to whoever was running the city. But he wasn't just out to protect his own hide. He'd watched things go from bad to worse, and he intended to change the government with strong leadership and a dynasty that would ensure the stability that Sun Acres needed.

Casually, he kept one eye on Avery. The old man had sparse white hair and plum-colored robes that had once been rich and impressive. Now they were wrinkled and stained. Because the fellow had no sense of pride. No ambition. He was content to serve others, as long as his life was reasonably comfortable.

As a boy, Falcone had been at the mercy of the Elders, just like all the other children with special talents. But he'd quickly started learning to use his powers and his political skills to advantage. He'd shown the guardians what he could do—while acting modest about his abilities—and that had earned him a place in the circle of power by the time he was twenty.

But he needed something more to take over the city. And he had figured out that the shape-shifter named Rinna was the key.

Falcone brought his attention back to Avery. The man sat very still, his head cocked to one side. He seemed to be listening to some inner voice or some faraway sound. When he shifted in his seat and made a small gesture with his hand, Falcone turned to him.

"You have something to tell me?"

"The trap is sprung, my lord," he said in a quavery voice.

Falcone studied the man. "I sense that you disapprove."

"You don't need my approval." Avery clasped his hands together in his lap.

Falcone leaned back into the soft cushions. "True." He gave the older man a direct look. "You're sure it didn't catch a deer or a bear or something else in the forest?"

"The teeth only open for a shape-shifter. Only one of their kind would be pulled toward the snare."

"Good." He felt a glow of triumph. The trap had done its work. He had Rinna firmly in his grasp, and she wasn't going anywhere until he released her.

He could scoop her up any time he wanted. First he would let her suffer for a while as the metal teeth bit into her flesh and the psychic probes sent needles of pain into her brain. Then he would haul her back where she belonged and make her sorry that she had ever defied him.

RINNA stood looking at the gray wolf who lay curled on his side, the cruel iron jaws holding his ankle fast.

He was in pain. And she could come up with only one explanation for his predicament. Falcone must have figured out where she had gone—and set up an ambush for her. But this other wolf had blundered into the snare.

Which could mean only one thing. He was a shape-shifter. And she thought she recognized which one.

Months ago, she had helped people from this world kill Boralas, one of the mind vampires, or Suckers as they were called. She had relived that battle many times in her memory. And she knew that this wolf had been one of the pack protecting the women who joined their minds to fight the monster. Then she and the wolf had been on opposite sides of the portal between the worlds. Now they met face-to-face, and the circumstances were the worst possible.

She had to put as much distance as she could between this trap and herself—and quickly. Because the longer she stayed here, the more chance she had of being dragged to Sun Acres in chains.

She took a step back, then stopped abruptly. She couldn't run away and leave this werewolf. He was in terrible pain—because of her. And when Falcone caught him, he would likely torture him to get information. The wolf couldn't tell him anything. He didn't know where she had come from or where she was going, but he would still die a painful death because of her.

No matter how desperate she was, her conscience wouldn't let her fade back into the forest, even though she was naked and unarmed—a woman at her most vulnerable in a land where she only vaguely understood the rules of existence.

Slowly she approached him, ready to jump back if his infirmity was just a trick.

But he only watched her with dull eyes, and she knew the iron teeth and the psychic probe embedded in the trap were sapping the strength from him.

Wishing she were wearing clothes, she went down on her knees beside the wolf. Even though the metal of the trap didn't touch her flesh, she could feel its power reaching toward her like a huge psychic spider sending out impulses to its prey—drawing her closer and closer to its web.

But now that she knew what it was, she could fight the pull. And the thing had already caught a victim, which lessened its power.

She forced herself to ignore her own terror as she spoke quickly and urgently to the wolf. "We have to get out of here before the warriors come. Falcone has adepts working for him. He'll know when the trap is sprung. So we don't have much time. You have to help me free you. You have to change."

He opened his mouth and closed it again, but he stayed in wolf form.

"Do you understand me? Do you speak my language?"

She thought he would. Back at the castle, she'd understood the women when they'd joined to fight the monster.

When he gave a small nod, she let out a sigh of relief.

Still, they didn't have much time.

"Change!"

He looked at her as though he wanted to ask, how? And she struggled to keep from shaking him in frustration. His mind must be too damaged by the trap to make the transition. Which meant she was going to have to help him—no matter what the cost to herself.

She whispered a prayer under her breath—a prayer to the Great Mother who had sometimes protected her, and sometimes not.

With shaking fingers, she cupped her hands around the wolf's head, stroking his cheeks, feeling the coldness of his skin beneath his fur as she gave him a direct order. "Change from wolf to man. Let me help you."

His lips moved and his body jerked.

She called on old powers that she had been afraid to use—with good reason. The moment she began to tune her thoughts to his, a great pounding started up inside her own skull.

The pain was Falcone's present to her. She struggled to break through the impediment he had placed in her mind, even as she fought the sickness rising in her throat.

At first, keeping her concentration on the wolf was almost impossible. But she fought to call on the skill that her teachers had helped her develop. Ignoring the pain, she forced her thoughts into the wolf's head and felt the substance of his mind, soggy with the poison seeping from the trap.

The poison sent out tendrils toward her, and she reared back in shock.

As her terror bubbled up, she pulled her hands away. Was this the real snare? This wolf, lying here on the ground. Had Falcone trapped him and laid him out for her to find—so that she would be caught in the same sticky mental fog that held him fast?

She could believe it, and she wanted to get up and run—as far away from the wolf and the trap as she could get.

But she stayed where she was and thrust the fear aside. Reaching for the wolf again, she forced herself back to the task.

"Change," she murmured. "Change to your human form. Do what you need to do."

In response to her words, he stirred on his bed of leaves, and she thought she caught strange syllables whispering in his mind. She didn't understand them, but she knew they must be part of his ritual of transformation. Not her ritual, but that didn't matter. He must use whatever worked for him.

Yet she knew the words were garbled in his thoughts, knew that he could barely put one syllable in front of the other.

Gritting her teeth, she helped him focus, forced him to stay with the task of changing from wolf to man, even as she sensed dark forces closing in around the two of them.

Under her hands, she felt the wolf's body shape begin to morph, and she moved her hands downward, sliding along his fur-covered body, skimming along his hip, avoiding the male part of him as she reached for the place where the metal jaws held his leg fast.

Thrusting aside her own fear, she fought to keep her

focus—her concentration on the task that she must accomplish—even when it felt like the cells of her brain were going to explode.

She sensed the crucial moment approaching. If she failed now, they were likely both doomed.

CHAPTER THREE

THE WOLF'S MUSCLES jerked as his skin flowed under Rinna's fingertips like heavy syrup flowing from a bottle.

She had made this transformation herself many times, but she had never felt the change take another living creature. It was a strange sensation, and she battled not to pull her hand away, because she must keep in close contact with him if she was going to act at the crucial instant.

In the fluid seconds when the cells of his body were neither wolf nor man, she jerked his leg out of the trap.

He screamed in pain, as the change rolled relentlessly on, transforming him from one form to another. They tumbled together into a pile of leaves, a tangle of arms and legs and other body parts. Flesh to flesh, his naked chest pressed to her breasts, his sex scrunched against her middle.

That intimate contact was too much for her. She gasped and thrust him away from her so violently that he fell backward onto the leaves, then lay sprawled on his back, gasping.

He had been a handsome wolf. He was a compelling man, with dark hair, nicely shaped lips, a blade of a nose and an appealing mat of hair on his chest.

In her mind, she pictured him reaching out one of his strong arms and pulling her to him, then reversing their positions and covering her body with his. But that was only an evil fantasy. He only lay where he was in the leaves, the breath sawing in and out of his lungs and his strong face contorted by pain, and she knew with a stab of remorse that she had hurt him by slamming him away with such force.

But she simply hadn't been able to deal with the sensation of his skin pressed to hers. Not when she felt his hard muscles and corded arms. He was naked, and her gaze was drawn to his groin. His penis was large. She imagined it growing hard and stabbing into her. Hurting her. Bending her to his will in the way that men had tamed women since the dawn of time.

She pulled herself away from the disturbing image. He wasn't going to overpower her. Not while he was fighting for his life.

When he turned his head toward her, the confusion in his eyes tore at her.

"I . . . I didn't mean to hurt you," she whispered.

"You saved me," he answered in a voice that told her that the pain in his leg still clawed at him.

The words and his effort to speak reminded her of where they were. In the forest, far from shelter and still in danger. Falcone would send men to bring her back, and she must be somewhere else when they arrived.

Again, she was tempted to leave this stranger and

run. She had gotten him out of the savage trap. He could fend for himself.

Even as she told herself that story, she knew it was a lie. Focusing on his leg, she saw his mangled flesh. She had freed him from the metal jaws, but he was in no shape to defend himself—or even run away.

"We have to get out of here," she said.

He pushed himself up, but sat where he was, dragging in drafts of air. "I have to rest."

"Later."

The thought of touching him again made her throat close, but she did it anyway, crawling toward him and slinging an arm around his shoulder, urging him to get up.

"Come on. We must leave."

"Who are you?"

"Rinna."

"Logan," he answered, then looked back to where the snare had held him fast. "What was that thing?"

"A trap. For shape-shifters."

She watched him take that in, watched his brow wrinkle. "Why?"

"We can talk about it later. We have to get away from this place—now."

He pushed himself to a sitting position and winced. "I . . . don't think I can stand on this leg."

"You have to. The man who set the trap will kill you."

"Why?"

"He'll be angry when he figures out he didn't catch me."

She gave Logan a minute to rest, then moved her arm under his, pulling him up.

He wobbled to his feet, then stood, leaning heavily

against her. She led him farther into the forest, toward a rocky outcropping.

She tried to ignore his naked hip brushing against hers as they made their slow way across the leaves. She wanted to hurry, but she knew he could barely walk. She wished she had clothing she could pull on. But that was one of the great inconveniences of transforming from animal to woman.

If you couldn't get back to where you'd changed, you would have to stay naked until you found something to wear.

She had become a master of stealing clothing—a skill she wasn't proud of. Yet it was necessary.

A familiar sound stopped her in her tracks.

Great Mother, no!

Her fingers digging into Logan's ribs, she pulled him behind an outcropping of rock. When he tried to speak, she clamped her free hand over his mouth.

From her hiding place, she saw four men burst from the other side of the rock and dash into the forest.

They were dressed like Sun Acres warriors with tight-fitting leggings, molded body armor and spears. They must be Falcone's men. Who else would dare to send troops through a portal and into this patch of forest?

She knew she and Logan had almost no time left.

Quickly and coolly she considered her options. She could stay on this side of the portal, but she knew very little about this place, which made that decision dangerous.

The man needed to rest—and heal. And she didn't know where to keep him safe in this foreign territory, after he passed out, which would surely happen in the next hour or so.

As the warriors took off through the trees, she made

a decision. They were going back to her world—if they could.

LOGAN gasped as the woman named Rinna pulled him forward. His leg could barely hold him, and he wanted to sink to the ground—then sink into oblivion.

But he forced himself to stay on his feet because he had heard men rushing past in the night. He was pretty sure they were the enemy—closing in on the trap to find out what it had caught. Leaning around the rock, he stared at their backs. They looked like a cross between Star Wars storm troopers and Roman soldiers.

In his present condition, they could mow him down like grass.

As soon as the men swept past, Rinna moved.

"Hurry," she ordered.

Catching the urgency in her voice, he struggled to make his body move faster. But he was almost at the end of his strength.

He had given up being ashamed to lean on her. And given up wondering what they looked like—a naked man and woman staggering through the Maryland woods.

If someone saw them, they'd probably think they'd been enjoying some wild drug party and taken the notion to get some fresh air.

He tried to put more weight on the leg, but it threatened to collapse, so he let her do the heavy lifting as they staggered through the trees.

It was hard to keep going. He did it by concentrating on the woman who had clamped her arm around him. He closed his eyes and let her guide him, focusing on small pleasures, like the soft pressure of her breast against his side and the way her brown hair swayed against his cheek.

She had been a beautiful wolf. She was an equally beautiful woman, with that fall of long dark hair, light eyes that he thought were probably green, and delicate features that nevertheless conveyed strength. He wanted to ask her how a female werewolf had come to be. She couldn't be part of the Marshall clan. So where had she come from?

His questions would have to wait for later. If there was going to be a later.

He was dizzy with fatigue—and whatever poison that damn trap had injected into his body. But as they headed for a rock outcropping, he saw a slit in the face and thought she might be going to hide in a cave.

He spared the breath to say, "If they come back we'll be trapped."

"No."

She tugged him forward, and at the last moment, the rock wavered like a doorway in a science-fiction movie. His next breath was a gasp as they walked through the rock—into another place he had never seen before. Or maybe he'd completely lost his marbles. Maybe his addled brain thought it was better to be somewhere else, anywhere else.

"Beam me up, Scotty," he muttered.

"What?"

"Forget it," he answered, as he looked around.

He understood the nuances of the Maryland woods. He knew the plants and animals in his environment because he spent so much time among them.

This landscape was completely unfamiliar. The hardwood forest was gone. In its place was a plain with charred tree stumps, bare dirt and what looked like buildings that had been badly damaged in a World War II bombing raid. A German city at the end of the war.

The buildings looked ghostly in the moonlight. And the air smelled rank and unhealthy. Not like the clean atmosphere of the forest they'd just left.

"Where are we?"

"My . . . country," she answered in her oddly-accented voice.

And what country was that? Denmark? Sweden? She sounded vaguely like she might come from the far north of Europe.

"How did we get here?"

"Through a portal."

"What happened to the buildings?"

"The wars. Stop asking questions. You need your strength for walking."

He pressed his lips together and continued to look around at the grim landscape.

Rinna steadied him, but he knew he couldn't go any farther.

"Let me rest," he gasped, striking out toward one of the buildings. At least it would afford him a little shelter.

"Yes. But only for a few minutes. I'll be right back."

They crossed hard, packed ground. When they had passed through a ruined doorway, she eased him down so that he was leaning against a half-destroyed wall. After giving him a critical look, she turned and trotted off. As she disappeared, he felt a jolt of panic.

From the other side of the building, he saw a flash of white. Blinking, he tried to figure out what it was, then finally realized it was a large white bird, taking flight. A hawk or an eagle. Nesting in one of the buildings?

Rinna must have frightened it.

He saw it rise high in the air, circling around the area where he was lying. Then it was gone, and he was alone again.

He fought to stay awake but couldn't muster the energy.

It seemed like an instant later when he felt someone grasping his shoulder, shaking him gently.

He woke to pain. And grim reality.

"We have to move. The area is clear now," Rinna told him. "But when the soldiers find the trap is empty, they will search for me. I don't know how long they will look in that area or when they will come back this way.

Questions bubbled inside him, but he didn't have the strength to voice them. And he certainly couldn't sustain any kind of discussion

She helped him to his feet, and he leaned on her again as they staggered forward. But they were still in the open when the leg that had been mauled by the metal teeth began to shake. He tried to take another step, but the knee buckled under him, and he sank to the ground.

"Get up," she ordered, her voice sharp and commanding.

"I can't." He looked up at her. "Go on. Save yourself. You don't have any obligation to me."

When she stepped away from him, he thought she might be taking his advice.

Then she was back, lifting his hips and slipping something that felt like a thin sheet of plywood under them. The wood scraped his flesh, and he wondered if he'd have a butt full of splinters when they got where they were going.

Before he could protest, she started to pull, dragging him like a sack of coal on a makeshift sled, with his legs dangling ignominiously behind him.

If there were any way he could have climbed off the piece of plywood and staggered along under his own power, he would have done it. But he'd used up the last of his strength.

He looked over his shoulder to see where they were going and saw another wall of rock.

Once again, it looked like they couldn't possibly get through the solid barrier. But she pressed her hand against the rock face, and it wavered. Then she pulled him forward. He felt resistance, but Rinna dragged him through, then let him flop onto the ground.

"Stay put. I'll be right back."

Yeah, right. He wasn't entering a dance contest anytime soon.

He saw her grab a broom made out of twigs that was propped beside the doorway. The opening hadn't closed behind her. As he watched, she hurried out and began sweeping the dirt back and forth, disguising the marks of where she'd dragged him into this shelter.

Looking around, he could see it was a cave with rough rock walls and a ceiling about ten feet high. Some of it seemed to be a natural cavity in the hillside, but there were places where the walls looked like they had been chipped away to enlarge the opening.

Water gurgled in the background. An underground stream?

He was still focused on Rinna when a shuffling sound from the back of the shelter made him realize he wasn't alone.

Turning his head, he saw a man with wild gray hair,

a wrinkled face, and stubby legs sticking out from beneath a short tunic made of animal skins.

The clothing made him look like a prehistoric man. But the knife in his hand was steel—and pointed directly at Logan's throat.

CHAPTER FOUR

NAKED AND ALONE, Logan returned the old man's malicious stare.

Gathering every drop of his remaining strength, Logan waited until the attacker was almost on top of him, then he rolled to the side, slashing out his arm as he moved.

He hit his assailant in the side of the head, and the man growled something that sounded like Carfolian Hell as he fell back a couple of steps. Logan tried to scramble back toward the door where Rinna had dragged him inside. But the man caught up with him, the knife raised to strike.

The best Logan could do was kick out with his good leg. But his feeble efforts only deflected the blade, which came down on his naked shoulder, slicing into his flesh like hot fire and drawing blood.

As the man swooped in for another thrust, Logan rolled across the stone floor with his attacker in full pursuit. He came slamming up against a wall, panting hard.

The knife was inches from his throat when a shout from the doorway stopped the action.

Rinna leaped into the room. "Haig, no!"

The old man stared at her. "How did he get in here? What in the name of the gods is he doing in this cave?"

"I brought him through the portal. Then in here. He was caught in a trap that Falcone set for me," she answered.

"You should have left him there!"

An expression of horror contorted her delicate features. "How can you say that? You're the one who taught me that the strong have to help the weak."

"He's not weak! He's well-fed and well-muscled. I'll wager he never went without a meal a day in his life."

"He's sick—from the trap." She gave Logan a good look and gasped. "You cut him!"

He made a grunting sound. "He fought me."

She advanced on the old man. "Put down the knife."

He glared at her, then dropped the weapon to the stone floor with a clatter.

She gave him one more warning look, then ran to the back of the cave. A minute later, she came pelting toward them, still barefoot. But she had pulled a tunic over her head. She also held a tray with a basin of water and a white cloth.

Kneeling beside Logan, she began to wash the shoulder wound. He winced.

"Sorry. I need to see how deep it is," she told him.

The old man was speaking again. "It could be a trick," he insisted. "Falcone could have sacrificed one of his men."

"He's a shape-shifter. That's why he's naked. I had to help him change to get him out of the trap."

"You *helped him*?" the old man breathed.

"Yes."

"That's an unacceptable risk."

"I'll be the judge of that." She spared him an angry glance.

"You shouldn't have left him in here. How was I to know he was okay?"

"Because I had to open the door to let him in. Now stop arguing, Haig." She turned back to Logan. "Come on."

When she dragged him up, the place where the teeth of the trap had dug into his leg bloomed with white hot pain, and every muscle in his body quivered with the effort to walk.

To his relief, she led him only a few yards farther into the cave, where she eased him down onto a narrow pallet.

He lay there breathing hard, watching Rinna while she leaned over him, examining the wounds; then she began to work on him, gently washing his leg and examining where the jaws of the trap had gouged into his flesh. The touch of her hands could have been sensual, until she uncapped a bottle of what smelled like alcohol.

"I'm sorry. This is going to hurt," she murmured.

When she drenched another rag with the pungent spirits and wiped his shoulder, he gritted his teeth to keep from gasping.

"It's all right to cry out," she whispered.

He kept the scream clamped inside himself as she did the same for the leg.

She pressed her fingers to his forehead. "You don't have a fever. That's good. Sleep will help you mend."

The injuries continued to throb, and he thought that sleep would be impossible. Reaching out, he clasped her hand. "Wait, who are you? You were in my mind, when I made the change, weren't you?"

She gave a small nod.

"You have to explain about that trap. And Falcone . . ."

At the mention of the man's name, her face contorted, and she pulled her hand away. "Later."

He realized he had asked the wrong question. *Damn!*

"Sleep," she said again, brushing the hair back from his brow as she whispered low, soothing words to him. He struggled to keep his eyes open and focused on her, but his lids grew heavy. It felt like she was sending him a hypnotic suggestion with her words and her voice and her touch. Or maybe she was just helping along a natural process.

Almost instantly, he dropped into blessed darkness.

At first, he was lost in oblivion. Then a dream grabbed him by the throat. A twisted version of reality.

He was running naked through the forest, pursued by men with ancient-looking body armor and leggings like aliens out of an old *Star Trek* episode. Lucky for him they had spears instead of ray guns.

The last time he'd seen them, it had been night. Now it was broad daylight, making him feel even more exposed.

He had no weapons, and he knew that if they caught him, he was a dead man. They would slash him to pieces with spears and knives. Or maybe they would drag him back to Falcone. He didn't know which was worse.

Falcone.

He imagined a giant of a man sitting on a carved stone throne. The figure was vaguely human. But he had devil's horns, cloven hoofs, and massive hands that gripped the high armrests of his chair.

He had teeth like the grooves on a saw blade. And his hollow eye sockets glowed red. That frightening image as much as the men behind him kept Logan running.

His breath was coming in great gasps, and he knew he was reaching the end of his strength.

Then a voice called to him through the trees.

"Over here. Hurry."

He saw a flash of white skin and dark hair. To his relief, Rinna stepped out from behind a tree. She was wearing a white gown like a Greek goddess. But she was flesh and blood. Swiftly she grabbed his hand, pulling him into the forest. They ran for their lives—first through the trees, then through a gauzy curtain into a dark cave.

They were both breathing hard from the run, but he managed to say, "We need light."

"Yes."

As she spoke, golden lights flickered around them, and he saw fat candles burning on stone ledges around the walls. In the center of the circular room was a bed covered with rich fabric.

Outside he heard the sound of men shouting, their tone desperate.

"Where in the name of Carfolian Hell did they go?"

"Hurry, we have to find them. Falcone will kill us if we come back empty-handed."

Every muscle in Logan's body tensed, but Rinna only tipped her head to one side, listening.

When the sound receded, a deep sigh of relief flowed from her throat, and he knew she wasn't as composed as she looked.

"Thank the Great Mother that you got here in time," she whispered.

"The Great Mother?"

"I pray to her, sometimes."

He studied her grave expression and the white gown she wore. It was soft and translucent, and he saw hints of her beautiful body through the fabric where it draped over her breasts and hips.

He wanted to reach for her, but she had been shy with him before. *Shy?* He laughed.

"What?"

"You could have stepped out of a Wonder Woman movie, but you're . . . nervous around me."

She looked away from him, and he hated the way she broke eye contact.

Slowly, giving her time to pull away, he reached out his arm. When she stayed where she was, he stepped toward her, moving quietly until he could wrap his arms around her. As she rested her cheek against his shoulder, he knew he had won a victory.

At the same time, in some inexplicable way, he felt as though he had finally come home to a long-lost lover.

"Are you the woman I've been looking for?" he asked, breathing deeply, taking in her delicious scent.

"I don't know."

He wanted to find out. So he changed the terms of the dream.

They had been running for their lives. Now that they had the luxury of time alone together, he was swamped by a host of sensations. The feel of her soft hair against his shoulder. The pressure of her high, firm breasts. And that wonderful scent that clung to her like a field of herbs and flowers. She was so exquisite that he could barely breathe. Yet he felt her uncertainty. She was as tense as when the soldiers were searching for them nearby.

"Don't be afraid of me," he murmured. Then he lowered his lips to hers. He was so hungry for her that he wanted to ravage her mouth, but he kept the kiss light and gentle as he explored her sweetness, rubbing his lips back and forth, then settling down for firmer contact.

She sighed out his name, and he struggled not to frighten her away because he understood that she was poised to flee if he made the wrong move.

It would be a mistake to hold her tightly. So he only draped his arms around her. The contact was light. Still, he grew so hard that he couldn't draw the line between pleasure and pain. In that moment, he knew that he must have her. But not yet. Not until she was as ready as he.

She seemed to know little about kissing. And he enjoyed teaching her, nibbling at her mouth, using the tip of his tongue to stroke the seam of her lips, gauging her response before increasing the pressure.

Finally, he couldn't resist taking her lower lip between his teeth.

"Don't."

He stopped at once, and she lowered her head, resting her cheek against his shoulder again. He wanted to go further, but he knew on some deep, instinctive level that she would turn and run from him. But he couldn't keep his hands off of her, so he stroked them lightly along her ribs, feeling her shiver.

He trembled, too. Sex had always been fun—and casual for him. He understood the charisma of the werewolf. The sexual attraction. Women sensed the edge of danger under the civilized exterior, and that turned them on. Not that he had pursued women with the wild enthusiasm of his brother Lance. But no woman he had ever gone after had turned him down. Still, it had all been a game, because he'd known instinctively that the relationship with the partners he bedded would never deepen.

This was different. More urgent. More real. More important.

"What do you want?" she asked in a barely audible voice.

"All of you."

"I . . . can't."

"I'll prove to you that I'm the right man—the man you can trust," he promised, because it seemed that was his only option. If she didn't trust him, that would be the end of it.

At the thought of endings, his heart lurched inside his chest. He wanted to take her by the shoulders, fix his gaze on hers and tell her that the two of them belonged together. He wanted to explain that he had been waiting for her all his life.

The words stayed locked in his throat. Words wouldn't work with her. Only deeds.

The right deeds.

He ached to kiss her again—and take the kiss from sweet to mind-blowing. But he was wise enough to hold back.

Later, he would put his stamp on her. She was his mate. Or she would be—when he finally made love to her.

For now, he contented himself with weaving his fingers through her silky hair, stroking his hands over her bare back, nuzzling his lips against the side of her cheek. Breathing in her sweetness. Marveling at the softness of her skin.

He found it wasn't enough. Not nearly enough. The contact made him tremble inside with a powerful urgency that was more than sexual.

He wanted to explain that she was his. But he realized that the claim would send her running. So he kept the knowledge to himself.

His hand dipped to her waist, stroking the indentation, memorizing her shape so that he could find her with his eyes closed. He wanted to slip lower and cup her bottom so that he could pull her more tightly against his erection. He wanted her to feel the power she had over him. But he managed to stop himself.

It was still early in the mating game, however he couldn't stop himself from raising one hand and gently cupping her breast. When he felt the nipple bead, he stroked her gently. There was no rush. They had time to get to know each other better before they made love.

If the soldiers outside let them. He had conveniently forgotten about the damn soldiers. And when he made a low sound of anger, she stiffened in his arms.

Instantly he was sorry he'd alarmed her. Wanting to let her know that the angry sound had nothing to do with her, he moved back a few inches. Then he forgot what he was supposed to be doing when she moved her shoulder, pulling the thin gown against her breasts, drawing his attention to their sweetly rounded shape and the rosy nipples, which he could see through the gauzy fabric.

The temptation was more than he could stand. Reaching out with his hand, he gently cupped her again.

"Oh!"

The warmth and weight of her felt wonderful. Just right for his palm. And when he began to play his fingers over the tight bud of her nipple, she cried out again.

"You like that."

She dropped her gaze and he knew that need and modesty were warring inside her.

That sweet reluctance made him want her all the more. His body tightened with need for her. They were in a bedroom. Because both of them wanted to make love. Even if she couldn't admit it yet.

But he would use his hands and mouth on her body—

with all the skill he possessed. And she would open to him.

"Don't be afraid of me. All you have to do is let me give you pleasure."

She looked around the room, as though seeing it for the first time.

"Why did you bring me here?"

"To please you. Only that."

Before he could drag her closer and pull her down to the surface of the bed, the wall shimmered and another man stepped into the cave.

"Take your hands off her. She's mine," a gruff voice commanded.

Logan turned to face the intruder. "Who the hell are you?"

The man laughed. "I own this woman. Get away from her."

"Falcone!" Rinna breathed, taking a step back, and then another, until her shoulders were pressed against the wall of the cave.

He was nothing like the monster Logan had imagined. He was young and handsome, with dark hair and piercing blue eyes. He raised his hand, and suddenly he was holding a sword. Logan backed away, knowing he would die if he couldn't find a way to defend himself.

"Reach for a weapon," Rinna shouted.

He didn't know what she meant. But he understood that his only chance was to follow her directions.

So he reached out his hand and felt his fingers close around something cold and hard.

The hilt of a sword.

Falcone made an angry sound and charged.

Logan jumped back, holding the blade in front of him. He'd never used one. His only experience with sword fighting was from the old movies he'd seen on television. He raised the weapon, parrying the thrust of the man who was now on the attack.

Miraculously, he seemed to know what to do. He beat the man back, pressed him against the stone wall opposite where Rinna stood. But Falcone lashed out again, striking Logan on the shoulder. As the sword slashed his flesh, hot pain shot through.

And suddenly he was on the floor, the intruder leaning over him, about to plunge the sword into his heart.

"No," Rinna shouted, and the man dropped his weapon, pressing his hands over his ears as though he could block out some horrible sound Logan couldn't hear.

Falcone turned toward Rinna, his eyes blazing. "Stop it," he ordered through gritted teeth. "Stop it. You're not allowed to use your power."

She screamed, her face contorting as she sagged against the wall. Then she straightened and focused her gaze on Falcone, and he fell back once again.

This was Logan's chance to get the guy. But when he tried to lunge forward, he found he couldn't move. And he couldn't call out. All he could do was lie paralyzed on the ground, waiting to see what would happen next.

Sickness rose in his throat as Falcone advanced on Rinna. He felt her fear and her revulsion. And he knew that the worst thing that could ever happen to her was to have this man touch her.

Falcone reached for her, and her scream rang in his ears.

Before it happened, Logan's eyes blinked open.

He was in a cave with Rinna all right. But not the place of his dream. He was lying on a pallet of rough blankets and she was leaning over him. Nearby, a hurricane lamp flickered.

Instead of a silky gown, she wore a much more practical shirt and britches. It was obvious that she had come to tend his wounds, because she had uncovered the leg that had gotten caught in the trap and was rubbing some kind of balm onto his flesh. But in his sleep, he had transformed the encounter into a scene where they were touching and kissing. And he had thought she was his life mate. Was she?

He was still caught in the reality of the dream.

When she lifted her head to look at him, he dragged in a shaky breath.

"How are you?"

"Better. Thanks to you."

"You have a strong constitution."

"How do you know?"

"Some people die from the bite of that trap."

"Oh, great."

He would rather think about life than death. He had gotten close to her in his imagination. And he wanted the same thing in reality. Clasping his hand around her shoulder, he pulled her toward him. Perhaps he caught her off balance, because she made a small sound as she came down hard on top of him.

He cradled her body against his, feeling her breasts press into him and the curve of her hip. "Nice," he murmured, nuzzling his lips against her cheek.

But she wasn't the woman of the dream. She struggled in his hold, and when she pushed against his shoulder, he gasped.

Her palm had come down on the cut, sending pain shooting through his shoulder.

"Sorry," they both said at the same time.

She sat up again, finding her balance.

He studied the haunted look on her face. Then her

expression turned practical. "Do you have to go to the bathroom?" she asked, and he knew she was deliberately putting distance between them.

"Yeah," he admitted.

He didn't love the idea of a woman helping him to the bathroom, but he wasn't going to ask the old guy for any assistance. So he let her get him to his feet, then lead him to an enclosure where they'd built a makeshift toilet just before the point where the fast-running underground stream exited the cave.

He managed not to fall into the water while he used the facilities, then staggered out again. It took all the strength he had left to make it back to bed. Once he was horizontal again, he felt her hands on his forehead, and he let her think he was slipping into sleep.

As he relaxed, so did she. When she pulled her hand away, he lay very still, his eyes half-closed. His thoughts were confused, dream and reality twisting together in a pattern he couldn't quite grasp.

But he could tell she was skittish around him. And she certainly hadn't enjoyed being naked in the woods once she had changed back to human form.

The casual thought hit him like bolt of lightning. This was no ordinary woman. She was a werewolf. How the hell was that possible? He'd never even heard of a female werewolf before—he hadn't believed they existed.

In the dream, he had thought she was his mate—the woman he had been longing to meet. And that longing seemed to have carried over into real life. Yet he knew almost nothing about her.

He ached to find out more, but instead of bombarding her with questions, he lay back against the pallet, letting his eyelids flutter, as though staying awake was too much effort.

As he pretended to drift into sleep, she sighed, and he thought he caught the edge of relief in that sigh.

When he'd first awakened, her hands had been light as they examined his wounds. Now that he was supposedly unconscious again, he felt her touch grow a bit stronger as she rubbed salve into the cut.

He struggled not to let her know he was reacting to the touch of her small hands on his flesh.

She made a low humming sound as she worked over him. Then she stood, and he heard her move a few feet away.

Apparently the old man had been watching the scene from somewhere nearby. Haig came forward, speaking in a low voice.

But Logan caught the words.

"I see he's housebroken."

"Of course!"

"Why are you getting so intimate with him?"

"I'm not! I'm tending his wounds."

The old man snorted. "I still think we should kill him."

CHAPTER FIVE

WHEN RINNA ANSWERED, her voice held as much sorrow as concern. "Haig, what's happened to you?"

He replied with an angry snarl. "I'm tired of watching my back all the time—and yours. I'm being practical. Like I said, he could be a spy."

"Let's assume he's an innocent bystander," she said gently.

"He could be a spy for another city. Maybe the Preserve at Eden Brook. Or White Flint."

"Then why hasn't he asked for information about Sun Acres?"

"He's waiting until he's sure we're not working for Falcone. Then he could ask us to join him."

She snorted. "We wouldn't be any better off in one of the other cities than at Sun Acres."

"You could set conditions for going there."

"I can't change my loyalty the way I'd change my dress. There are people at Sun Acres I care about, like my mother."

"We have enough problems without taking care of someone else. You never should have brought the man here."

"I couldn't leave him."

Haig made a harsh noise. "Too bad they taught you all that conscience stuff in school." They moved off, and Logan couldn't hear the rest of the conversation.

He opened one eye, trying to judge the distance to the door. Could he get out before the other two people in the cave caught him?

But how? The door seemed to have disappeared.

FALCONE had worked hard to make himself a powerful force in the political life of Sun Acres. His parents had left him a considerable sum, and he had increased his wealth by buying and selling slaves and also by setting up a private army that provided security services to other wealthy households.

He'd confiscated his mansion from a former council member named Blaine, who had been caught in secret negotiations with the Preserve at Eden Brook. The spacious residence had come completely furnished, so that all he had to do was move in.

He'd brought along his own slaves, who kept the place in smooth running order, and he'd sold off most of the staff he'd inherited from Blaine. But he'd tried out the women first and kept the ones who made good bedmates.

His staff was wise in the ways of the city. Even when staples like coffee were not available in the marketplace, his household knew where to get them. And with his own connections, he had picked up choice antiques to replace lesser modern furnishings.

Today he sat in a comfortable leather chair in the reception room off the front hall, waiting for news.

The house had been built before the change. The walls were solid, and the ground floor windows were covered by grillwork that was decorative as well as designed to repel thieves and assassins—an occupational hazard given his position on the council.

A whip lay on the glass-topped table in front of him. He wanted to pick it up and slap it against the arm of the chair. But he kept his hands lying easily in his lap because he didn't want Avery to know that his nerves were jumping.

A loud knock sounded at the door, and Martin opened it. In the hallway, he heard a brusque exchange of words between the head of his personal guards and a newcomer.

Finally! News from the other side of the portal.

But when Calag, the captain of the search team, stepped into the room, Falcone knew that he wasn't going to like what he heard. The man's features were rigid, and his gaze lodged somewhere over Falcone's shoulder, because the fellow didn't have the guts to look him square in the eye.

"What happened?" Falcone asked in a voice that was calm yet edged with steel.

Calag swallowed, then replied, "The trap was empty."

Falcone's head whipped toward Avery. "You said the woman was caught in the snare."

"She was," the adept insisted. He looked toward the man who had come in with the bad news. "Were the teeth of the trap open or closed?"

"Closed."

"Then how did she get away?" Falcone demanded.

"She must be stronger than we thought. Only the most powerful mage could have gotten out of that snare."

"Yes," Falcone hissed.

"When you find her, you must kill her."

He gave the older man a sharp look. "I don't take orders from you."

Avery's voice immediately turned conciliatory. "It wasn't an order—it was advice."

"I don't want to kill her. I want to use her."

The adept's face had solidified into grim lines. "But she is stronger than you. Stronger than any of us."

"And I have a way to make sure she retains only the powers I want her to have," Falcone clipped out. What he planned to do was illegal, but that had never stopped him before. He had been yanked away from his parents at the age of eight and thrown into a brutal environment. A school where all the children had special talents. And he had been expected to be one of the best—because of his highborn status.

At the end of term competitions, Rinna bested him more than once. She'd humiliated him in front of the whole school. He'd managed not to let his feelings about it show. He had figured out how to get along with the guardians—and how to make himself the leader of the children his age. The lessons he had learned in that childhood environment had served him well in adult life. Except with Rinna. He silently acknowledged that his anger with her had simmered below the surface all these years. He'd handled things wrong with her. And she'd run away. Now he was expending a lot of energy chasing after her.

He turned his thoughts back to Sun Acres. It was a city of great contrasts. You could live a miserable existence and sleep at night on a straw pallet with a rough blanket, or you could enjoy power and prestige and sleep on a soft mattress with crisp sheets. He had seen the depths, and he had worked hard to stay at the heights.

From his platform on the ruling council, he'd figured out how to rise to a whole new level.

Only he needed Rinna for the plan to work, and she had slipped through his hands.

He kept his face bland. And his mind bland, too, on the off chance that Avery was skillful enough to poke into his head and read his thoughts. He had learned from grim experience, starting when he was a child, that the only person you could trust was yourself. That was the key to survival in Sun Acres—and the rest of this miserable world. Nobody else must know what he was thinking and planning.

The captain of the crack military team he had sent out was still standing at attention, probably wondering if he was going to be beaten—or worse. Falcone considered various options, but in the end he decided that punishment would only salve his own pride and waste valuable time.

He had sent five men to bring her back. He would need more to find her now.

"You and five others go back through the portal, but make sure you come back before sunrise. I want ten more men searching on this side of the portal. She's resourceful, but she can't get far. Not with the poison from the trap in her leg."

From the corner of his eye, he saw Avery shift in his seat.

"What?" he bellowed, then instantly regretted the tone. "What?" he asked again, in a more moderate one.

"If she got out of the trap, then perhaps she has drawn the poison out of her flesh."

"And perhaps not," he answered, punching out the words.

LOGAN'S eyes blinked open again. He hoped against hope that this whole episode had been a dream, starting with the trap and ending with the old man.

Rinna was another matter. He wanted to hang onto her. As he looked around the cave, he saw that he didn't have a choice about keeping the good parts and discarding the rest. He wasn't in Maryland anymore. He was in a primitive environment like something out of the History Channel.

Oil lamps flickered in holders fixed to the stone walls, giving out enough light for him to see that he was in the same damn cave where he'd fallen asleep. Half a dozen yards away, the old man was fiddling with some sort of equipment. Like a toaster oven or something. It didn't seem to go well with the oil lamps.

Under the covers, Logan moved his shoulder. It felt tight and a little sore but not hot, which he took to mean that the knife wound was healing and not infected. He eased his leg toward his middle and stretched down his hand, probing at the place where the teeth of the trap had bitten into this flesh. That injury seemed to be healing, too.

When he hauled himself to a sitting position, the old man's head whipped around.

"I'm just going to use the facilities again."

He got to his feet slowly, partly because he wasn't sure of the leg and partly because he didn't want to look like he was on the attack.

"How long have I been out of it?"

"Two days."

He grimaced. It seemed more like a few hours, but he accepted the assertion that a lot of time had passed.

"I don't suppose there's anything I can wear besides this blanket?" he asked.

"She left clothes in the bathroom. She said she thought they'd fit."

"You're Haig, right?"

"Yes."

Haig got up, and Logan tensed as the man approached him. But he only lifted a hurricane lamp out of a wall holder and offered it to Logan.

Light in hand, he headed for the enclosure at the side of the cave, still moving slowly. But he was delighted to find that the leg supported his weight with no problem.

After closing the door behind him, he used the toilet. A basin of water sat on a table. On the wall above it was a broken piece of a mirror. Clothing lay folded on a wooden stool.

He stripped off the blanket and hung it over the free-standing rack along the wall.

Once he was naked, he looked down into the small river that ran along one side of the room. It might be a way out—if he wanted to leave. Quickly he washed with soap and cold water, wishing he had something warmer.

When he looked at his face in the mirror, he grimaced. His left cheek was abraded. Deep circles shadowed his eyes, and beard stubble darkened his cheeks. Looking around for a razor, he found one—an old-fashioned straight blade like you only saw in cowboy movies. Could he shave with it and not cut his throat? And in cold water to boot.

* * *

THE white wolf stopped silently behind a tree. In the clearing ahead, she could see a rabbit munching on greenery. The animal would make a good dinner for Haig, Logan, and herself. They needed food, and she focused on the small animal that didn't know it was being stalked.

As she hunted, her mind was still working on what had happened between herself and Logan. The intimacy in the cave made her nervous. But the worst part was the dream.

She had imagined herself in his arms, and she had the feeling that it had been no ordinary dream. It had felt so real, and she had awakened hot and needy.

That was more frightening than the simple physical part of the encounter. He had aroused her.

She didn't want to desire him—or anyone else. If she hadn't brought him through the portal, she could have walked away from him. But he was in her cave. And she had made him her responsibility.

So now she was plowing herself into catching dinner and trying to wipe away the tingling sensations that assaulted her body.

She sprang from behind the tree, leaped across the clearing and grabbed the rabbit by the back. She broke its neck, putting it quickly out of its fear and misery, because she understood what it was like to be caught and helpless.

As soon as she had made the kill, she picked up the animal in her teeth and started back to the cave. Falcone would have men out looking for her, and she'd better pay attention to her surroundings.

Because her wolf senses were sharper than her human senses, she stayed in animal form, scanning her surroundings carefully.

When she got close to the cave, she changed back into a woman, then washed her mouth in a stream and put on the clothing she'd discarded behind a rock.

She dragged in a deep breath and let it out before marching toward the entrance. Maybe Logan was still asleep, and she could avoid him for a few more hours.

WHILE he washed, Logan tried to figure out where he was. Not just in a cave. In a world that wasn't much like home.

What had happened to create the destruction he'd seen as they'd crossed the plain?

Rinna had said something about a war. What war? When? How?

Could there have been a disaster in some isolated part of the United States that created primitive conditions?

That might be pretty difficult to hide in today's media age where reporters jumped with both feet on every chink in the government's armor.

But maybe the government could pull it off. How? With a force field? He'd never heard of anything like that in real life, but it could be some kind of scientific test.

Maybe they were running an experiment to see what happened to people in here. Yeah, right!

He hated to think that was the case. But if it was true, how had Rinna gotten out? And not just her. Let's not forget about the guys who were chasing her. She'd talked about some kind of portal. From where to where?

He started letting his imagination run wild to the science fiction and fantasy novels he'd read when he was in his teens. The fantasies had included mythical creatures, like werewolves. And it had reassured him to know that writers had imagined men like him, even if the werewolves weren't necessarily the good guys.

So was this like a fantasy? Or was it more like science fiction? Had he gone back in time? Forward in time to some era where people were living after a disaster had wiped out most of the population? That might account for the ruined buildings he'd seen, and maybe Rinna and Haig had taken refuge in this cave.

He didn't like that explanation. And what were his chances of getting back from the past—or the future?

He took comfort in the knowledge that Rinna had moved through some kind of portal to his patch of Maryland woods. Then she'd brought him back here.

As he thought about her vaguely Scandinavian accent, another idea struck him, and he stopped in midstroke of his soapy hand across his chest.

What if this were a parallel universe? A few months ago he would have dismissed that notion out of hand. Then his brother Lance had asked him to help drive the monster Boralas back to where he came from. After that, he'd done some reading about string theory—the new physics that postulated universes parallel to ours.

So was he now in another universe—a universe that was Boralas's home base? Was he going to step out of the cave and meet something like the monster?

He hadn't seen any enemies besides the storm troopers and the old man. But he'd better be prepared for anything.

He shuddered and began to wash more quickly, thinking he'd feel less vulnerable when he got some clothes on.

After drying off with a rough towel, he decided to let the beard go, then pulled on a navy blue T-shirt and a pair of sweatpants that looked like they had come from his world. No underwear, but he did find a pair of gray socks. The running shoes were a size too big, but he figured that was better than too small.

When he came out of the bathroom, the cave doorway was open again and he felt every muscle in his body tense. Maybe this was his best chance to get away.

CHAPTER SIX

AND MAYBE HE was dashing headlong into disaster. Logan hesitated a split second, then decided to stay where he was.

He was glad he'd remained in the cave when Rinna stepped inside. She was dressed in a rough tunic, leggings, and leather boots. And her magnificent dark hair was hidden under a leather cap.

In one hand, she held a limp, furry body. A rabbit, which she handed to the old man.

"Dinner."

Her gaze shot to the pallet, then to him, and he saw her shoulders go rigid. As he took a step toward her, she took a quick step back.

"You should be lying down."

"I'm feeling well enough to get up, but not well enough to chase you around the cave." When he saw her face go tense, he added, "That was a joke."

She nodded tightly, then turned toward Haig. But it

was several seconds before she spoke. And not to Logan. "Did you offer him something to eat?"

"No."

"Give him some of the soup you made."

The old man scowled, then took a crude mug from a shelf along the wall and dipped it into a pot that sat on a burner. He held it out to Logan, who crossed the stone floor and accepted the food from the old man.

Probably it wasn't poisoned. Still, Logan's first sip was cautious. He found the soup was made from vegetables and meat stock and expertly seasoned. The first taste made him realize he was starving. He wanted to gulp down the whole cupful, but he drank slowly because he hadn't had anything in his stomach in days.

The door in the rock had closed, and he drifted casually toward where it had been. As he drank the soup, he leaned his shoulder against the wall. It felt solid, yet he could detect a background buzz that vibrated against his nerve endings.

On some level he could feel where the doorway was. Now he just had to figure out how to get through it.

He looked up to find Haig watching him.

"You're a good cook," he complimented.

The old man only grunted.

Rinna handed him the rabbit, then tidied up the cooking area. They had a working rhythm that spoke of long association. Logan wanted to know more about what they meant to each other, but he was sure neither one of them would appreciate his prying.

Haig began to expertly skin the rabbit, probably with the same knife he'd intended to use on their unexpected guest.

Logan edged closer to Rinna, but she avoided eye

contact and headed for the bathroom, perhaps as a way of getting away from him.

He'd never ambushed anyone at the bathroom door before, but he lurked just outside, resting his shoulder against the rock wall again because it was an effort to stay on his feet.

FALCONE had repaired to the dining room, determined not to let the household know that he was upset. That was one of the disadvantages of living with people who didn't have your best interests at heart. As they went about their daily business, a lot of his slaves were probably giving out reports on his activities, and he wanted to make sure that they were positive.

So he and Avery sat at the table, waiting while servants brought choice morsels from the kitchen.

His chief cook knew that he liked the tender breast meat of doves, so she had cooked up a plate of the delicacy for him. And Franz had gone to the greenhouses and brought back ripe tomatoes and basil.

Falcone politely handed the plate of dove meat to his guest and waited while Avery served himself.

Then he took a portion. He was washing down a bite with some white wine when Calag came to the door.

"Excuse me," Falcone said to Avery. Getting up, he left the room and stepped into the hall.

"Have you found her?" he asked.

Calag shook his head. "There's a new development," the man said in a low voice.

"Spit it out."

"It looks like she wasn't alone."

"What?"

"We've taken another look at the trap. It appears that

another shape-shifter was caught. And Rinna got him out."

"Gods! How could that be true?"

Calag shrugged. "That's the only conclusion—if you're sure that the trap only catches shape-shifters."

"I am," Falcone answered. At least, that was what he'd been told. Perhaps the maker had lied to him. He'd have to question the man carefully.

"You're saying she wasn't injured?" he asked.

"We don't think so. But the other person seemed to be in physical distress. She had to hold him up so he could walk."

"How do you know it was a man?"

"His feet are large. And his weight dragged her down. We were able to follow their trail back through the portal and into the badlands. Then we lost the trail."

Falcone clenched and unclenched his fists. "I suppose they were going to some hiding place where the old man was waiting for her." When Rinna had escaped from the city, she had taken Haig with her. He looked toward Calag. "How far did you follow the trail?"

"Half a mile into the badlands."

A plan began to form in Falcone's mind. He went back and explained the situation to Avery. "I want you and Brusco to close that portal so she can't get back to the other world."

"If we close it, it may not open again."

"I don't need it," he said, keeping his voice even. "I want her trapped here so I can scoop her up."

WHEN Rinna finally opened the bathroom door and focused on Logan, he saw her draw in a quick breath. "Didn't your mother teach you manners?" she snapped.

"Of course. But she also made it clear that I have to protect myself. We have to talk."

She glanced over her shoulder at the old man, who stuck the rabbit carcass onto a spit and inserted it into the metal box that looked like a portable oven.

As Haig stared at it, the interior glowed red. He didn't appear to be paying any attention to the other two people nearby, but Logan was willing to bet he was hanging on every word.

Rinna must have had the same thought because she jerked her head toward the back of the cave, then turned and walked into the shadows.

He watched the rigid line of her back. A very smooth and feminine back, as he remembered.

Grimly, he followed her until they turned a corner into a part of the cave where there was almost no light.

Logan looked back, seeing the old man focused on the cooking rabbit. Gesturing toward him, he said, "I don't see any flames. Or any electric outlets. Or any portable gas tank. Where does the power come from?"

He felt Rinna's gaze on him, and the look in her eye made his stomach clench.

"The power comes from his mind."

"Do you expect me to believe that?"

Her voice was cool and controlled. "Believe what you want."

"Okay . . . his mind," Logan answered. "What does that mean, exactly?"

She raised one delicate shoulder. "You have the ability to change from man to wolf and back again. He has different talents."

Under other circumstances, Logan might have dismissed the explanation. But he'd already had evidence of Rinna's psychic powers. Also, he knew that some of the women who had married his brothers and his cousins had paranormal abilities that had nothing to do with shape-shifting.

"Can Haig change to wolf form, too?" he asked.

"No."

"But you can."

When she didn't comment, he asked, "Are there a lot of people around here who have psychic powers?"

"Yes." She sighed. "I'm sorry that you got caught in a trap that was meant for me. I'm going to try and help you get home."

"So I won't be your responsibility anymore?"

She raised her chin. "Haig and I have enough problems without having to worry about you."

"I'll get out of your way, then," he said gruffly, starting back toward the front of the cave.

She grabbed his arm. "You wouldn't last ten minutes out there."

"Oh, thanks."

"Get your strength back. Then we'll talk about getting you home."

"Sure," he answered, struggling to keep any note of sarcasm out of his voice. He returned to the pallet, not because he wanted to rest but because he had decided he might as well look like he was cooperating. But he was getting the hell out of this cave the first chance he got. He had a good memory. He thought he could follow the landmarks he'd seen when they'd first come in here. Then he'd look for the portal she'd told him about. The question was—would it lead him back to the same time period he'd left? Or was there some trick to it?

He struggled to repress a shudder. He knew he was overreacting again. Maybe he should wait and see how things shook out. Or maybe he could persuade Rinna to come back home with him. Did she really like living in a cave with a surly bastard? Surely Logan could offer her something better.

Haig opened the door of the oven and took the rabbit out. He poked it with a fork, then cut off some of the meaty parts and left them to cool on a large wooden plate.

After a few minutes, Rinna picked up one of the pieces and brought it to Logan along with a cloth to wipe his hands.

"Thanks," he said, trying to judge her mood. The meat was tender and delicious. He'd had rabbit before, of course. But never cooked.

While he ate, Rinna walked to the spot that the door occupied when it was visible. He watched her press her hand against the rock to open the door. She stepped out. And he counted the seconds before it closed again. Ten. Not much time.

Haig cleaned up and wrapped the remains of the rabbit in cloth.

"Have you lived here long?" Logan asked.

"That's none of your business."

"Just making conversation."

"Or gathering information."

Logan closed his mouth, and the old man worked in silence for several minutes. Then he raised his head as though he were listening to something.

Logan heard nothing. Was it something subliminal?

Haig set down the bowl he was holding with a thunk and pressed his hands over his ears. Clenching his teeth, he stood rigidly for several moments. Then he paced toward the place where the door had been.

Raising his hand, he started to press the spot. Then he jerked his hand away. Breathing hard, he turned and whirled back toward the cave interior, his hands clenched.

He looked terrified.

"What's wrong?" Logan asked.

His only answer was a low growl. Then he whirled away and rushed toward the wall, where he pressed the rock. As soon as the door opened, he dashed outside.

Logan had only seconds to act. Before the door closed, he sprang up. At the last second he grabbed the knife off the low table. Then he leaped out the door.

When he hit the opening, something stopped him in his tracks, and he felt panic well in his throat. Then he remembered when he'd come inside. Something viscous had held him back, and Rinna had pulled him through.

She and Haig had passed easily through the force field or whatever it was that protected the entrance to the cave.

But the damn stuff must not be tuned to Logan's body—or however it worked. Determined to get through, he kept pushing and finally emerged into the open air. By the time he reached the area in front of the cave, the old man had disappeared.

"Oh, great," he muttered aloud.

Earlier he'd thought about getting the hell out of Dodge. But now it seemed more important to find the old man—for Rinna.

There were many directions the guy could have taken. Logan picked a path that hugged the rocks and disappeared into a trail through the boulders.

Sparing a quick look over his shoulder, he saw the rock where he'd left the cave shimmer and solidify. Going back was no longer an option.

He stayed in the shelter of the boulders for several minutes, getting the lay of the land. Then he wound his way through the rocks until he came out on a flat plain with more of the ruined buildings he'd spotted when he first arrived in this place.

Doggedly, he set off across the open space.

When he heard the sound of many tramping feet, he took off at a trot for the closest shelter—a low, partly burned structure. By the time he reached it, he was breathing hard. Leaping around the corner of a crumbling wall, he leaned against the bricks, trying not to give himself away with any gasping breaths.

From his vantage point, he saw a troop of people walking toward him. Three men at the rear and three men at the front of the column were dressed much like the soldiers he'd seen previously and armed with swords and whips. Between them walked twenty bedraggled men and woman wearing rough tunics. They were dirty and barefoot, their hands were tied, and they were joined together with a chain.

They trudged along, heads down, feet shuffling. When a woman fell, one of the men with whips rushed forward and began to beat her. The woman next to her pulled her to her feet, talking softly to her, and the column staggered on, with one of the guards cracking the whip on a few bent backs as they went.

Logan stared in horror at the scene, hoping he might be caught in the grip of a nightmare. But he was sure that he wasn't dreaming. Were these people the spoils of war? What?

Standing in the watery sunlight, he decided that his best chance of getting home was to change to wolf form so he could detect his own scent and follow the trail back to the portal.

Of course, as a wolf, he couldn't carry the knife. But he'd have his teeth and claws.

Just as he bent down to put the knife on the ground, two men wearing animal skins stepped around the corner of the building.

Logan took in details in an instant. Both of them had long, greasy hair. One had a scar that ran from under his left eye all the way to the corner of his lips. The other was missing several front teeth. They both had broad shoulders and thick forearms. One carried a club that looked like it had once been a heavyweight baseball bat. The other carried a spiked ball on the end of a stout stick.

They weren't the soldiers he and Rinna had avoided yesterday. These guys were freelancers.

As the one with the bat spotted Logan, he stopped short. "Well, well. Fresh meat."

Logan would have backed up, but he was already pressed against the wall.

"I can take him," the guy boasted, stepping forward and raising the club.

Logan might not have all his strength, but his reflexes were good. He ducked to the side to avoid the blow, then thrust up with the knife, catching the guy in the gut. The man bellowed, but he was tough, and he swung the club again.

Shouting a string of what must have been curses, his friend sprang forward, but Logan pushed the first guy into his companion.

They both went down. The one with the knife wound stayed on the ground, blood oozing from the front of his shirt. The other picked himself up and faced Logan, his eyes narrowed and his face red.

"This is where you die," he growled, raising his weapon and slashing downward.

The spikes grazed Logan's arm, and he winced in pain as he dodged aside. He was in no shape to fight this guy in human form. Taking a chance on his other alternative, he danced back a few yards, then dropped the knife and began ripping off his shirt.

"Oh, shit," Baseball Bat muttered.

Ignoring him, Logan began to say the words of transformation.

"Taranis, Epona, Cerridwen," he intoned, then repeated the same phrase and went on to another.

"Ga. Feart. Cleas. Duais. Aithriocht. Go gcumhdai is dtreorai na deithe thu." He was still wearing his pants, but he knew from past experience that the wolf's body could slither out of them.

The man gasped and took a step back. Logan tried to focus on him, but it was hard to see as the structure of his eyes changed.

He felt his muscles contort, his jaw lengthen. The change was always painful, but the place where the jaws of the trap had dug into his flesh throbbed with agony.

Baseball Bat could have run. Instead he chose to stand and fight. Even before the transformation was complete, Logan felt the guy leap forward, knocking him backward.

Snarling in pain and anger, Logan went for the man's arm, his jaws clamping down.

The assailant screamed, flailing at the wolf with his good arm, desperation fueling the attack.

Logan felt his strength ebbing. He wouldn't have bet that a man could win a fight with a werewolf, but knew it was happening.

CHAPTER SEVEN

LOGAN CLAMPED DOWN with all his strength on the man's arm. If he was going to die, he would inflict as much damage as possible before he went out. Just as his jaws began to slacken, he saw a figure leap from the shadows.

It was Rinna.

She came up behind the assailant and brought a massive rock down on his head. A crude but effective maneuver.

The man went still, and Rinna yanked him off the wolf, then tossed him to the ground.

"Come on," she shouted.

When she took off in the direction of another ruined building, he was right behind her, running on all fours.

In wolf form, he should have been able to outrun any human. But he had trouble keeping up with Rinna, and his lungs were burning by the time they ducked into the shelter of another bombed-out structure.

Panting, he lay down on the pieces of charred wood that littered the interior of the building.

Rinna let him rest for a few moments. Then said, "What in the name of Carfolian Hell were you doing outside?"

He didn't like getting chewed out—not when he'd almost gotten killed. And, of course, he couldn't answer in his present form, so he stood up. Taking a step back, he said the words of transformation in his head, feeling the change take him again.

The pain in his injured leg was worse now that he had disturbed the tissue. But he gritted his teeth as he faced Rinna.

She had something in her left hand, and when she tossed it toward him, he realized she'd snatched up his pants before dashing away.

He pulled them on.

"How did you get outside? And what were you doing out here?" she repeated.

"I followed the old man through the entrance. Something was wrong with him."

"You're lying!"

"No."

"Haig wouldn't go outside with you there."

"See for yourself."

"I will."

She turned and started running back in the direction of the cave, looking left and right as she went.

Luckily no other enemies sprang up during the short trip back to the shelter.

Logan kept up with Rinna as best he could. As soon as she reached the rock wall, she pressed her hand against the vertical surface.

The door opened as he had seen before, and she

dashed inside. He followed, and this time he understood better how to ignore the sensation of the force field trying to hold him back.

Rinna looked wildly around the front area of the cave, then charged to the back. When she returned, her eyes were wild.

"He's not here. What have you done with him?"

"What? You think I attacked him?"

"I . . . don't know."

"He went out, and I followed him."

"But where would he go?"

"You're asking *me*?" he answered sharply, but the look of terror on her face softened his heart.

"I'm sorry. I know you're upset."

"Upset!" she echoed.

"Before he left, he looked like . . ." Logan stopped and swiped a hand through his hair, wondering how to describe what he'd seen.

"Like what?" she demanded.

"Like he was listening to something I couldn't hear."

She gasped. "No."

"You know what was going on with him?"

Her face had taken on a look of alarm. "I . . . not for sure," she said in an uncertain voice.

"Are you thinking he'd rat you out?"

"No." She raised her chin, apparently eager to go back to her previous theory. "What really happened. Did he go after you . . . and you killed him?"

"Jesus! All you want to do is blame me."

She took her lower lip between her teeth. "I'm sorry," she said in a small voice.

He took the opportunity to ask a question. "You've been with Haig a long time?"

"Since I was a little girl."

"He's your father?"

"My friend." She gave him a direct look. "Why did you go outside? I told you it was dangerous."

"Like I said, I tried to follow Haig. But he disappeared before I could get through the door. When I couldn't find him, I tried to go home."

"You can't. Not without my help."

"That's just great! Where the hell are we—I mean, what world is this?"

She swallowed. "A universe parallel to yours."

He wasn't exactly surprised, yet the confirmation shook him.

She glared at him, but below the anger, she looked shaken.

Now that he had her talking, he kept probing for information. "You say it's dangerous. Give me the tools to cope with this world. I saw men herding people along, people chained together. Who were they?"

Rinna swallowed. "Slaves," she finally said. "And if you don't want to end up as one of them, you'd better try not to get caught. If those guys could have subdued you without damaging you too badly, they would have sold you to the highest bidder."

"Sold a werewolf?"

"That makes you especially valuable."

Before Logan could respond to that observation, a low buzzing sound made Rinna's gaze shoot to the place where the door was located. "Carfolian Hell."

"What?"

"Somebody's out there."

"It's just Haig coming back."

"No. It's someone who isn't keyed to enter." She moved to a spot along the wall where a chink in the rock let in light from the outside. When she looked through, she gasped.

"Slavers?"

"No, Falcone's men."

"Can they get in?"

"I hope not."

Logan moved to the spy hole. He could see a man on the outside of the rock, moving his hand along the flat surface, probably looking for the mechanism that worked the door.

"Interesting coincidence that Haig goes out and soldiers show up right away," Logan muttered.

"He wouldn't turn me in," Rinna breathed.

"Then how did they find us?"

"I don't know," Rinna snapped. But her insides were churning. Turning away from Logan, she looked toward the place where the door would open, struggling not to let her panic drown out rational thought. She'd told him he could end up as a slave. She hadn't told him how bad it could be.

"If they get the door open, they have us," she whispered, hearing her voice shake.

Logan's expression had turned hard. "We could change to wolf form and fight."

"There are too many of them. And . . . and you still aren't up to full strength."

"Unfortunately." Logan looked over his shoulder. "Is there another way out?"

"No."

"What about the river?"

She stared at him. "What about it?"

"It flows out of here."

She thought for a moment. "I never tried to figure out where it exits. I don't even know how long it goes underground. It could be miles."

"Or not. I'm a landscape architect. Part of my job is studying the contours of the land. I think the river goes through the rocks. How big is the outcropping?"

"Not wide," she said in a low voice.

"Can you swim?"

"Yes. But I wouldn't say I'm good at it." Glancing toward the rock that blocked the doorway, she saw the stone beginning to thin, and she knew someone on the outside was melting his way through the barrier.

When she and Haig used the psychic key, the opening appeared almost instantly. The men out there hadn't found exactly the right combination yet, but they would get through eventually.

If she didn't want to get caught, she'd have to take her chances in the water. Even if she drowned, that was better than falling into Falcone's clutches again.

She and Logan rushed to the side of the cave where the river flowed through the bathroom area.

"I'll stay with you. Take off your clothes," he ordered.

She gulped, then turned her back and began tearing at her clothing.

"When we get to the other end, you'll have to lead the way to someplace safe."

Behind her, she heard loud voices. The warriors! They'd made it through the barrier.

She took a gasp of air, then dove in, the icy water shocking her body.

Above the roaring in her ears, she thought she heard the voices of the men shouting to each other, but she couldn't be sure.

She sensed Logan enter the water beside her. But the current pulled him away, and in the blackness she couldn't see him.

Struggling not to panic, she let the river carry her downstream. She felt something long and hard bump against her side and might have screamed if she'd had her head above water. A spear. One of the soldiers had thrown it at her retreating form.

The water flowed out of the cave and into a narrow passage, increasing the speed of the current and rushing her along. She cursed herself for not counting the seconds. In the black, watery environment, she had no idea where she was, how long she had been in the tunnel, or even if Logan was with her.

As the river carried her along, her shoulder bumped against an outcropping, and she scraped along the rock, feeling her skin abrade.

Repositioning herself, she struggled to stay in the center of the stream, but twice more the water banged her into a rock.

She knew she was collecting scrapes and bruises, but they were the least of her worries. Her lungs were going to burst if she didn't get some air. Swimming toward the surface, she was relieved to find that there was just enough room for her mouth and nose to poke above the water. She might have stayed above the surface, but she was afraid that she would hit her head in the dark and get knocked unconscious.

So she plunged under again, then kicked toward the surface when she needed air again, only this time there was no room for her head. She was stuck under the water.

Fighting panic and the pressure inside her chest, she looked ahead of her and saw a spot of light.

Thank the Great Mother! The river must be coming

out of the underground passage—if she could only last long enough to reach it.

Focusing on the brightness, she struggled to increase her speed, kicking with her legs and stroking with her arms, trying to get out of the tunnel as fast as she could.

Finally, she burst into the open, broke the surface of the water and gasped in blessed air.

Her relief was short-lived, however. A hand closed around her ankle, pulling her under again before she had a chance to scream.

CHAPTER EIGHT

RINNA SHIFTED TO her right and saw one of the warriors had her in his grasp.

As she struggled to get away, the soldier grunted, and the hand loosened. The man began to thrash beside her. Twisting around, she saw Logan struggling to pull the attacker off her.

Trying to help, she grabbed at the soldier's hair, angling his head back. Together, they held him under while taking quick gasps of air themselves. The struggle seemed to take forever. Tired from the long swim, she felt her own strength ebbing. But finally, the man's body went limp. When she and Logan let go, the current carried him away.

Dragging in drafts of air, she let Logan take her arm and steer her toward the shore. But the rock walls along the banks were steep, so he kept going, looking for a place to get out.

She was beginning to think they would have to drift

along for miles when they finally came parallel to a sandy beach. Logan began to tow her toward shore.

They both crawled onto the sand, where they lay panting. When she shivered, Logan rolled toward her, lifting his arm to gather her close.

It was a natural response to their chilled circumstances, but she couldn't stop herself from flinching.

She was angry with herself for the reaction. This man had proved that he had her welfare at heart. Of course, she could have said the same about Falcone—not so long ago.

He had seemed to care about her. When some of the members of the council had voiced concerns about her power, he had told them she was useful. He had sent her out of the city to fight the Suckers. Partly to get her out of sight. And she had proved that she could track the mind vampires and drive them back to the world where they had originated. That was when she had first seen Logan. She had been tracking a Sucker and found it had gone into his universe.

She kept her head turned away from him, still remembering Falcone's betrayal. She had thought he was her protector. And he had proved her so wrong.

Logan was speaking, and she struggled to focus on his words. "You're hurt," he said, touching the place where the rock had scraped her shoulder.

"So are you," she said, staring at the ripening bruise on his muscular thigh where he also must have struck a rock. At the same time, she was trying not to stare at his sex. He was magnificently naked, and so casual about his body as he lay sprawled on the sand.

She should be just as casual. A woman who often found herself inconveniently nude when she changed from wolf to human could ill afford to be modest. Yet she couldn't stop herself from scooting a foot away from his large body, scraping her bottom on the rough sand as she went.

A flash of movement in the water caught her eye, and she went rigid. Great Mother! It looked like Logan was the least of her worries.

As she watched, another of Falcone's soldiers bobbed to the surface of the fast moving stream. Apparently more than one of them was willing to risk his life to bring her back.

Luckily, the man was turned away, scanning the bank on the other side of the river. Logan had followed her gaze, then grabbed her hand and pulled her off the beach and around a pile of boulders, shielding them from the river.

Climbing up on the nearest rock, he reached down to help her up. They ascended about ten feet above the river, into an open space.

Behind them, Rinna heard splashing noises. More warriors.

"If they find the beach, they'll see our footprints," she gasped.

"Shit! I wasn't thinking about that."

"There wasn't anything we could do about it. Not if we wanted to get out of there fast."

Exclamations from below told her they were almost out of time. "Hurry," she urged. But as she looked around, she saw that there wasn't much chance of a quick escape. They'd have to keep climbing. And when they did, they would stand out against the rock walls.

On the other side of the open space, two rock outcroppings created a crevice.

One wall had a ridge that jutted out like a roof, darkening the space inside and giving a good deal of shelter.

But it would also be one of the first places the soldiers looked.

Still, it might be their only chance.

"We'll be trapped," Logan whispered when she started toward the crevice.

"Maybe not. Maybe I can do something." She pressed a hand against his shoulder. "You go first." She could leave him now. Maybe she could even get away, if she was by herself. But she wouldn't abandon him to the mercy of the warriors.

Logan gave her a doubtful look. But as they heard the sound of men scrambling up the rock, he backed quickly into the space until he was hidden by darkness.

She followed, then turned to face the doorway, focusing her thoughts on the opening. By herself, she couldn't create a force field like the one that had protected the cave. But perhaps she could make a mental curtain.

Moving closer, Logan cradled her in his arms, his naked front pressed to her back. It would be easy for him to take advantage of her here. He could let his hand drift downward, onto her breast, and she took her lip between her teeth as she realized how vulnerable she was. She couldn't run. And she couldn't fight him—if she wanted to keep the two of them hidden from the soldiers.

To her vast relief, he kept his fingers cupped over her shoulders.

Lowering his mouth to her ear, he spoke in the barest whisper, and she knew he was thinking about their situation—not about overpowering her. "If they find us, we can change and fight them."

Depending on how many, she thought.

She pressed her lips together when she heard a voice below; one of the pursuers was calling to the other.

They both went still as they listened to the shouted conversation.

"Are you all right?"

"Yeah. But I thought I was going to drown."

"Where's Terrell?"

"I didn't see him."

Terrell. Was that the guy they'd killed in the water? She'd prefer not to know his name. He had nothing personal against her. He was just trying to survive in the service of a ruthless man.

"Maybe he didn't make it," another voice said.

"I thought he was a good swimmer."

"Maybe Rinna and the guy drowned."

At the sound of her own name, her heart started to pound even harder. Logan stroked her neck, her hair, but he said nothing.

"We could go back and say that's what must have happened."

The first speaker made a harsh sound. "You want to tell *Falcone* that we lost them?"

"Gods, no."

"They're both shape-shifters. They could be long gone."

"Still, we'd better search. Falcone was sure they'd be in the cave."

Rinna felt her throat close.

Logan pulled her farther into the shadows of the rocks, as far back as they could go.

It was dark inside the crevice. She couldn't see Logan, but she could feel him. They had been close together before. Now her body was wedged against his. His skin had warmed, maybe because the two of them were generating heat in the enclosed space.

He lowered his head again, stroking his lips lightly

against her neck. As footsteps approached their hiding place, she pressed the back of her head into the dark hair on his chest.

When she heard a soldier climbing toward them, she went absolutely still as she formed an image in her mind. An image of the cave entrance and the cavity beyond. It was dark and scary inside. And it was impossible to see more than a few inches into the darkness. Probably there were cougars inside. Or bears. Or maybe even a fire-breathing dragon.

She felt Logan shiver, then lower his lips to her ear. "Are you doing that?"

"Yes," she murmured.

One of the warriors came close to the cave, and they both stopped breathing. Rinna could see the man staring into the darkness of the crevice.

Did he have a flashlight? They were very rare because it took some psychic ability to operate them. But this man might have been trained to do it.

She tensed, waiting for a beam to strike a shoulder or a leg. But apparently the man lacked that skill, and with the terrifying images she had called up, it seemed that he didn't want to take a chance on creeping into a tight space where danger might lurk.

After several moments, he moved off, and Rinna let the air trickle out of her lungs.

She would have pulled away from Logan, but he held her fast.

"I think they're gone," she whispered, reaching backward to press her hand against his shoulder. "We should get out of here."

"Not yet."

She couldn't see him, but alarm sizzled through her as she felt him turn her in his arms.

"I dreamed of kissing you," he said. "Was it real?"

"How could it be real if it was a dream?"

"But do you remember it?" he pressed.

She gulped. Lying was never easy for her. But there was no way she could tell him the truth.

"No," she whispered. She remembered sharing a kiss with him. Not just a kiss. He had touched her, stroked her body and she remembered waking—out of breath and wanting him. Then she'd gone right to him and tended his wounds.

They had been in an opulent bedroom. Now they were outside, wedged together in a crevice in the rock.

Before she could drag in a breath and let it out, he lowered his head so that his lips skimmed hers, brushing back and forth, and she felt a thrill along her nerve endings. Like in the dream.

She didn't want it to be true. She wanted to remain aloof from him. She thought of standing very still and simply letting him kiss her as though she were a statue. If she didn't respond, he would get the message.

They were both naked, and she felt a dart of fear when his penis stirred against her middle.

"I won't hurt you," he murmured. "I only want to find out if the dream was my imagination."

Suddenly she knew she'd trapped herself. If she'd told him the truth, perhaps he would turn her loose now. Or would confession only have made it worse?

He rubbed his mouth against hers again, creating a kind of heated friction. When she made a small sound, he pressed more firmly, moving his lips against hers as though he were speaking to her in a language only the two of them could understand. When she accepted that much from him, he took the intimacy to another level, his tongue playing along the line where she had her mouth sealed closed.

She had never realized there were so many subtle nuances to a kiss. And maybe she wasn't as opposed as she thought because she allowed the tip of his tongue to work its way to the inside edge of her lips, teasing and persuading.

He was gentle yet convincing. When he lightly stroked the sensitive inner surface of her mouth, then slowly swept his tongue along the line of her teeth, it felt good, which was as alarming as his naked body pressed to hers. Something about this man drew her. Some inner voice urged her to let down her guard with him. Only him.

Yet the thought of being at the mercy of any man tightened her chest.

She made a small sound, and he took advantage of that opening, deepening the contact, finding her tongue with his, delicately stroking the side.

He seemed to have turned kissing into an art form that a man and woman could appreciate together.

His tongue withdrew, and he used only his lips again, sipping from her as though her mouth tasted better to him than fine wine.

She was dizzy, swaying against him, his crisp chest hair making her breasts tingle. He stroked his hands up and down her arms, then slid lower, tracing the indentation of her waist and the curve of her hip, his fingers trailing heat over her skin.

It felt right. And good beyond belief. Yet there was no way she could relax in this situation. And the spreading warmth in her body changed to panic when she felt the hard shaft of his erection rising between them.

He was aroused. And his touch grew more urgent as

he reached to stroke the sides of her breasts, then slid his hands inward toward her nipples.

"Don't."

He didn't seem to hear her, and that fueled her fear, so that she pushed sharply against his chest.

As soon as he felt that pressure, he dropped his hands to his sides and lifted his mouth away from hers.

Though she couldn't see his face, she knew he was looking down at her. When he spoke, she heard confusion and disappointment in his voice. "You wanted me to kiss you. You were enjoying it."

This time she found she couldn't lie to him. "Yes."

"It stopped feeling good?"

"I . . ."

She wanted to tell him she was frightened—of him and of herself. But admitting so much would put her at his mercy. And she knew what it was like to be at the mercy of a man.

When she didn't speak, he went on in a gritty voice. "I wasn't planning to take advantage of you."

Words rose to her lips. Words she wanted him to understand, yet at the same time, she couldn't speak.

Unable to tell him what she was feeling, she turned the subject away from what they had been doing and to the danger around them.

"We have to leave before more soldiers come. We should climb the rock wall and see what's on the other side. If you can get down as a wolf, then we should change," she said.

To her relief, he agreed. "You're right. I guess I stopped thinking clearly."

She had done that, too. But she didn't admit it.

As they moved toward the light, he cleared his throat. "How did you do that trick with the cave entrance?"

"You saw the image?"

"Yes. How did you do it?"

"In school we had classes where we learned to project scenes," she answered. "Sometimes I can do it."

He tipped his head to one side, studying her. "What kind of school was that?"

"For children with psychic talents," she answered in a clipped voice.

"Magic school, like in *Harry Potter*?"

"There was no one in my school named Harrypotter."

He laughed. "He's a character in a book."

"Oh." She dragged in a breath and let it out. "Some people call it magic. I call it talent."

"Okay."

As they approached the entrance to the cave, he held her back, then stepped in front of her, inspecting the area around the hiding place before stepping out.

Once they were in the open, he moved to his right. She followed and saw that there was a rough trail through the rocks.

"We should change," he said.

"We won't be able to talk."

"Unfortunately. So tell me where we're going."

"I'll know better when I figure out where we are. You stay here and wait for me."

"I'll stay with you."

Perhaps he could. And perhaps he couldn't. She'd find out in a few minutes.

When he said, "I'll change first, then guard you," she nodded.

She might have said she didn't need guarding, but she knew that was false bravado.

He walked to the front of the outcropping and turned to face her—his gaze seeking hers.

In her experience, changing was a private matter. But it was obvious he planned to do it in front of her—again. Was that the way with his people?

The last time he had done it, he had gone from wolf to man. Now she heard him chanting low, unfamiliar words and realized they must be part of his ritual. Not her way of changing, but she hadn't really expected him to be like her.

As she watched, his body began to flow and transmute into its wolf form. It was a strange—and fascinating sight. And somehow it made her feel closer to him because this change from human to animal was something few people understood. When he had completed the transition, the wolf turned so that he could guard her, and watch the water.

She stayed where she was, letting her mind flow into the animal shape that was part of her being.

Not a wolf this time. She had two nonhuman forms she could take. And the other shape that she had been granted by the gods would be more useful now.

Her thoughts helped form her body into a large white bird. And she had the satisfaction of seeing the wolf gape at her. From his expression, she gathered that he had only one form, and she had surprised him by taking this alternate shape.

LOGAN stared in astonishment as Rinna transformed—but not into a wolf. He'd expected to see the white wolf he'd first encountered in the Maryland woods.

Instead she became a large white bird. Some kind of hawk or eagle, he thought, but he wasn't sure.

As she leaped into the air, he realized that he'd seen the bird before. In the badlands, Rinna had gone behind the ruined house, and he'd seen the bird rise into the air. He'd thought she'd startled it. Now he understood the truth.

She rose gracefully as her wings beat the air. After circling him once, she took off toward the mountain of rocks from which the river emerged.

His stomach knotted as he watched her go. She could leave him here, if she wanted. But he hoped she was coming back.

She was a brave warrior, yet so shy and inexperienced as far as man-woman relationships went. He knew she had enjoyed the kiss, but she was afraid of where it would lead. Could he chance to change the equation between them? He ached to do it—if she gave him the chance.

Out of necessity, it seemed she had learned to take care of herself in the wild. He could do that as a wolf. But he hadn't spent much time living rough as a man. Sure, he'd been camping out when they'd first met, but he knew that if he wanted a hot shower, he could always check into a hotel or go home.

But she was the real deal. A woman at home in a primitive setting. And on top of that, she was a magical creature with many talents. Well, not magical. She'd objected to that characterization. So what did she call herself? A witch? A mage? An adept?

As he watched Rinna disappear, he ached to know her. And he wanted answers to all the questions that had piled up in his mind, if she would give them to him.

RINNA flew away from the river. She saw that Logan had been right. They had traveled less than half a mile from the entrance to the cave, and she was tempted to head back that way. But she knew that it wasn't safe. The soldiers must have been briefed about her appearance. And if they were waiting back at her old refuge, they would recognize her bird persona.

She was sure of that much. But she had no idea what orders Falcone had given the troops.

When she'd escaped from him, she'd known that he wanted her alive. But was that still true? Had his plans changed? Had he come to the conclusion that eliminating her was the better course?

The cave tugged at her. She ached to go back and look for Haig, but that would be a fatal mistake.

At first she'd thought one of the mind vampires had gotten him. Now she was pretty sure Falcone had put him under a compulsion. She shuddered. They had talked about the theory in school. No one she knew had ever attempted it. But it looked like Falcone had gotten desperate enough—and succeeded.

She flew onward, looking at the plain below her and the buildings.

Satisfied that she saw no enemies, she started back. She was almost to the river when she saw a flash of movement from the ground. In the next second, a rain of arrows shot upward, heading straight toward her.

CHAPTER NINE

AGAINST THE DEEP blue of the sky, Logan saw the white bird winging its way to him and felt his spirit leap.

But before she reached the clearing where he waited, arrows shot into the air.

His heart wedged in his windpipe as his gaze locked on the bird. Incredibly, she dodged and wove through the air, avoiding the onslaught of arrows.

From his position above the river, he could see three soldiers crouched behind boulders.

They had each launched an initial arrow. They followed with more shafts

Three against one. Not good odds, considering that the wolf had been wounded a couple of days earlier, then gotten himself into a nasty fight not far from the cave. But he was already running down the rocky incline with no thought of turning back.

He felt the familiar animal savagery take him. With a snarl the wolf leaped from the rocks, landing on the closest shooter. He went for the man's throat, feeling satisfaction surge through him as he chewed through flesh and bone and tasted warm blood spurting into his mouth.

The archer made a gurgling sound and dropped the arrow he'd been about to mount on the bow string. Next to him, his comrade pulled a knife and rushed the wolf.

For long seconds, the third man was too stunned to move. Snapping out of his trance, he drew a sword and dashed to his comrade's aid.

Unfortunately, the odds were even worse than Logan had thought. Two more men had been crouching out of sight. As they leaped forward, Logan wondered if the target really had been the bird. Maybe they'd worked up a plan to get him to attack.

And he'd done just what they wanted—rushing right into another trap like a wolf bent on self-destruction.

Only he was going to take as many of them with him as he could. One man was on the ground, probably dying from the wound to his neck. But the three additional soldiers moved into position, surrounding Logan. He whirled to snap at the one coming up behind him with a sword, and the guy to his left lashed out, slashing with the knife.

He was barely able to avoid the two blades. Grabbing for the knife hand, he bit down, hearing the satisfying sound of bone crunching.

A sword thrust aimed at his side slid along his flank, cutting into his flesh, but his thick fur prevented major damage.

He saw the soldiers' eyes. Two of them were scared. The other was angry.

At the wolf? Or at the orders he was forced to carry out?

It didn't matter. They would kill him in the end. He

charged the soldier with the sword, coming in low, throwing the man off balance. He got in a killing bite as he heard the two men behind him charge.

The next sound he heard was a scream.

Whirling away from the man he had just vanquished, he saw the white wolf come down on a soldier's back, teeth clamped on his neck.

Rinna! She had changed form and come to his aid. But had she ever been in a fight like this?

Logan leaped to defend her, chomping down on the wrist of the man with the knife. He cried out and dropped the weapon.

The soldier who was still standing went for Rinna. Logan whirled toward the man, knocking him off his feet.

The white wolf leaped on the attacker, tearing at the man's scalp with her teeth.

When the guy went still, the white wolf lifted her head and looked around as though stunned that the ground was littered with bodies.

Her gaze met Logan's. He saw her triumph in addition to her shock. And he wondered what she saw on his own face.

He'd hunted and killed plenty of animals, but he'd never killed a man before today. He was sure the soldiers back at the river hadn't survived the fight. Maybe that was even true of the two men who had attacked him after he'd left the cave. But in both cases, it had been their lives or his and Rinna's.

He longed to change to human form, run to her and hold her close. But they had to get out of this area before reinforcements showed up.

He didn't know much about warfare in this world. He wanted to find out if the soldiers had some means of communicating with each other in the field. Would they send reinforcements? What?

Rinna stood stock-still in the middle of the carnage. Making his way around the bodies on the ground, he came up beside her. When he butted at her with his head she looked like she was coming out of a dream.

He touched her with his muzzle, trotted a few feet away, then shifted his head to the right several times.

She followed slowly at first, but as soon as they were out of the little area where the soldiers had been grouped together, she picked up her pace, then quickly sped past him.

Good. She knew that they had to get the hell out of there.

He followed her through the rocks and out into the open. He wanted to tell her they were too exposed out here. If other men were coming, they'd see the wolves dashing away. They should head for the woods, where there was more cover. But she kept a steady course toward a ruined building.

They stopped in the shadow of a crumpled wall, and she pawed the ground, then blocked his body with hers, and he got the idea that she wanted him to wait.

No way was he going to let her take off on some dangerous mission on her own, so he stayed with her as she dashed into the open again.

She turned and growled at him, but he kept pace with her. When he saw her roll her eyes, he grinned.

There were more destroyed structures ahead, so there was some shelter. But when she came to one of the buildings, she stopped short.

Again, he heard her growl, this time low in her throat.

He followed her gaze and saw a group of men standing about a hundred yards away. They were grouped at the side of a half-standing building. Ten of them were soldiers. But two of them didn't fit the pattern.

One was an old man with white hair and a scraggly purple robe. The other was younger with close-cropped blond hair.

Falcone?

If so, he looked a lot less formidable than Logan had imagined.

Rinna slunk back, her fur bristling. She bared her teeth, then gave Logan a long look.

When she turned and dashed away, he followed. Maybe she couldn't talk, but he got the message.

Sticking around here was dangerous.

She took off across the plain, running fast, making for one refuge, then another. Each time she rested, she stopped and looked back.

They were both breathing hard, and Logan knew he couldn't keep up the pace for long.

Finally, she led him toward a much larger building.

To his astonishment, it looked like a cathedral.

A cathedral? That was the last thing he'd expect to find here. But he had given up trying to figure out what to expect in this crazy world.

The closer they got, the more massive it looked. Part of the roof was missing, but the walls were mostly solid. She bypassed the imposing main entrance and led him around the side where a partially intact wall enclosed what had once been a formal garden with flagstone paths and planting beds. Many of the paving stones had been removed and the beds were full of weeds, but he recognized a climbing rosebush. And some straggly thyme and lavender plants.

He watched Rinna trot down one of the uneven paths, thinking that the garden must have once been magnificent. She stopped beside an ancient-looking fountain, then changed from wolf to woman.

He made a similar change, pushing past the ritual of transformation. The shadows were lengthening and the wind was picking up. Maybe that was why this place felt ten degrees colder than the air outside the enclosure.

He saw Rinna shiver. She was a naked woman again, and he couldn't stop himself from taking in the way the cold had contracted her nipples. But he ruthlessly thrust aside the physical, since they had more important things to deal with.

He wanted to know how he'd gotten into this mess in the first place. She'd been evasive with him since the beginning. Now he asked a direct question.

"I take it you turned around because you saw those men."

"Yes."

"Who were the two guys who weren't soldiers?"

"Avery and Brusco. Falcone's men. If they were there, he sent them to close the portal."

He wedged his hands on his hips. "You were taking me there. Then you changed directions when you saw them. Were you planning to send me home, then disappear?"

She raised her chin. "Yes."

"Because you couldn't handle getting close to me?"

"Because it's a lot safer for you back in your own world."

"Stop lying to me!"

"I . . ." She started to answer, then closed her mouth and looked away from him. He wanted to take her by the shoulders and shake her. But he stayed where he was. "Just for fun, see if you can give me some straight answers. Why are they after you? Did you steal something? Kill someone?"

"No."

"Then what?"

She sighed. "The man I talked about—Falcone. He wants to take me captive."

He wanted to get more information, but he realized he didn't have the luxury of interrogating her out here. Every minute they spent where someone could spot them increased their chances of being attacked again. But one more question burned inside him. "So . . . are you still defending Haig? Do you still think he didn't turn us in?"

"He didn't want to!" she answered.

"Then what?"

"Falcone worked a compulsion on him."

"Why now? Why not earlier?"

"Because he needed power for it. Power from the death of an innocent."

Logan sucked in a breath. "Are you saying he killed someone to get the power?"

"Yes! He killed a child. That's illegal. But he did it anyway. So you'd better hope he doesn't catch up with *you*."

"I'll keep that in mind," Logan answered, looking up at the massive building. In a more even tone, he asked, "Why did you come to this place?"

"Because it's forbidden. Falcone thinks I wouldn't dare come here."

"It's cursed or something?"

"It's from the old religion."

"You mean . . . Christianity."

"Yes."

"What religion do you have now?"

"There are a lot of . . . sects. Lots of gods. People pray to the ones they believe will help them."

"You spoke of the Great Mother. If you believe in her, do you believe she's the only God?"

"I hope she is."

He wanted more facts. About this whole damn world. But that couldn't be his priority.

He took a step toward the edifice. When she didn't move, he said, "It will be dark soon. We need to find shelter and clothing."

She shuddered. "I don't want to go inside. A wolf can travel at night."

"Yeah, but I've got to rest after that fight."

She grimaced. "Sorry. I wasn't thinking. You've been out of bed less than a day."

"I'm not afraid of a building, especially not when it's a good place to shelter," he said. This time he took the lead, ushering her toward a side door, not allowing her to hang back.

Inside, he looked around and found a table that held several oil lamps, which he recognized because he'd seen them in a museum display. They were shaped a little like gravy boats, with an elongated body and a handle. But instead of a pouring spout, they had a smaller opening where the wick came out. He picked one up and shook it, hearing the oil slosh inside. "Too bad there's nothing to light them with," he said.

Rinna gave him a quick look, then took one of the lamps and held it in front of her. As she stared at the wick, a flame sprang up.

He blinked. "How did you do that?"

"That's one of the talents I discovered in school."

"Did it get you into trouble?"

She made a small sound. "No. I told you, all the children in the school had psychic talents. Actually, that's why we were there—to find out what skills we possessed and develop them to the fullest."

"How old were you when you first changed form?"

"Eight."

He looked at her in surprise. "You didn't have to be . . . sexually mature to do it?"

"No. Morga was my guide."

"Who was Morga?"

"One of my teachers. She was strict, but she taught me a lot. Without the school I never would have . . ." She let the sentence trail off.

"Wouldn't what?"

"Wouldn't have found out everything I can do," she answered, but he suspected she had changed what she was going to say. She was telling him more than she had previously, but she was still hiding information from him.

"Can you light another lamp?"

She handed him the one she was holding, then picked up a second vessel and sparked the wick.

Logan held his in front of himself as he walked toward another door and pulled it open.

He was thinking how strange it was to step naked into the sanctuary. In the shadows, he couldn't see much. But he caught the feel of the massive high-ceilinged room. There were no chairs or pews inside, only a great expanse of open floor.

Some light came in through the elongated windows. They had retained much of their stained glass, but the wind whistled through a number of holes in the glass and in the ceiling high above the stone floor.

A whirring sound made Logan's head jerk up. Beside him, Rinna had gone rigid.

He turned and pulled her close, cursing himself for putting her in danger.

Were they under attack again? What?

Then he saw a large flock of pigeons flying upward and out through holes in the high windows.

"Sorry, I'm jumpy," he muttered.

"Both of us," she whispered. "I feel ghosts here."

"You believe in ghosts?"

"Yes. Don't you?"

"I'm not sure."

He draped his arm around her shoulder, feeling her skin quiver. He wanted to turn her toward him, bury his face in her thick hair and breathe in her wonderful scent.

But because he wanted her to feel comfortable with him, he kept his touch light and his gaze on the building. His mother had tried to cultivate his belief in religion. His father had scoffed at what he called superstitions.

Logan had gone with his father's teachings because they seemed to make more sense to his werewolf mind. And since he'd first changed from teenager to wolf, he hadn't been inside a church. But even in its ruined state, the cathedral conveyed a feeling of majesty.

Rinna's reaction was quite different. Beside him, she drew in a sharp breath.

"What?"

"So many people gathered together in one place," she murmured, her voice hushed.

He also kept his voice low. "You don't do that?"

"It's dangerous."

"Why? Does it spread disease?"

"Someone could attack. Or something."

"What do you mean, something?"

"A Sucker could have found this place. One of the mind vampires."

A connection suddenly clicked in his head. "A mind vampire?" He stared at her. "You were there when we fought Boralas, weren't you?"

"Yes."

He studied her with new understanding. "I didn't get a good look at you. And your hair was shorter."

"Yes. Falcone had it cut—to punish me." She stopped short, looking like she wished she hadn't shared that bit of information.

He didn't press her on that. "Why didn't you tell me we'd . . . met?"

"We didn't. Not really." She lifted her chin. "Was it important?"

"You know it was." He kept his arms at his sides, when he wanted to reach for her. "You've learned not to trust anyone."

"I trust Haig," she shot back.

"But not me?"

"I hardly know you."

"But you saved my life. You could have left me in that trap. At the river, you could have flown away."

"I couldn't leave you to die. Not when that trap was meant for me in the first place."

"Like when you were under attack, and I stopped the soldiers from shooting. Does that count for something?"

She swallowed. "Yes."

"But?"

"Trust is hard for me."

"Then I'll earn it," he promised.

He reached for her hand, and felt her give a little start as he knit his fingers with hers.

When she tried to pull away, he kept her hand in his grasp. "If it's dangerous here, we must stay together."

She stopped arguing and he cast her a sideways

glance as he led her toward the back of the building. He didn't mind the view of her naked body, but he suspected she hated the situation.

At the rear of the structure, he found a flight of stone stairs leading to the basement.

"We might as well go down."

"We could get trapped."

"But you can walk through walls."

She snorted. "You mean at the cave?"

He nodded.

"That's not exactly what it seemed. Haig set up a field that looked like a stone wall. It wasn't really solid."

"Haig did it?"

"He has a lot of talents," she said with a hitch in her voice. "And he would have stayed with me—if he could."

Changing the subject, he said, "What about the portal? You said they closed it."

"We may be able to find another one," she said, but she didn't sound too hopeful.

"Explain the portals to me."

She sighed. "I don't understand it well myself. I think there are some naturally weak places in the plates between the worlds. If you find one, it's not too hard to open, with the right powers. With more power, you can open a portal almost anyplace. Theoretically," she added.

"Theoretically?"

"It wouldn't take a lot of energy. From more than one adept."

"So you can't do it by yourself?"

"No."

"If we can't get through a portal, we need to find a place to hole up," he said.

She nodded, and he held the lamp high as they went

down, then stopped short when he saw mud on the floor. "Somebody's been down here."

He took a quick look through some of the empty rooms and saw nothing, but it was obvious that there were too many chambers to search quickly.

Rinna looked around nervously. "I want to make sure there's another way out."

"Yeah."

He led her along the hallway, his senses on alert. When he saw another flight of steps going up, he stopped.

"We'll go up and make sure we can get out, then come back and find a place to camp out," he said.

"Okay."

As they hurried up the stairs, he turned to see her following him, the light from her lamp showing the strain on her face.

His chest tightened. Maybe she wouldn't be in trouble at all if she hadn't stopped to get him out of that trap.

At the landing, he turned and walked a few steps across the room and found a closed door, it led to a hallway and a door to the outside, much like the entrance where they'd first come into the building. Which meant that they had two ways to get out.

They went back down.

He thought Rinna was right behind him. But when he turned, she wasn't there.

CHAPTER TEN

LOGAN'S HEART STOPPED, then started to pound in double time.

He wanted to call out to Rinna—but if someone had grabbed her, that would give him away.

Or maybe she'd found that getting close to him too threatening and had fled.

Because he didn't know if someone was going to jump out of the shadows at him, he divided his attention between the area at midlevel and the floor. When he spotted Rinna's footprints leading toward another doorway, he breathed out a sigh.

But just before he reached the entrance, he heard her make a strangled sound.

Heedless of what might be on the other side, he charged through the door and found Rinna standing in front of a closet, perhaps where the priests had hung their robes. Instead of religious garments, he found something else—men's clothing, neatly folded or draped over hangers.

He rifled through the garments, seeing sweaters, jeans, loafers, cowboy boots, work shirts, khakis. The normal clothing of everyday life in the world where he came from.

In addition to clothing, he found money—good old U.S. currency.

"What the hell is this?" he growled. "Have you been playing some kind of trick on me? Are we really in some part of the United States?"

"No," she whispered.

"Then what?"

"I . . . don't know," she answered, her voice quavering.

"I think you do. But you're clamming up, as usual." He made a sound of frustration. "Well, with all this clothing here, I'm damned if I'm going to stand around naked."

His jaw set, he put down his lamp and began rifling through the stacks of pants and found a pair of jeans his size. Then he pulled a button-down shirt off a hanger and jammed his arms into the sleeves. Finally he grabbed socks and a pair of size nine running shoes.

When he looked up, Rinna had pulled on a T-shirt. It was much too large, but she could probably get away with the baggy look.

As she began searching for pants that would fit her, he pulled out several and held them up. They were all too big, but she stepped into one, then tried to drag the zipper up. After watching her yank fruitlessly at the tab, he reached for her hand.

When she felt his touch, she jumped.

"Let me show you how to do it."

She gave a little nod.

"Like this."

He leaned over and held the bottom of the fabric to

stabilize the zipper, then slowly pulled up the tab. He was just helping her dress—like he'd help a little kid. But he felt her hold her breath as his hand traveled over her center.

He made an effort not to press against her. But it was impossible to avoid all contact. He concentrated hard on the simple task because he wanted to show her he could touch her so intimately without getting aroused. He was only partially successful.

She started to step away and tripped over the pants legs pooling around her feet.

His hand shot out to steady her. "We need to roll those up."

Again she gave her assent with a nod, and he hunkered down in front of her, keeping his head bent as he folded up one pants leg and then the other.

When she swayed on her feet, she reached out a hand to his shoulder to steady herself. He wanted to press his face against her middle, but he kept methodically working, evening out the cuffs of the jeans as though her life depended on the exercise. And perhaps it did, he suddenly realized.

"Maybe this isn't such a good idea," he said.

"Why not?"

"You're not used to wearing this clothing are you?"

"No."

"Will it get in your way if you have to fight?"

"I don't know." She whirled away from him, moving her hands in the air, making some impressive martial arts moves.

He watched her focus on the drill, watched her graceful moves, knowing she was using the exercise to distance herself from him.

"You need shoes. But none of them are going to fit."

He searched through the shelves and found some running shoes in a mens seven and a half. With a thick pair of socks, they stayed on her feet.

He let her move around in them for a few minutes, then stopped her with a gruff order. "Enough."

Her head jerked toward him.

"Tell me what all this stuff is doing here."

She swallowed. "I don't know for sure. Anything I tell you will be . . . speculation."

"Let's have your best guess."

"Falcone is planning an invasion," she said, speaking very fast as though she wanted to get the words out before she lost her nerve.

He wedged his fists against his hips. "An invasion of what?"

"Your world," she said in a barely audible voice.

"Maybe you'd better explain that."

She made a broad sweeping motion with her hand. "This place is a mess. I don't mean this room. I mean this whole . . ." She gave a little shrug. "This whole universe. It's a lot like where you come from," she went on. "You can breathe the air. You can eat the food. We even speak your language. But there are things that are very different between the two worlds. I found some of your history books. You have something called the atomic bomb, don't you?"

"Yes," he said, still trying to grasp where this conversation was going.

"We don't have that kind of science. Something happened here to make us develop differently."

"What?"

"I can't give you a history lesson right now. The important point is that a lot of people have more psychic powers than in your world. Some of us have . . . psychic jobs."

"Like what?"

"Like running machinery. The way Haig did with that oven. But psychic powers are also used as weapons. That's how everything turned into such a mess. People like Falcone wanted to rule, so they got groups of psychics together to fight each other."

She stopped abruptly, watching his face. "That's the truth. But it looks like you don't believe me."

"It's hard to take in. You said something about a change. Are you saying there's a specific time when your world changed?"

"After 1893," she said promptly.

"Jesus! You have the same dates we do?"

"Yes."

"And you can pinpoint it that accurately?"

She nodded. "Our historians can."

"What happened in 1893?"

"Eric Carfoli started the psychic revolution."

"Okay," he answered, since there was no way to prove the assertion either way. He was sure as hell going to dig up more information about this Eric Carfoli. But the present was more important at the moment. "I haven't seen any evidence of . . . psychic wars," he challenged. "The soldiers who have come after us seem like ordinary guys."

"A lot of the psychics killed each other off. Which is why most of the fighting is done by conventional troops these days. The men you saw are Falcone's private army. A few of them would have talents, though. Like communications officers who can relay messages over long distances. Or men who could sense the presence of an enemy."

He looked from her to the store of clothing. "And Falcone is bringing them into my world?"

"Yes. Haig never wanted to believe that there were portals to other worlds. But I read a lot about it . . . in the vaults at Sun Acres. Scholars debated about it, and I wanted to believe it. I looked for ways to prove it. And I found them. First we saw the monster, Boralas, in your world. Then I showed Haig that there were ways for people to cross from one . . . time continuum . . . to the other."

"What were you doing in my world when you found me in the trap?" he asked

He saw her features tighten. "I was looking for a place to hide from Falcone. I thought he didn't know how to open a portal. But he must have figured it out. Or, more likely, one of his advisers did—maybe Avery. Falcone knows this is a horrible place to live. He's thinking he can set up an outpost in your world, then conquer your people and enslave them."

"Aren't you making a lot of assumptions?"

"I've known him for a long time. I never underestimate his power—or his greed."

She was about to say more when they both heard a noise on the upper level.

Rinna sucked in a sharp breath. "They found us."

He wanted to deny it, but as troops crossed the floor above, he was pretty sure she was right.

"There are two ways out," he reminded her, but even as he spoke, he was afraid that wasn't going to do them any good because he could hear footsteps coming from both directions. "I'm sorry. I trapped you," he bit out, wondering how long they had before the bad guys came down here.

"Maybe not. Maybe he closed that other portal because he knew there was another one here. If he's stockpiled supplies for an invasion, this is the logical place for him to go through."

She looked wildly around, then moved quickly to the wall, running her hand along the rough stones.

"Can I help you?" he asked.

"How?"

"When I was in the cave, I felt the entrance, like a tingling against my skin."

"Okay. Yes. Search for that," she said hurriedly as she moved from one section of the wall to another.

He stepped into the next room, braced for the soldiers to pounce on them at any moment.

Moving to a dark corner, he pressed his palms against the rock and felt nothing besides cold stone.

Unbearable tension coursed through him. He had to find the opening. But at the same time, he had to be prepared to whip around and fight off an attack from trained soldiers. He would have to kill again. But he had come to realize that this was war.

He thought about changing to wolf form. That was a better fight mode for him. But he had learned when they fought Boralas that a wolf didn't have all the same abilities and vulnerabilities as a man. In that fight, the monster had been able to reach into human minds, but the wolves had been immune.

That made him think he might need to be human to sense the hidden doorway. So he kept working—all the time listening for the sounds of the soldiers bursting through the doorway.

Methodically, he moved around the room, until he felt that strange tingling sensation that he had experienced when he'd leaned against the hidden opening in the cave.

Because he couldn't risk a shout to Rinna, he darted back to her and closed a hand over her shoulder.

She whirled, ready to attack, then saw it was him.

"I think I found it," he told her in a harsh whisper, then heard men coming down the stairs.

Quickly they both turned and rushed back to the place where he'd been searching.

He stared at the rough walls and fought panic when it all looked the same.

Damn! He should have marked the spot.

But Rinna began sliding her palm against the stone, then stopped and gave him a quick, grateful look.

"Here," she whispered.

When she'd brought him from his world to hers, he'd been too sick to watch what she was doing. Now he tried to follow the steps, but it looked like she was working mumbo jumbo.

He listened to the footsteps coming closer, wanting to yell at her to hurry.

But he knew he'd only distract her—and alert the bad guys.

Finally, after what felt like centuries, a portion of the wall began to waver. What he saw on the other side made him blink, and he tried to figure out where it was. Not out in the woods.

"How do you know it's my world?" he demanded.

"I don't. Not for sure. But I think that's what it is."

When the wall disappeared, Rinna grabbed his arm, urging him through but kept in back of him.

"Do you have some idea of staying here?" he growled, turning to hold on to her so that he could pull her through with him.

She didn't protest, and he suspected she'd only been trying to get him to safety first. Damn the woman.

Once they stepped through, she turned to reverse the process. He also turned. Through the doorway, he saw a man's arm and leg coming around the corner of the wall.

The breath froze in his lungs, and he tensed for another battle. Hell, it seemed like every time he turned around in this world, he was fighting someone off.

What would it be like to grow up in such an environment?

To his vast relief, the wall solidified before the soldier came around the corner. Or at least Logan hoped that was what had happened.

Agonizing seconds ticked by. When the wall stayed solid, Logan breathed out a sigh. They were back in the United States of America—he hoped.

IN the basement of the old cathedral, Calag studied the marks in the dust. The man and woman he sought had been here. They'd walked around on the ground level, then come down the stairs, probably looking for a hiding place.

But they'd come up again so that the trail was messed up.

His men were searching now. Twelve trained fighters and two with extra talents—Balfer and Darnet. He'd kept those two with him while the others spread out.

When he stood still and concentrated, he was pretty sure that the fugitives were no longer in the area. But his psychic powers were minimal, which was why he was leading a group of Falcone's soldiers rather than sitting with him at the dining room table like that old fart Avery.

Still, Balfer and Darnet had qualified at the second level of training. Not a great recommendation, but maybe good enough for his purposes.

He looked at the two men. "I think they're not here. But see if you can tell me where they went."

They both saluted, then stood still for several seconds, looking like they were listening. Darnet walked to the shelves of clothing and began fingering the garments, trying to get an impression from something one of the fugitives had touched. Balfer walked into the other room.

Calag watched him retreat, wanting to give more specific directions. But he'd learned not to interfere. He could break the man's train of thought, and some twinge of information he might have picked up might be gone.

So Calag crossed his arms and stood rigidly to keep from tapping his foot in impatience, staring at the oil lamps the fugitives had left on the shelves.

He didn't have one of those things you wore on your wrist to tell time. But he had been taught about seconds ticking by. And he had learned to count silently in his head.

He reckoned that about five minutes passed before Balfer returned. His face was tense.

"You lost them?"

The man pressed his hands against his sides and looked down at the floor. He had been born a slave and he was always ready for punishment.

"Speak up!" Calag snapped.

"I think they went through the portal."

"Carfolian Hell!"

"Can we go after them?"

"We should get authorization. Can you send a message back to Sun Acres?"

"We're too far away for me to make the contact by myself. But I think Darnet and I can do it together."

Calag thought about his options. If he waited, they could lose the man and the woman. But Falcone had given specific orders that nobody was to go through a portal without authorization.

"Darnet!" Calag called. "Get in here."

The other adept came running.

"Yes, sir?"

"Lander is waiting at Falcone's residence. I want you and Balfer to send a psychic message to him immediately.

He watched the men stand so that their shoulders were touching, watched them link hands.

They might be able to get through. Or they might not. And if they couldn't, it was Calag's head on the chopping block.

CHAPTER
ELEVEN

LOGAN HAD BEEN so focused on the soldier that he hadn't been paying attention to where they had landed. Then he felt Rinna's fingers grip his arm.

He swung toward her and found her staring around in wonder—and also alarm.

They appeared to be in a convenience store, the kind of place where customers dashed in for some product they needed right away. Or where they came to get coffee and a premade sandwich.

"We're safe," he told her, thinking that they had just gone from a crisis into a safe harbor. Then he reminded himself that he was the only one who had stepped into a familiar environment.

Her voice quavered as she moved closer to him and whispered, "Is this a storehouse?"

"No. It's a convenience store. There's nothing to worry about here. Why does a storehouse frighten you?"

She loosened her grip on his arm and gestured with her hand. "There's never enough of anything where I come from. Food. Medicine. Clothing. The rich can buy those things and store them for when they're needed. But they guard them jealously. And they kill if they catch you trying to raid their private stock."

"We don't have that kind of violence here. This is a place where ordinary people come to buy things they need," he said, keeping his tone reassuring, trying to remind himself how strange her world had seemed to him. She must be having the same problem—in reverse. "This is a public place, not a rich man's storehouse. Anyone can come in and shop here."

She seemed to relax a little. "Like the marketplace, you mean. Only inside?"

"Yes."

She took another look at the well-stocked shelves. "And we're in the back where the merchant hides his best things and brings them out for the rich people."

"It's not like that here," he answered. "If you have the money, you can buy it."

She nodded, but she looked like she didn't really believe him as she took a step along the aisle where they stood.

"Does Falcone have control over where this portal comes out?" he asked.

"I don't know. I don't think so. Probably Avery and Brusco took advantage of a weakness in the plates. The way Boralas did."

"A store isn't such a hot place to land," Logan muttered, then amended the comment. "Well, I guess it depends on whether the clerk is paying attention to who goes in and out."

Rinna was moving her hand along the shelves, touching products. She picked up a jar of spaghetti sauce, shaking it gently and looking through the glass at the contents before putting it back. Moving farther down the aisle, she scooped up a bar of bath soap and slowly read the label.

"This is to wash your body?"

"Yes."

"They taught me to read in the school when I was a child," she murmured.

He stared at her. "Not everyone can read?"

"Most slaves can't," she said, then turned her head quickly away.

Most slaves.

She'd said it casually, but the words sent a small shiver traveling over his skin. Had she been talking about herself? He looked at her with fresh awareness as he watched her turn the bar in her hand, then bring it to her nose.

Strong emotions welled up inside him. His life mate looked so feminine, yet he sensed an iron core at the center of her being. And he had seen her in a fight. She knew how to defend herself. In her world, she had been the one who knew exactly what to expect. Here, the tables were turned. Could she trust him enough to rely on him?

His life mate?

Good Lord. He'd used the term without even thinking about it. Yet he knew in the secret depths of his soul that it was true. He'd bonded with her. Even if she didn't know it yet.

"This must be expensive," she murmured.

He blinked, bringing his mind back to the conversation even as he struggled to keep his voice steady. "No. It's ordinary."

She gave him a startled look, and he wondered if she heard the emotion in his voice.

But her words were still about the product in her

hand. "Not in my world. A woman who had this would be of very high rank."

"Things are different here. You'll have to let me guide you," he answered, thinking how much pleasure it would give him to teach her the things she needed to know to get along here.

"Yes," she agreed, but was she just giving an automatic response?

She moved farther along, and he saw that her eye was drawn to a selection of brightly colored boxes with smiling men and women on the outside of the packaging.

Condoms. He swallowed, wishing she'd focused on something else, because he was immediately aroused as he pictured the two of them making love.

She picked up one of the packages. It said, "Extra long." She shuffled through other types and brands, slowly reading the attributes. "Ribbed for her pleasure. Prelubricated." Turning to him, she asked, "What are they?"

"Condoms," he answered brusquely.

"Which are?"

His throat had tightened, but he managed to say, "Something a man uses when he makes love to a woman—to keep her from getting pregnant."

He saw her flush. "Oh."

He wanted to tell her they wouldn't be needing any. A werewolf wanted to get his mate pregnant to perpetuate his species. That was programmed into his genes.

Then he realized how far he was getting ahead of himself. She didn't even understand that they had bonded, which meant he could hardly start making demands.

Unaware of the turmoil roiling inside him, she put the box back and took a deep breath. "They have coffee here? In a public place?" she murmured.

Delighted to find another focus for his thoughts, he answered, "Yes."

Again her surprise showed on her face. "And it's not expensive?"

"No." He laughed. "But the stuff they have in a place like this probably isn't very good, either."

"Ersatz coffee," she murmured.

"Real. But not the best quality."

She tipped her head to one side, considering. "They have good soap but bad coffee?"

"Soap comes from a factory. They brew the coffee right here," he answered, knowing he couldn't explain. Especially when he didn't drink the stuff. He was only going on what other people had told him.

"Oh."

His chest tightened as he watched her gravely studying each new thing she encountered. There was so much she didn't know, so much he wanted to tell her. Not just about this world—but about the two of them. He ached to cement the bond between them by making love with her.

But he knew on a gut-wrenching level that she had spoken the truth earlier. She was not a woman who gave her trust easily.

They were still standing at the back of the store. He hadn't been paying attention to anything besides Rinna and his feelings for her. But just then, something else caught his attention. The dumpy woman with gray hair tending the cash register. He'd seen her before—in this store.

And suddenly, to his relief, he knew where he was. At the Easy Shopper where he'd stopped on the way to his campsite, when he'd remembered that he'd needed flashlight batteries.

He was about to turn toward Rinna and tell her they were no more than twenty miles from home when a customer came in and approached the clerk. He was a young man with weedy hair and a plaid shirt. Something about the way he walked and the way he looked put Logan on the alert.

"Can I help you?" the woman asked.

"Yeah." The answer came out high and aggressive.

Sensing that something was wrong, Logan cupped his hand around Rinna's shoulder, drawing her behind the end of an aisle.

As he watched in sick fascination, the man drew a gun and pointed it at the clerk. "Hands up. Into the back," he ordered.

Rinna threw Logan a look of shock.

He pressed his finger to his lips, then brought his mouth to her ear and spoke in the barest whisper, "He has a gun. It's a deadly weapon."

Had she ever seen a pistol? Did she know how much damage it could do?

He thrust her behind himself as the thug moved toward the back of the store. He could feel her tension—and his own.

After the clerk and the man with the gun passed, he and Rinna could run out of here and call the cops. But by the time they arrived, the woman might already be dead.

Rinna took the decision away from Logan. He felt her move, and before he could grab her, she was creeping silently around the other end of the aisle. She turned and stared at him, then toward the clerk and her captor. He knew she was telling him that they could take the guy by surprise.

She didn't even know the clerk. But she was going to the woman's aid.

He was pretty sure she didn't understand how much damage a firearm could do. And he couldn't warn her, not without giving the two of them away. So he picked up a can of pork and beans, ready to hurl it and duck back as the man passed him.

Before he could act, all hell broke loose.

Part of the wall to his right wavered, and he knew in a moment of sick fascination that the portal was opening once more.

His assessment was confirmed when he looked through and saw the stone chamber from which he and Rinna had escaped. But the chamber wasn't empty.

In the next second, two of Falcone's soldiers burst through. They had exchanged their comic opera costumes for twenty-first century American civilian clothes, but their unkempt look gave them away. Also their weapons. One held a spear and a knife. The other had a bow and arrow and a mace.

The man with the gun saw the soldiers at the same time Logan did. "What the hell?" he shouted, turning and firing several shots in rapid succession.

One of the men went down. The other kept coming.

Logan saw Rinna gasp as she took in the scene. Falcone had sent his warriors after her—and they had stepped into a situation that they could hardly understand.

"Go. Get out of here," he shouted.

She hesitated.

"Go. I'll meet you outside."

She gave him a long look, then ran for the wide doors at the front of the shop and ducked out.

He jerked his attention back to the interior of the store as the robber's gun discharged and a jar of grape jelly exploded, spraying glass and grape-colored goo.

The clerk screamed and kept screaming. The man with the gun kept shooting and the other soldier went down.

While the thug was occupied, Logan came up behind the robber, then slammed the can of beans he was still holding into the man's skull.

In the distance, he heard the sound of police sirens. Obviously the clerk had been able to press a concealed alarm before the assailant had hustled her off to the back of the store.

The woman was staring at him as though coming out of a daze. "Help is coming," he said.

"Don't I know you?"

"No."

"You were in here before."

He repressed a curse. "You're mistaken," he said firmly as he turned and walked away.

Across the parking lot, he saw a white hawk perched on the branch of a tree. Thank God, Rinna was safe. But they had to get away from the scene before the cops arrived. No way was he going to get caught in this situation and have to explain about portals to another world.

Once he reached the door, he bolted across the parking area, putting a couple of parked cars between himself and the building. When he reached the woods, he began to chant, tearing off his clothes as he said the words of transformation.

He landed on all fours, leaving his clothing behind as he sped into the woods, just as two cop cars with their sirens blasting rounded the corner.

Rinna flapped after him. He kept running through the woods, thankful that they were in a fairly rural area, which was good for the wolf and the bird.

After ten minutes, he realized he was winded, and he

remembered that he was still recovering from a bad injury. But he pushed himself because he wanted to put distance between himself and the store. He kept going until he finally stepped on something sharp with his right forepaw.

He yelped and sank to the ground. Turning up the paw, he saw an embedded thorn, which he extracted with his teeth. Then he forced some blood from the injury to help prevent infection. After that, he tried to push himself up, but he was too tired to go on.

The bird flew to his side, tipping her head as she looked at the wound. He couldn't talk, couldn't tell her what to do, and when she flew off, his heart leaped into his throat.

Logan scanned the sky, looking for the bird. When she failed to return, he felt his throat close. At first he hadn't trusted her. But that hadn't stopped them from growing close in a very fundamental way.

He had longed for a mate. Perhaps that was why they had bonded so quickly. Or was it always like that for the Marshall men? They met the right woman—and the process started.

He'd like to ask one of his older brothers or his cousins how it had been for them. At the same time, he couldn't quite picture himself revealing so much. Maybe Megan or Antonia or Savannah would talk to Rinna about it, and she could tell him. *Yeah, right.* He was getting ahead of himself again.

Still breathing hard, he curled on his side, closing his eyes, wondering if his possessive thoughts had driven Rinna away. When he got some strength back, he would look for the bird. Or would that do any good if she didn't want to be found?

With his heart aching, he considered what he knew

about the family history. He'd overheard the women talking about how his brother Grant had lost his life mate. He'd been suicidal until Antonia had brought him back to life.

When he'd heard the story, it had just been words without his being able to truly key into the emotions. Now he could understand.

Rinna was his mate, and if he lost her, he would lose his sanity. Perhaps even his life.

CHAPTER
TWELVE

HIGH ABOVE THE trees, Rinna looked down, searching for the spot where she had left Logan. She had flown away, thinking that if she wanted to keep going, she could fly off into the distance. Fly far north or far south where Falcone would never think to look.

But she had known she would not leave, could not leave. Something had happened between herself and this man, and she ached to know what it was, even if she was also afraid of where the connection would lead.

So she circled the area. First she flew back to what he had called the convenience store and watched uniformed men bring out a man on a cart, the one who had the weapon that sent the deadly missiles into goods and people. He looked pale and sick. The men in uniform could have killed him in there. But he was still alive.

That was not the way of her world, and she struggled to understand. If warriors in Sun Acres had caught a man who was robbing and killing, they would likely execute him on the spot, unless they thought he could give them information. Maybe it would turn out that he hadn't been doing anything wrong. But by then he would be dead.

Too bad for him.

Less than a mile away she saw a house with a line in the rear yard and laundry flapping in the breeze. Nobody was there and she swooped down, inspecting the clothing.

She saw T-shirts and short pants. Diving at the line, she pulled out some of the pins that held the clothing in place, then tossed items of apparel to the ground—one eye on the house, lest someone come outside with one of those weapons and shoot at the bird thief.

But nobody came, and she was able to take away her booty. The clothing was short and thin. But it was enough for modesty.

She gathered the items in her beak and rose into the air, striking out for the tall pine tree where she had left Logan. It was farther than she thought, and she felt panic rise inside her when she thought she might not be able to find him again. Then she saw the tree and circled overhead.

When he heard her wings beating the air, he sat up and raised his head, scanning the sky. She landed lightly beside him and set her offerings on the ground.

She wanted to nuzzle her beak against his fur, but she only snatched up a shirt and a pair of very short pants, then flew low to the ground, landing behind a tangle of brambles where she could have some privacy.

Once she was alone she took a moment to catch her breath and prepare her mind. After silently offering a prayer to the Great Mother, she sent her thoughts into the pattern that she had been taught as a little girl.

Not the pattern of a bird. The pattern of her human self. And her body flowed into her woman's shape.

She flexed her arms and legs, stretched her muscles, then, conscious of her nudity, snatched up the shirt and pulled it over her head. Once she'd also climbed into the pants that barely covered her butt, she looked down at her body. The clothing was very skimpy. She could see her breasts through the thin fabric of the shirt. And because the air was chilly and the wind was blowing, she could see her nipples standing up. Logan had seen her naked. Now she was covered up. But she knew from watching men and women that a little covering could draw a man's interest more than nudity.

When she returned, Logan had finished with his own ritual—the chant he said to change—and had pulled on another pair of the short pants. They were a little too tight and gave her a good view of his body through the fabric as he flexed his arms, pulling on the shirt. It fit him better.

They stood facing each other, and she knew he was looking at her the way she was looking at him, taking in physical details. She struggled not to fold her arms across her chest or to clench her fists at her sides. Months ago she had made the decision that getting close to any man near her age was dangerous.

Logan had made her want things she had denied herself, yet she still didn't know if she could trust him. Or trust herself.

He broke the silence by saying, "Thank you for bringing the clothes—and for coming back."

She hadn't known for sure whether he'd understood her fear. Now she gave a small nod, unable to move closer and unable to move away, either.

He was the one who took a slow step toward her. When she didn't back up, he dared another, then another. And when she stayed where she was, he closed the remaining distance between them and gathered her into his arms.

She was afraid. Yet his embrace felt right in some deep, fundamental way that she couldn't describe. Like when she'd been a little girl and Haig had hugged her to take away hurt or sadness.

Only this was different. Her closest relationship in all the world had been with Haig, but she knew that what she felt for Logan was more than that. For one thing it was sexual.

As she considered that component, she acknowledged fear simmering below the surface of all the other emotions. But she had learned to deal with fear, and she could deal with it now. She had to, because she wanted to reach out to Logan in a way she had never reached for Haig. He was like a father to her. Logan was— She couldn't allow herself to finish the thought.

Instead, she sighed out his name as she buried her face against his shoulder.

"Rinna. Thank you for coming back," he said again.

"I think I had to."

He tipped her head up, so that he could meet her eyes. "Don't hide from me."

"I . . . I'm trying not to," she said in a shaky voice. "But maybe I'm not the woman you need," she heard herself say, because honesty had become as important as anything else that existed between them.

"Don't lie to yourself or to me," he said gruffly, then claimed her mouth. Before, his kiss had been gentle. This kiss was charged with power. It should have alarmed her, instead it was the most natural thing in the world for her to open her lips for him.

He made a gratified noise and angled his head, deepening the contact, and as his lips moved over hers, she was swamped by a raft of sensations. The feel of his hard muscles. The subtle scent of his body. And the exquisite mouth-to-mouth contact. Waves of heat seemed to come off of him, heat that should have seared her flesh and her mind. But it didn't burn. Well, not in a painful way. Instead, it made her own temperature rise in response.

His kiss was hungry and possessive, and she knew in that moment that she had been waiting for him all her life.

When he realized she wasn't going to pull away, some of the desperation went out of him. He nibbled at her mouth, gauging her response before increasing the pressure, taking her lower lip between his teeth, then easing up so that she was astonished to hear herself making a small sound of protest. Was she begging for more? It sounded that way to her own ears—and surely to his.

He drank her in for long seconds, then drew back, his eyes meeting hers.

He held her gaze for a charged moment, then dipped his head again, feasting from her mouth as his hands stroked up and down her back.

She knew they were the two halves of one whole. And she had been incomplete all her life without him.

He swirled his tongue over the sensitive tissue of her inner lips, then probed more deeply, claiming possession in a way that thrilled her. She felt herself giving over to the heat he kindled in her body. Her nipples grew hard. And with the tightness came a kind of yearning ache high up between her thighs.

Still, a frisson of alarm crept into her mind.

She knew he didn't understand that part. He only knew that she was responding to him sexually, which made him confident that she wanted the same thing he did.

One of his hands tangled in her thick hair. The other slid under her shirt and stroked up and down her back. When she swayed on her feet, he steadied her, then moved back, propping his hips against a tree trunk and splaying his legs so that he could equalize their heights.

With a sound of satisfaction, he cupped his hands around her bottom and brought her aching center against the hard shaft of his erection.

That was the instant when full-blown panic came leaping to the surface. She stiffened in his arms. "No. Please. No."

Maybe he had been waiting for that to happen, because he dropped his arms and raised his head, looking down at her.

"Every time we get close, you back away," he said in a gritty voice.

"I don't want to," she managed to answer, astonished that she had voiced her own thoughts so accurately.

"Tell me what's going on."

She wanted to turn away, instead she stayed facing him, struggling with too many emotions. And because she saw the wounded look in his eyes, she forced herself to be brutally honest. "I know you won't hurt me. Somewhere in my mind I know that, until the scary part takes over."

He dragged in a draft of air and let it out in a rush, his gaze never leaving hers. "Rinna, did someone . . . force himself on you?"

She wanted to look away. She wanted to deny the shameful secret that she hadn't even shared with Haig. But she knew that lying to Logan would be the worst thing she could do. "Yes," she answered in a barely audible voice.

"Who?"

Still she had to look away when she said the name. "Falcone."

"The bastard. I'll kill him."

"Stay away from him. He'll kill *you,*" she cried out. She was still grappling with her own emotions. She had told her terrible secret to Logan, and she waited for the world to fall in on top of her. When heartbeats passed and she found the earth was still solid under her feet, she let out the breath she'd been holding.

"Can you tell me about it?"

"Not yet," she answered, then took a step back, looking up at the night sky. It was cloudy and she smelled rain. When Logan raised his head and sniffed the air, she knew he did, too.

"We need to get inside."

"Where?"

"I'm not sure. I think we're too far to make it home from here before the rain."

Casually, he reached for her hand, and gave it a squeeze before leading her through the woods.

"Thank you for trusting me enough to tell me why you keep backing away," he said. Then, to her relief, he dropped the subject. "Where did you get the clothes?" he asked as they walked.

"From someone drying them outside. I guess they're going to get wet."

"Yeah."

She swallowed. She had her own questions. And she might have been afraid to ask them, except that she was discovering that nothing was forbidden with this man. "Back at the convenience store . . . the man with the weapon . . . you said there was no violence here." The sentences came out disjointed and jerky, and she wondered if they sounded like an accusation.

Logan didn't break his stride. "Not as much as in your world, but there is always violence in any society. Sometimes it comes from inequality. Sometimes from bad people. Or greedy people. So I'd say it was just bad luck that we arrived at the Easy Shopper when we did."

"The Easy Shopper?"

"That's the name of the place."

"Oh." She swallowed. "That man, the robber. I felt the desperation and the hatred inside him. I think he would have killed the woman who owned it."

"She probably doesn't own it. More likely she was working for someone."

"Um," she answered, assimilating that new piece of information. Someone trusted the woman enough to leave her with all those goods.

In her memory, Rinna pictured the scene again. "Then cars came with flashing lights."

He turned his head toward her. "The cops. That's slang for the police. Like soldiers. They keep order. But I don't think it's like in your world. We have soldiers, too. But they don't operate in the civilian world here unless there's a national emergency." He sighed. "That's probably getting too complicated."

"I know you're trying to give me the . . . the short course."

"Yeah. We have laws, and most citizens obey them. If you break the law, the cops come after you."

"And throw you in a dungeon," she said promptly.

"Well, not a dungeon. Jail. Which I assume is a little more humane. And what happens depends on how bad the crime was. You might get caught stealing—and be able to put up bail. I mean, you give them money that says you will stay in town until your trial. You get a lawyer, and you are presumed innocent until proven guilty. I get the feeling that in your world, you are presumed guilty unless you can somehow prove you didn't commit the crime."

"Yes," she whispered, still trying to process a bunch of new concepts. But there was something else she needed to understand. "Tell me about the weapon the robber had. I've heard of something like that, but I've never seen it."

"A gun."

"It hurts worse than a knife. And you don't have to be close to the person to use it?"

"It may not hurt worse, but it can do more damage inside the body."

She shuddered. "I think we used to have those."

He nodded, then asked his own urgent question. "Can the soldiers figure out where we've gone? Do they have a way to track us? With smell, for example?"

She considered the possibilities. "If they brought a shape-shifter, he might track us. But shape-shifters aren't all that common. I don't think Falcone has one."

"That's good."

"What about that trap that Falcone used? Could he get us with that?"

Again she tried to come up with a logical answer. "He thought he would find no shape-shifters here. When he caught you, he probably reconsidered the wisdom of using it."

" 'Probably' being the operative word."

"Yes. We can't be . . ."

"Careless," he finished for her.

They had come out of the woods and were facing a narrow road. The middle was paved with a smooth black material. As they started walking to the right, the gravel at the sides dug into the bottoms of her feet.

"We need shoes," she murmured as she stepped from the gravel to the level black surface.

"How do they get it so smooth?" she asked.

"Machines with big metal rollers that press it down."

As she tried to imagine that, rain began to fall, first lightly and then with more force.

"I don't know about you, but I've had it for tonight. I need a place to rest and get out of the weather," he said.

Behind them something roared. Then she heard a loud horn. Logan pulled her off the road, and a huge vehicle hurtled past.

A car. She had seen them before when she'd come to this world, but she had never been this close to one that was moving.

"That could kill you," she whispered.

"Yeah. If you got hit. Which is another reason we need to get off the road."

"Is it against the law to kill with one of those?"

"Of course!"

"But we're not supposed to be walking on the road, are we? So if we got killed, it would be our fault."

"You're still not supposed to kill anyone," he muttered.

They passed several narrow lanes leading to the left and right. Logan kept trudging past them. But when he came to one with what looked like white logs lying on the ground, he stopped. When she looked more closely, she could see they were made of some material that was rolled up with a transparent coating around them.

"Newspapers," Logan said, seeing her eye them. "A lot of them. Which usually means someone is out of town. Away from home," he clarified, then opened a metal box on a short pole and looked inside. "And a bunch of junk mail."

"Junk mail?"

"Advertising circulars."

"Like when a merchant has something to sell, and he wants to let the rich people know?"

"Exactly. Here they pay a government service—the post office—to deliver them."

He closed the box and turned back to her, his expression serious. "I told you about the law and the police. We could borrow the house. But if we go inside, we're breaking the law."

"Like when I took the clothing off the line?" she asked.

"Yeah."

"People just hang it out like that? In the open. Not behind a fence. They're not afraid anybody will take it?"

"Most people around here don't need to steal laundry, so there's no threat in leaving it out. Generally, it's not okay to steal. But when we're naked with no chance to get back to our own clothing, we don't have much choice."

She was still thinking through the whole situation. "And the houses are so far apart," she said. "With no guards."

"They might have a security system, an electronic device that lets the police know if someone's broken in."

"So we can't do it," she said.

Logan gave her a long look. He'd like to leave her where it was safe. He was sure she wouldn't agree. "Let's find out."

They started up the driveway, shoulder to shoulder, the rain turning their clothing soggy. Casting a sidewise glance at her, he noted how the soaked T-shirt was clinging to her skin. Of course, maybe the shirt was an advantage. If a guy was home, he'd focus on her boobs, and Logan could coldcock him.

They rounded a curve, and she caught her breath as she stared at the house. "It's a palace. Only a rich person could live here."

"It's not all that grand," he informed her, then shot her a speculative look. "How long had you been in this world before you found me in the trap?"

"I came a few times," she said defensively.

He didn't bother saying that she hadn't picked up a lot of information. But then, how would she—completely on her own?

He studied the setting. The house was on a wooded lot, and he couldn't see any nearby neighbors.

At the top of the hill, the driveway opened out into an empty parking area in front of a two-car garage.

He walked to the garage. There was one car inside, but the adjoining space was empty. As he watched, a light blinked on in an interior room. He tensed, and Rinna jumped.

Ducking low, he hurried to the window and looked inside. A lamp had come on in what looked like a den, but nobody was in the room. Which suggested that the lamp was on an automatic timer.

But he didn't abandon caution, even when they were both starting to shiver from the cold and wet. Carefully he walked around the perimeter of the house, checking for signs of occupation. Finally, he approached the back door and began looking for a good place to hide a key. It was under a fake rock.

As he inserted it in the lock, Rinna came up beside him. "Why lock the door if anybody can get in?"

"They think nobody will find the key."

She snorted, then followed him inside.

After making sure the house was empty, he took Rinna upstairs and began looking for something to wear besides gym shorts and T-shirts. A man and a woman lived in the house. No children, which was a relief because the idea of a family walking in on what they thought was a burglary made his stomach knot.

Rummaging in closets and drawers, he found suitable clothing for both himself and Rinna. The women's shoes weren't even a bad fit for her.

She looked slightly dazed as he presented her with the booty, then led her to the bathroom.

He stroked his hand up her arm, feeling her cold skin. "You need a hot shower."

"You make the rain hot?"

"No. There's a shower stall in the bathroom. You don't have hot water in your houses?"

"Not unless you heat it over a fire."

He turned on the water, adjusted the temperature, and showed Rinna the soap and shampoo—and how to turn the water off again without getting burned.

As she stood looking at the modern marvel, he pictured himself stepping under the hot spray with her, heating her up in more ways than one. But he knew she wouldn't react the way he wanted, so he left her alone.

Probably she was thinking that he'd walk in on her because she was finished in record time, then scurried into the walk-in closet in the master bedroom to towel off and change into the knit top and pants he'd selected for her. He took his own quick shower. By the time he emerged, she'd gotten her hair almost dry with the towel.

Twenty minutes after they'd entered the house, they went back down to the kitchen, which he saw had been recently remodeled. The cabinets were of warm oak, and all the appliances were sleek stainless steel.

While he checked provisions in the pantry closet and

the refrigerator, Rinna tiptoed across the ceramic tile floor, exclaiming over the equipment.

She tapped a toaster oven that looked like the one Haig had used, only it was plugged into the wall.

"This heats food?"

"Yes." He picked up a bag of bread from the counter, took out a slice, and put it on the rack. He pressed the on button, and the elements heated—then toasted the bread.

Opening the door, he used a fork to pick up the bread, which he offered to her. "Careful, it's hot."

She took it gingerly, then nibbled at the edge. "Do your people like bread this way?"

"I guess it's an acquired taste." He opened the refrigerator, found the butter, and cut off a pat, which he spread on the toast.

She tried it again. "It's good now." She turned back to the refrigerator. "That keeps the butter cold?"

"Uh huh."

"How do they work? And the oven?"

"Don't ask me for a technical explanation." He gestured toward the range. "This is the main cooking appliance. It's connected to natural gas lines, and the refrigerator works by electricity."

He watched her look around uncertainly. Probably she expected the homeowners to come back at any moment. He was pretty sure they wouldn't.

"While you were in the shower, I found a calendar in the upstairs office. The people who live here aren't scheduled to come home for another three days."

"Good," she murmured. Of course, breaking and entering wasn't the only thing bothering him. He and Rinna had started a conversation they needed to finish. So he pulled a can of beef and vegetable soup from the pantry and a hunk of cheddar cheese from the refrigerator. He would have preferred a rare steak, but the soup and cheese would do.

While he worked on the simple meal, he tried to think of how to talk to her about the two of them. He might only have known her for a few days, but he knew she was his life mate. And he wanted her to understand that they belonged together. But he suspected that she didn't see herself belonging to any man.

She watched him cut some chunks of cheese, then heat the soup in a saucepan.

"I should help you, but I'm afraid I'll break something."

"You can help wash up," he said as he carefully poured the soup. "If we clean up very well and put everything away where we found it, the owners might never know we were in here."

"I hope not." She looked around the room. "How long are we staying here?"

"Part of the night. After I get some rest, we can head back to my campsite."

They sat down, and he took a sip of soup. She nibbled on a piece of cheese.

He managed to take a couple more swallows before saying with studied casualness, "You'll feel better when you tell me about Falcone."

CHAPTER THIRTEEN

LOGAN SAW RINNA almost choke on the piece of cheese in her mouth. Deliberately she chewed and swallowed, probably to give herself time to think of what to say.

He wondered where his last line had come from. It hadn't been what he'd planned. He'd wanted to tell her how much he cared. He wanted her to understand that they had bonded. But he'd never practiced in-depth man-woman communications. So he'd stuck to business, and the words he was thinking had popped out of his mouth. Probably from her point of view, he'd issued a challenge.

She folded her hands in her lap before asking, "Why will I feel better?"

He turned his spoon over and examined the back. "Because when you hold bad stuff inside, it eats at you. It affects your mind and your body."

She tipped her head to the side, watching him with unnerving intensity. "You know that from personal experience?"

"Yes." He wanted to look away, but he kept his gaze fixed on her. If he could show her he wasn't afraid to share his painful memories, maybe she would, too.

"From when I was a kid. My father was a hard man who expected that his sons would do what he ordered and not buck his authority. I had a lot of questions about what it meant to be a werewolf, since the only werewolves I knew of were in the Marshall family. And we hid that trait from the rest of the world. But I kept my feelings bottled up because . . ." He shrugged. "Dad never brought up that kind of stuff."

He shifted in his seat and went on. "You said you first changed to another form when you were a little girl. But in my heritage, we don't change to wolf form until we're sexually mature. It's a big deal not just because it means we've turned from boy to man. Unfortunately, half of us died trying to make the change."

She gasped. "Why?"

"Nobody knew. That's the way it was, through all the generations. My cousin Ross's wife, Megan, says it's hormonal. She thinks she can fix the problem for . . . the children. But when I was facing the change, I got more and more upset and angry because I was sure I wasn't going to make it. I thought I was going to die because three of my brothers before me had already bought the farm. It all came to a head one day when I was helping my father clean out the garage of all things. I threw down the armload of fireplace wood I was carrying and started screaming that I wasn't going to do it."

He saw that she was hanging on every word. In truth, he had always been ashamed of the way he'd taken out his fear on his father. Dad hadn't set the rules. He'd just had to live by them the way all the Marshalls had.

But that outburst had truly wiped the slate clean in an odd sort of way. And now Logan seized on the confession as a way to deepen his relationship with Rinna. So he kept talking.

"My father understood why I exploded, and he calmed me down. He said he'd felt the same way when he was facing the change. He told me how sad and angry he was that my brothers had died. For the first time in our lives, we had a really good talk. He explained about our heritage, and he gave me some ways to get through the transformation. Just having that conversation with him—man-to-man—made me feel a lot better. Maybe it even saved my life."

"You chant when you change?"

"Yes."

"What does it mean?"

"It's in an old language. Gaelic. It's asking the gods for special favors. My cousin, Ross, figures some long-ago Druid ancestor asked to become a shape-shifter, and he got his wish. The gift, or the curse, has been passed down through the men in my family."

She nodded, then asked, "What about the girls?"

He hadn't planned to get into so much detail on the Marshall curse. But he answered the question. "For us, the werewolf trait is sex linked. So all of the girl babies died at birth. It's different now. Megan and Ross have a daughter. That's a big milestone for our family."

"So the wives of your brothers and cousins don't have psychic powers?' she asked.

"Actually, a lot of them do. I think we've gravitated toward talented women."

She pushed back her chair and got up, and for a heart-stopping moment, he thought she was going to leave the room. But she only walked to the sink and began playing with the lever that turned on the water, making it run, then stopping it again.

With her back to him, she said, "A free man might take a slave as a concubine. But he would never marry one."

"You were a slave?"

Her shoulders tensed. "Yes."

"And you think I care about that?"

"Don't you?"

"I don't give a damn about where you came from. I care about who you are now and what you've made of yourself. I come from a society where everyone is free to live up to his or her full potential—if they have the drive and the know-how. You obviously did."

"I was living in a cave!"

"Living free in a cave."

She ignored that and went on, "Falcone had no plans to marry me, but he wanted me to bear his children—children that would have powerful talents. He wants to found a dynasty that will rule Sun Acres for generations to come."

"Why is he so sure his children would be talented enough to stay in power?"

"It's not just my psychic abilities that would make the difference. He has great talents—more than most men and women."

He stared at her rigid back, grappling with his surprise. "You're saying Falcone has psychic power?"

"Yes. That's how I met him. At school." She turned back toward the table, leaning her hips against the sink cabinet. "In Sun Acres and in the other cities, they test children for psychic abilities. If you have them, they take you away to a special school, even if you are a slave."

"And when you graduate?"

"It depends. You could tell the future for a rich man. You could run the equipment in the kitchen, like what Haig did. Or you could be used for an assault on another city. It depends on your status and how gifted you are."

"Both men and women go into battle?"

"Usually only the boys."

"And not the highborn children?"

"They might be generals. And in school, they think they are better than the slaves, even when they have less talent. Or sometimes because they know they have less talent, so they do things to us when they think the teachers aren't looking. Probably the teachers know, but they don't interfere unless things get too bad, because they don't want to offend the highborn families."

He tried to imagine it. "Falcone was older than you?"

"Yes. He was a couple of years older." She swallowed. "I never knew how he was going to act. Sometimes he was the leader of the gang who teased me. And sometimes he made them let up on me."

"It sounds like a miserable childhood."

"It was better than what I would have had if they hadn't discovered my potential. At least I had enough to eat, I learned to read and do math, and I didn't have to do menial work." She laughed. "Well, I do. But not for someone else."

Leaning forward, he asked, "Is that what your mother did?"

"No. My mother was the concubine of a rich man named Jandor. He's on the council. He's got a wife and three children, but he always had concubines, too. My mother's life with him was comfortable, and when he got tired of her, he got her a job in . . . in a place where they cut the hair of rich women and do beauty treatments for them. She does fortune-telling there while they get their hair and nails done. Or while they are relaxing after the treatments. She's very good, so the women like her. Jandor was clever about placing her there. He also uses her as a way to get information about what other men on the council are doing. That part can be dangerous, but she does what he asks because he could yank her out of there and send her somewhere much worse."

"I'm sorry."

She shrugged. "That's the way it is in Sun Acres."

"Jandor is your father?"

"Yes. After I was born, he made my mother have an operation so she wouldn't have any more children."

"Christ!"

"It could have been worse."

"And it could have been a lot better. Here nobody owns anyone else."

"But some of your people have better status than others."

"That's always going to be true. The communists tried to change the equation. Their way didn't work, either."

"The communists?"

He laughed. "Let's not go off on them. We should talk about us."

"Us," she repeated uncertainly.

"I want you for my wife," he said. He hadn't intended to say that so soon—but it had come tumbling from his lips.

She stared at him wide-eyed. "You don't even know me."

"I know what's important about you."

"I'm a slave," she said again.

"No. You had the courage to free yourself."

She turned over her arm and pointed to the wavy lines below her elbow. "That's Jandor's mark."

"Not anymore. We can have it removed."

"It's still . . . in my head."

"You'll find out that in this world, it doesn't matter where you came from or what you were. We have a saying here: This is the first day of the rest of your life."

Before he could say more, a ringing sound made her jump in her seat.

"Falcone!"

"No. The telephone."

She looked wildly around, trying to identify the source.

He got up and hurried to the end of the counter, pointing to a phone with a built-in answering machine. "Don't answer it. It's probably someone calling the people who live here."

"I don't know how to answer it."

A woman's voice came on the answering machine. "Bart? Helen? Are you there?" The caller sighed. "I guess not. This is Terry. Give me a jingle when you get in. We have a problem with the duplicate bridge date." The line clicked off.

"What was that?"

"Someone named Terry calling them to talk about bridge."

"To cross a river?"

"No. There are bridges to cross rivers. But she's talking about a card game called bridge. Do you play cards?"

"Rich people do."

"When Terry didn't find Bart and Helen home, she left a message."

"Okay."

He picked up the portable receiver and brought it to her, dialing back to the previous call on the caller ID. "This is the woman who called. Terry Maxwell."

She stared at the readout and nodded, then said, "Why is it buzzing?"

"That's the dial tone. It means you could make a call to someone else. You also pick this up to get a call. You put this part to your ear and speak here." He dialed the weather and held it to her ear.

She listened.

"He says it's going to stop raining. How does he know?"

"We have weather satellites. But don't worry about that right now."

She sighed. "It's complicated."

"You're smart. You'll get the hang of it. And you don't have to do it all at once." He put the receiver back, then stood beside her so he could stroke her shoulder. "Right now we need to keep you safe from Falcone. My family will help us."

"Why?"

"Because you're my . . ." He stopped short.

"What?"

"Life mate. That's what we call the woman who bonds with one of the men in our family."

"Aren't you forgetting something?" she asked, her voice taking on an edge he didn't like.

He pressed his hands against her sides. "I guess I must have, if you're getting ready to tell me about it."

"I think you've noticed that when you . . . when you get close to me, I pull back. How can you have a life mate who can't make love with you?"

"I think we can work on that together."

"Falcone . . ."

He could feel his expression turning fierce. "I'm nothing like him. So don't bring him into the room. This is between you and me. Let's talk about what it feels like when I touch you and kiss you."

He watched her face soften.

"Does it feel good?" he asked.

"Yes. But then I get scared."

"You won't, if I prove to you that I'm not going to grab you or hurt you or do anything you don't like. If you're willing to try."

He held his breath until she answered with a little nod.

"Come back to the table and eat."

She sat down opposite him and picked up her mug, taking a quick sip.

"Tell me about Carfoli," he said because he wanted to switch to a subject that would be less threatening to her. "You said he's in the history books."

She thought for a moment. "In your world . . . did you have the White City?"

He sucked in a sharp breath. "The White City—1893. You mean at the Chicago World's Fair?"

"You know it?"

"Of course. I should have recognized the date when you told me before. I'm a landscape architect. Frederick Law Olmstead planned the city. It was all classical Greek and Roman architecture. And it was full of exhibits from around the world. They had everything from elephants and gondolas to Greek statues and a dancer called Little Egypt. But I never heard of anyone called Carfoli."

She took a sip of soup, then said, "Maybe he didn't show up in your . . . timeline. He had an exhibit where he said he could give people psychic powers. And . . .

he did. People left his building with abilities they never had before."

"How? Why?"

"He had some kind of machine that did it. Nobody knows how it worked. Some historians think it enhanced natural talents that were already present. The important thing is that it was very popular, so a lot of people did it. They went home being able to do things like move objects with their minds. Or see the future. Or view a remote scene. It caused all sorts of disruptions in society. Those without the powers ganged up on those who had them. But the people with the powers fought them off. It was a very bad time. Cities were destroyed. A lot of people were killed. The people who were left gathered together in gated communities for protection. And some of them used the opportunity to take over the leadership. Some of them might be good leaders. But others were ruthless."

He nodded, trying to imagine the chaos. "And if you got psychic abilities from his machine, you could pass them on to your children?" he asked.

"Yes."

"And how did people end up as slaves?"

"Sometimes they were captured in wars with other city-states. Or they might have been the people in the city with no status."

"It's hard to believe. It sounds like Carfoli created chaos. Lucky for us he wasn't in our world."

"Or maybe he was and his machine didn't work."

"Or they ran him out of the fair."

"Or he was a space alien—and he went back where he came from earlier in your world."

"You believe that?"

"Some people do."

They talked about what might have happened over a hundred years ago—and its present effect. Then, while they cleaned up after the meal, she asked him questions about the owners of the house.

"Won't they notice that we took some cheese and soup?" she asked. "And some of their clothing?"

"They probably won't miss the soup, if we take the empty can with us. I'm hoping that they won't remember how much cheese was in the refrigerator. And if we take some of their oldest clothes, maybe they won't look for them for a while. Or they won't remember if they gave them to a charity."

She nodded, and he didn't know whether she understood the reference. But she would, because he was going to teach her everything about this world so she'd feel comfortable here.

More comfortable than in the horrible environment where she'd been born.

FALCONE was lounging on a comfortable couch, sipping a goblet of wine that was spiked with a drug that amplified his mental powers. Few people in Sun Acres had access to the drug, but he could get anything he wanted, if he was willing to pay for it.

His abilities were already strong, of course. Thanks to his native talent and his training. When he'd been a boy, he hadn't wanted to leave his comfortable home. So they'd dragged him kicking and screaming to that school for children with psi powers. But after a few months, he'd silently conceded he was learning something valuable. And he was one of the best students in the school.

Rinna had been stronger, of course.

He clenched his teeth.

Rinna. He wanted her back, and he wanted her to know that she had made a bad mistake by defying him.

So he took another sip of the drink—to give himself the extra power he needed, while he debated his best option: He had Haig in captivity. He could interview the man in the stinking dungeon. Or he could have him brought up to the reception area where they could have a nice civilized chat. After thinking about his own comfort, he decided on the reception area.

He had given orders that the old man should not be injured. Haig was expendable. But until he fulfilled his purpose, he needed to be in shape for a trek across the countryside.

So he still had all his finger and toenails. His face was unbloodied. And nobody had chained him to a post and given him fifty lashes. Nevertheless, he was about to find himself in severe pain if he didn't cooperate.

Falcone gave a clipped order. Three minutes later, two guards hustled the prisoner in, then stepped toward either side of the door—not that the captive was going to bolt.

Falcone evaluated the man, as he sipped his wine. His head was bowed and his shoulders slumped. At the moment he wore filthy animal skins for clothing. They'd have to find him something more appropriate, when he agreed to cooperate.

Finally, Falcone spoke. "Thank you for joining us, Haig. And for leaving a trail my soldiers could follow to your cave."

The old man sucked in a sharp breath but said nothing.

"Answer me when you are spoken to," Falcone demanded. He hadn't used his special powers in a few days. Now it felt good to focus his inner vision and send a jolt of mental pain into the prisoner's brain.

Haig screamed and went down on his knees, clamping his hands over his ears as though that could shut out the pain.

Falcone kept up the invisible dagger of agony for several more seconds, then abruptly stopped, leaving the man rolling on the floor.

He waited until Haig was capable of listening again. "There's more where that came from," he said.

"What do you want?" the man croaked. "Why did you . . . compel me here?"

"You know what I want. I want Rinna. And as you can see, I'm willing to use any method available to get her back."

Haig raised his head. "If you compelled me here, you killed an innocent."

"So what."

"You have no regard for the law."

"I am the law! And you will find Rinna for me."

"If she wasn't in the cave, I don't know where she is."

Falcone gave him a knowing look. "But the bond between you is strong; you can surely find her for me."

"Noooooooo." The denial ended on a wail of pain as Falcone sent Haig another jolt of mental energy.

Falcone looked up, seeking out one of the guards whose features had turned to a mask of fear.

Good. It was an advantage to have men quaking before your power. The guards didn't have to know that the drug in the wine gave Falcone that extra edge.

He leaned back, looking down at the man on the floor. "You can go back to your cell for a while," he said. "And think about your best course of action. I'll have you brought in later so we can talk again."

He gave a signal with a flick of his hand, and the guards rushed forward to haul the prisoner to his feet, then drag him from the room. The mental thunderbolts would leave him weak for a while, but he'd recover.

Of course, too many sessions would lead to permanent brain damage. But Falcone hoped they wouldn't have to go that far. He wanted the old man awake and aware of his betrayal.

"CAN you finish cleaning up while I try to figure out the best route back to my camp?" Logan asked Rinna.

She looked at the dishes in the sink. "Wash these in the soapy water. Then rinse them with the clean water?"

"Yes. And dry them with a dish towel."

He grinned as he watched her turning the lever on the faucet from hot to cold and back again. He could have showed her the dishwasher, but it already had dishes in it. If he washed the whole load, the homeowners would wonder who did it. While she was playing with the water, he went searching for a phone book. He got the address of the house they'd broken into by looking at some of the mail piled up in the mailbox.

He would have liked to use the household computer. But he figured it was better not to turn it on. So he rummaged through the den and found a map of the area, which showed the address in relationship to the campsite.

"Good news," he called out as he came back down the hall.

When he entered the kitchen, he found Rinna standing at the counter, contemplating the toaster oven. She had pulled the plug from the socket and was examining the prongs.

Before he could stop her, she dropped the cord and picked up a fork. His heart leaped into his throat as she poked the tines at the socket from which she'd pulled the plug.

CHAPTER FOURTEEN

"NO!"

Logan leaped across the room, but he was too late. She had already poked the fork into the electrical socket.

He saw a blue spark arc toward her. Screaming, she dropped the implement. And he thanked God for that, because he didn't know what would have happened if she'd managed to hold on to it.

He reached for her, folding her into his arms, feeling her tremble as she laid her head on his shoulder. His arms went around her, and he held her close.

"What was that? What happened?" she gasped, looking dazed.

"You got an electric shock." He reached for her hand and turned it over, finding her fingers were reddened where she'd gripped the fork.

"That's going to blister unless we treat it right away," he growled, turning on the cold water, then thrusting her hand under it.

"Can you stand up okay?"

"Yes," she answered, but she leaned against the sink, her head bowed.

"I'll be right back."

He eased away, opened the freezer, and took out some ice, which he wrapped in a dish towel and pressed against her fingers.

"I'm sorry. I was trying to see how it worked."

"Never poke anything into an electric socket. It could kill you, especially if you're standing in water. Or if you're wet." The advice came out more sharply than he'd intended.

She gave him a wounded look. "Why do they have it, if it's dangerous?"

"Because they want the convenience. And children are taught never to do what you just did."

"I guess I'm stupid," she said in a small voice.

He turned her toward him, his fingers digging into her shoulders. "Of course not. You're inquisitive. Which means you're smart, in case you haven't figured that out. But you don't know enough about this place. Just like I didn't know enough about your world to stay out of danger. Ten minutes out of the cave, and I almost got caught by slavers."

She pulled away from him, and he wished he had stayed in the room with her. But he hadn't realized the kind of trouble she could get into.

"We should rest for a while, and then leave around four in the morning. We'll travel as wolves. I'll set the timer on the stove, so we can get up in time. Hopefully my car and money are still where I left them."

"You drive one of those things . . . a car?"

"Most people do. You'll learn."

She looked doubtful, but he was sure that she'd change

her mind. Getting a driver's license would be more of a problem. They'd have to get a false identity for her. But maybe Ross could help with that.

He knew he was getting ahead of himself once again. They had to make sure Falcone wasn't a threat before they could settle down to any kind of normal life. But he couldn't stop himself from making plans for the future.

"Let me see your hand."

She unwrapped the towel, and he saw that he'd prevented her fingers from blistering. "It looks pretty good. But keep the ice on it for a while."

"Okay," she said in a small voice.

"Don't beat yourself up over it."

"I keep wondering what else I'm going to do."

"Nothing!" An idea struck him, and he walked across the kitchen. "You can find out more about our world from television."

"What is it?"

"Moving pictures that companies send through the air."

She gave him a doubtful look.

"Sit down."

"Why?"

"It might startle you. Some people are startled because it's so bad." He laughed.

"That's a joke I don't get," she said, as she dropped into the nearest chair.

"You will. But maybe not right away."

He picked up a remote and pointed it toward the small television on the kitchen counter.

When the picture sprang to life, Rinna gasped.

"It's okay. It's normal here." He peered at the screen. It was an MTV video.

"What are they doing?"

"Dancing. I hope. Let me find you something you'll like better."

He pushed the up button on the remote and found a decorating show where a designer had swooped into a couple's life to resolve the differences between her taste and his.

Rinna stared at the picture as though he'd opened up a window into another universe, which, in a way, he had.

She looked from the screen to the device in his hand. "What's that?"

"A remote. Or as my nephew calls it, a turner. It changes the channel. Changes the sound level." He demonstrated, then put the remote on the coffee table. "I'll be back. I need to get some stuff."

He wanted to sleep downstairs, in case they had to make a quick getaway, so he went to gather blankets, which he spread out in the family room.

When he came back, he saw that Rinna had changed the channel.

Now her breath was shallow as she watched a drama. Moving closer, he saw that it was a cop show, with a hostage situation.

"Shit!"

Her head jerked toward him. "What?"

"That's too violent for you."

Ignoring the comment, she gestured toward the screen. "The man is going to kill that woman," she breathed. "He wants them to give him an airplane."

"It's just a story. A cop show. It's not real."

"But it must happen in real life, or they wouldn't have gotten the idea."

"Not often."

"Like people don't often rob stores?"

"People watch police shows because they're dramatic," he said, wishing the world were a safer place, for Rinna's sake.

"What's an airplane?"

"A car that flies," he snapped as he took the remote away from her and searched the channels. Apparently she read his body language because she didn't ask any more questions about the hostage situation.

He found an *I Love Lucy* rerun. The one where Ricky and Fred try to be housewives and burn the pattern of an iron on their shirts—among other disasters.

"Men want to act like women here?" Rinna asked when he came back from making up a bed on the rug. "They want to stay home and do the housework?"

He laughed. "Not usually. It's just a joke."

"You have dramas and jokes."

"Yes. Comedies. And reality shows where people eat . . . worms."

She grimaced. "Why?"

"For money. And to show they have guts."

"Oh." She shook her head, then looked up and saw that he had made a bed on the floor near the fireplace.

"I want to sleep down here. So we can make a quick getaway—if we have to. It's not a real bed, but it's probably more comfortable than the cave," he said, as he started walking around the kitchen, wiping all the hard surfaces.

"What are you doing?" she asked.

"Wiping away our fingerprints."

She walked to a kitchen counter and stared. "I can't see them."

"But the cops can use a special powder. So we have to wipe them up."

"Okay." She helped, and when they'd finished the first floor, he wiped down the bathroom and the drawers where he'd gotten clothing.

When he came back, Rinna was standing at the side of the room, eyeing the blankets and pillows.

She looked up as he approached, her expression uncertain. "You're planning to sleep next to me?"

"I'd like to."

"Just sleep?"

"Well, I was hoping for a little more," he admitted. "You can decide how much."

He saw her swallow. Making himself busy, he turned off the TV, then the lamp, leaving the hall light on so that it provided some low light.

After kicking off his shoes, he lay down with his clothes on, his breathing shallow as he watched her think about her next move. Aware of her tension, he stacked his hands behind his head, trying to look as casual as possible.

When she sat down gingerly on the edge of the blanket, he made no move to reach for her.

In a conversational voice, he said, "You told me it felt good when I kissed you and touched you. I was hoping you might do that to me."

"What do you mean?"

"Turn the tables. See how it feels to be the one in charge."

He lay without moving, hoping she'd accept the invitation. And when she moved closer, he grinned at her.

"I won't move my hands," he promised. "You're free to do anything you want—or not."

She looked like she didn't quite believe him.

"You won't reach for me?"

"Cross my heart and hope to die."

She made a small sound. "We say that!"

"Something we have in common."

She bent her head, and he saw her looking at his lips. He closed his eyes, waiting, struggling to keep his breathing even.

When she leaned over and gently brushed her mouth against his, he made a sound of encouragement. She moved her head back and forth, her lips butterfly light.

"I'm not very . . . experienced," she whispered.

"Just do what feels good to you."

"How do I know it will feel good to you?"

"Because that's the beauty of it. The things you like doing, I'll like, too."

She pressed her lips more firmly against his. Then drew back so she could stroke her tongue along the seam. When he opened for her, she slid her tongue just inside, caressing the inside of his lips. He felt his breath quicken, felt his body harden.

It took every ounce of willpower he possessed not to reach for her and pull her body against his, but he kept his hands where they were behind his head.

He heard her breathing accelerate as she sucked on his lower lip, then left his mouth to string kisses over his cheek and jaw, and he was glad he'd shaved while he was upstairs.

"What should I do now?" she whispered.

He cleared his throat. "Well, I've been lying here hoping you'd roll up my shirt so you can play with the hair on my chest and my nipples. Or the hair under my arms. That would feel good, too."

"It would?"

"Oh yeah."

He felt her fingers trembling a little as she carefully rolled up his shirt, her hands stroking his chest as she worked. She combed her fingers through the dark, crisp hairs she found there.

"That's nice," he murmured. And when her fingers glided over his nipples, then plucked gently at them, he heard a sound of appreciation rise in his throat.

"You like that?"

"Yes."

She leaned over, touching one nipple with her tongue before sucking it into her mouth, and he clenched his fingers so as not to break his promise and pull her down on top of him.

Raising her head, she stared down at him. "It makes me . . . hot and tingly to do that."

"Me, too. When you touch me like that, it makes me want to do the same things to you. And I know you want that, too. I can see your nipples standing out against the front of your shirt. They're tight and throbbing, aren't they?"

When she didn't answer, he went on. "Don't be afraid of the good feelings. Don't be afraid of what you want to do with me. When a man and a woman care about each other, making love feels very, very good."

"It already feels good. But . . ." She lowered her eyes, focusing on the lower part of his body where an erection strained behind the fly of his jeans. "I made you . . ."

"Hard," he finished. "Because of what you were doing."

Her shoulders tensed. "And now you want to put that thing inside me, don't you?"

"There's no use lying about it. You know I want you. But my penis, that 'thing' as you call it, doesn't control me. I wouldn't want to be inside you unless that was what you wanted, too."

She was staring into the distance with unfocused

eyes, and he didn't know if she'd heard him or not. "You could hurt me now," she whispered.

"But I won't. Never." He had told her to leave Falcone out of the conversation, but he heard himself say, "I need to ask you something. Did Falcone force himself on you more than once?"

"Only once. I . . . ran away after that."

He breathed out a sign. "Good." Clenching his hands behind his head, he said, "Did you know that the first time a woman has intercourse, it's likely to hurt? No matter if she wanted to do it or not. There's a membrane that has to break the first time. And usually that hurts."

He saw a flush spread across her cheeks. "I . . . didn't know. Nobody told me. I thought every time would be like that."

"No. The next time you do it, it will be because you want to. And it will feel good."

She looked like she wanted to believe him.

"Less talk and more action," he said.

She answered with a nervous laugh. "What should I do?"

"You want suggestions?"

"Yes."

He swallowed, wondering how far she trusted him. "I'd love it if you took off your shirt, so I could see your beautiful breasts. And I'd love it if you'd lean over and brush them against my chest."

Her breath caught. "You could grab me."

"I won't. I'll keep my hands behind my head . . ." He laughed. "Even if it kills me."

She hesitated for a long moment, staring off into space. He watched her take her bottom lip between her teeth.

"Don't do it if it scares you."

"I want to . . . be close to you."

"Good. That's all I want from you. As close as you want. When you want. And how you want."

She focused on his face, watching him carefully as she fingered the button at the top of her shirt, then slipped it open. She worked her way down the placket and sat with the front hanging open.

He barely breathed, waiting.

Finally, in one quick motion, she pulled the shirt off.

Her breath was rapid now, and she looked like she was getting ready to leap away from him.

He tried to look relaxed when every muscle in his body was rigid with need.

"You are so beautiful," he whispered.

"Am I?"

"Oh yeah. Your breasts are perfect. And I love the way your nipples look. All puckered. It makes me feel powerful to know I did that without even touching you."

She swallowed and gave a small nod.

"If you want to, I'd love to feel them against my chest."

She hesitated, and he knew that she might not be able to go any further. Not tonight.

Keeping her eyes on him, she slowly leaned over so that she could brush her nipples against his chest, the hardened tips like fire against his skin.

"Lord, that's good," he gasped out and fought to keep his hands where they were.

She made a small whimpering sound, increasing the pressure a little, driving him insane with need. But he didn't move a muscle, only let her do what she wanted. At her own speed.

She kissed his cheek, them moved back a little, pressing her hand to his chest. "Your heart is pounding."

"Yes."

"You want . . ."

"Everything a man and woman can give each other," he answered. "But not until you're ready."

She dragged in a shaky breath.

He knew he shouldn't press his luck, but he heard another request tumble from his lips.

"You could lie on top of me. With our pants still on. I'd like that, if you want to do it. It would feel good—to both of us."

She looked down at his swollen cock, standing out against the fabric of his slacks.

He held his breath, waiting to see how much she trusted him. But as he lay there in the semidarkness looking at her, he heard something outside—the sound of voices.

He went rigid.

Rinna tensed, then leaned away from him and snatched a kitchen knife from under the edge of the blanket.

Gripping the weapon in her hand she climbed to her feet, her body coiled in a defensive crouch.

Logan stared at the knife. "Put that away."

"We have to fight."

"We're the ones trespassing here. We don't have the right to kill anyone." Before he could stop himself, he asked, "Were you going to slit my throat if I did something in bed that you didn't like?"

She gulped. "I . . . I had to know I was safe . . ."

They'd have to discuss that later. Meanwhile, they had to get out of the house.

"Run upstairs," he told her. "Open a window and fly away. But wipe your prints off. I'll get out down here and meet you in the woods. Look for a wolf," he added with a rough laugh.

So much for making sure nobody knew they'd been here, he thought as she dashed for the stairs, her steps a lot lighter than his would have been.

He watched her disappear down the hall as he considered his options—and who might be outside. The homeowners coming home early? A neighbor who had seen someone in the house? The police?

The cops would be armed. Would the neighbors or the homeowners?

He hoped not, because if push came to shove, he would defend himself. But he'd rather not get into anything heavy.

He made a split-second decision. A wolf couldn't open the door, and if they closed it behind them, he was trapped. But a wolf might look like a German shepherd. And maybe they wouldn't shoot at a cowering animal.

Hoping that Rinna was already out the window, he tore off his clothing and tossed the shirt and pants into the corner.

Then he walked to the wall beside the doorway where he'd have the most shelter, already saying the words of transformation, pushing past the change as rapidly as he could.

Before he was finished, he heard footsteps coming down the hall.

"I don't see anything," a man called out.

It sounded like the homeowner. Didn't he have sense enough to wait for the cops if he thought something was wrong?

The man clattered into the room. He was short and stocky with a fringe of dark hair around his bald head. Logan cowered back like he was only a frightened dog.

"Jesus Christ," the guy exclaimed. "A dog got in here."

Logan fought the urge to attack. He could take this

guy so easily. But the man was an innocent bystander who had come home to find a dog in his house. So Logan played the part he'd assigned himself, ducking his head submissively and edging toward the side of the room, hoping he could make a break for it.

"Good doggie," the man said.

The woman rounded the corner. She was taller than her husband, with red hair and a big bust. Both of them looked to be in their midfifties. Too bad they'd decided to come home early.

As the lady of the house took in the scene, she gasped. "That's no dog; it's a wolf. Shoot it, Bart. Shoot it."

Logan felt his heart start to pound.

The guy moved toward a drawer in an end table that Logan hadn't searched. When the man drew out a gun, Logan howled, then turned and ran down the hall.

Unfortunately, he'd only run into a trap. The door was closed, and he stopped short. He could turn and attack. Or he could run up the stairs.

He chose to run.

At the top of the stairs he turned right, dashed into a bedroom, and found the window closed. It wasn't the room Rinna had used as her escape route.

Downstairs, he could hear the woman shouting out advice. "Stay away from it. It could be rabid."

"What do you expect me to do?"

"Call the police."

He didn't hear the end of the conversation because he was already out of the room and into another. To his vast relief, one of the windows gaped open.

Sticking his head out, he saw that it opened onto the front porch. When he climbed out, he almost lost his footing.

Above him he could see a white bird circling the house.

Rinna. She came down low, then landed a few feet away.

He wanted to shout at her to get away. But he couldn't talk. All he could do was say the words of transformation in his head.

In the distance he heard a siren. The cops were already on their way.

He pushed a curse out of his mind and focused on the chant. He could see flashing red and blue lights by the time he made it to human form. The pain of changing quickly twice in rapid succession made his head spin, but he knew he didn't have much time.

Rinna hovered around him, her wings frantically beating the air as though she could somehow help him.

With a grimace, he stumbled toward the edge of the roof, then hung by his hands and let himself fall. He hit some bushes, scratching his legs and his ass. Ignoring the scraped skin, he staggered away from the house.

A car door slammed.

"What the hell?" somebody shouted.

Either the cops or the homeowner must have seen a naked man dashing for the woods. Maybe they thought the house had been invaded by a druggie and his dog.

Behind him he heard the beating of wings, then a man's voice rang out, his voice sharp and frightened.

"Get the hell off me. Get off!"

And Logan knew the bird had attacked.

CHAPTER FIFTEEN

LOGAN STOPPED SHORT and started to turn, until the bird came flapping toward him, squawking. Knowing that he was making them both a target, he doubled over, feeling like he had a bull's-eye on his ass as he pounded toward the woods, gritting his teeth as stones dug into his feet.

He chanted as he ran. He'd never changed on the run. And he had never transformed from man to wolf to man and back again so many times in such a short period.

The process was always painful. But tonight his muscles and ligaments screamed in protest. Jaw clenched, he ignored the agony because he knew he couldn't outrun the cops if he remained in human form. And the next time the bird attacked, she could get shot.

Praying that they couldn't see him change in the darkness under the trees, he kept going, hitting the ground on all fours and stumbling before he got his footing again.

Somehow he kept running, and then there was another wolf keeping pace with him, a white wolf.

He stopped, dragging in air, fighting the pain in his side. Rinna came up beside him, nuzzling her muzzle against his face. He turned his head and licked her, wishing he could talk.

He wanted to tell her how glad he was that she was there, and at the same time, he wanted to scream at her that she'd taken a damn stupid chance by flying at the cops.

Probably it was better that he couldn't berate her, because he knew she was defending her mate—even if she didn't understand that yet.

After a few minutes' rest he started moving again, not quite so fast, pacing himself. He was damn glad he'd looked at the map earlier. When they came out on the road, he turned left, trotting along the shoulder until he came to a cross street.

He recognized the name and turned right, heading for the patch of woods where he'd left his tent.

Once Rinna left his side, and he wondered where she was going. She came back with a rabbit in her mouth, which she dropped at his feet.

He might have been embarrassed to tear the animal apart in front of her. But he needed the nourishment. So he ate what she offered, then cleaned his mouth at a stream.

He had a good sense of direction. He only got turned around a few times.

Rinna stayed beside him, stopping when he had to rest, pressing her flank against his and waiting until he could travel again.

Finally he came out into the small clearing where

he'd left the tent. To his vast relief, it was still there. He crawled inside and threw himself on the sleeping bag. When he thought he was strong enough to take the pain, he changed once more, gasping as he resumed his human form. After he could move, he pulled on jeans and a shirt before opening up the sleeping bag so Rinna would have some place to lie, if she dared to rest beside him.

She stuck her head inside the tent, and he saw that she had changed, too.

"Are you all right?" she asked, her voice urgent.

"Yes. But I need to sleep."

"I'll stand guard. Do you have something I can wear?"

He handed her sweatpants and a button-down shirt before falling back onto the sleeping bag.

RINNA had been near this place before, when she'd found Logan in the trap, but now it felt like alien territory. She'd been so naive when she'd come through the portal, thinking she could get along in this world. She'd found out how wrong she was. All you had to do was poke something into a little hole where the electricity came out and you could get killed.

She looked down at Logan. He must have thought it was safe to sleep. But what if he was wrong? What if someone came along and attacked them with that weapon—a gun? Was it all right to fight them off? Kill them?

She didn't know the rules, and the frustration bubbled inside her. That and other frustrations.

Back at that house, she'd gotten close to him—physically close. And it had felt so good to do those things. She wanted more of that with him. But she was still too afraid.

She clenched her fists. She didn't want to run away from the feelings building inside her. But she didn't know if she could let him . . . She cut off the thought. All she had to do right now was keep him safe until he woke and hope she didn't make any mistakes.

And what if Falcone's soldiers came along? That possibility had her fighting panic.

He had used the trap and found her once. But he wouldn't risk it again, she told herself, not when he might catch the wrong shape-shifter. But there was still Haig. He must have given away the secret of the cave. What else would he do under Falcone's orders?

She tried to put Haig out of her mind, as she looked through the equipment Logan had brought, handling each item carefully. He had a flashlight. Was it valuable here, or just ordinary? And what about the folding knife with a bunch of other funny parts that opened up? And he had a lot of supplies. Like in the convenience store. They represented a fortune back home. But probably not here.

He also had boxes with plants that he'd dug up. For his job, she supposed. He was like the gardeners who worked for rich men. But she suspected that he was paid well for the service.

After she'd inspected the things in the camp, she climbed back inside the tent and lay down next to him.

It flashed through her mind that he could wake up and grab her. Although she resolutely pushed that idea away, she took a knife with her when she lay down beside him. Not to protect herself from him, she assured herself—but in case someone came along who might try to hurt them.

She had hours to think—about Logan. About what he wanted from her. And what she dared to want from him. Finally, after a long time, he stirred. Still when she saw his eyes blink open, she felt her insides clench.

He stared toward the flap at the front of the tent, then turned his head and looked at her.

"You can put the knife down. I'm not going to attack you."

"How do you know I have a knife?"

"Intuition."

"I wanted to be prepared if someone came."

He dragged in a breath and let it out. "I'd like to say you don't need to carry a weapon in this world. But I'm not sure it's true anymore."

When she answered with a little shrug, he changed the subject. "What time is it?"

"Afternoon."

"I was . . ."

"Exhausted."

"I was going to say I was no help for the past few hours."

"Everything's fine."

"Good."

She had been waiting to ask him questions about what had happened.

"Those people back at the house; they found a wolf in their . . . family room?"

"Yeah."

"And then?"

"The nice lady wanted to shoot me."

She dragged in a shuddering breath, then let it ease out of her lungs. "Shoot you. Like the man at the convenience store?"

"Yeah. Only she was defending her home, not robbing someone." He sighed. "We've got too many guns in this world. Or . . . too many people using them."

"I was scared when you didn't come out—for you," she whispered.

"I was scared—for you when I saw you flapping around that cop."

She lifted one shoulder. "I was trying to distract him."

"You could have gotten hurt."

He rolled toward her, lifting a hand to stroke her cheek. "I'm sorry. It was pretty hairy back there."

She tried to figure out what he meant. "Hairy?"

"Dangerous. Frightening. I guess we shouldn't have stayed in that house."

"You thought it was safe, and you needed to rest."

"Bad judgment. But the emergency's over."

He gave her a long look, then his gaze drifted to her lips. "Rinna, let me kiss you. Just kiss you."

He had kissed her before and shown her he wasn't going to hurt her. She was still worried, but she wanted to feel his lips on hers, so she gave a tiny nod.

When he brought his mouth to hers, she sensed that he was trying to keep the contact light and nonthreatening. But deep emotions flowed through the kiss. Emotions that made her heart swell.

When he lifted his head, his eyes were very clear and as bright as new coins. "I love you," he said in a thick voice.

Shocked, she reared back. "You don't have to say that!"

"Right. I don't have to. But it's true," he growled. "And don't give me any of that slavery crap. I don't care who your mother and father were. I fell in love with the warrior woman you are. Well, warrior woman, wolf, and bird of prey," he amended, as he kept his gaze firmly on her.

When she couldn't speak around the lump in her throat, he added, "It's going to work out okay."

With all her heart, she wanted to believe that. But she had to be realistic. "We're so different."

"No. We're a lot alike."

"Even if that's true, it doesn't matter. Unless we can . . ." She stopped and started again. "Unless we can neutralize Falcone."

He studied her face, and she wanted to look away. But she kept her gaze steady.

"You were going to say . . . 'kill,' weren't you?"

Wondering what he would think of her, she answered, "Yes."

"Don't worry about the sentiment. I know he's worth killing. Not just for what he did to you. It sounds like he's bad for Sun Acres."

Again, she forced herself to be brutally honest. "Maybe not. The city needs a strong leader. If not him, then some other man with power who can protect them from invasion."

"You have a cynical view of the world."

"A realistic view," she corrected. "Even the nobles accept limits on their freedom in exchange for protection."

"How did there get to be nobles? There weren't any around here in 1893, were there?"

"I think the rich people . . ." She shrugged. "I think they gave themselves that title."

He snorted. "So much for the American experiment of equality. Do they have other titles? Like 'duke' or 'lord' or anything?"

"I never heard anything but 'sir' and 'noble.' "

"Well, maybe one of them is strong enough to protect Sun Acres. Because I plan on wiping Falcone off the face of the earth."

Those were brave words. She wondered if they were realistic.

"He's powerful," she warned. "Not just psychic power. Because he's been successful, he has a lot of support."

"But you know his weaknesses."

"And he knows mine." She gulped. While she'd lain beside Logan, she'd thought of what else she needed to tell him. "He did something to me . . . something besides . . ." She had thought she could say it, but the words simply stopped.

"You don't have to tell me anything you don't want to talk about."

She looked down at her hands and spoke rapidly, before she could lose her nerve. "In school they discovered I had a talent few people possess. It was a . . . big event. I was being chased by a bunch of the older boys, and I made them stop and turn around. The teacher saw it, and she realized I could . . . influence people. Put suggestions into their mind, and they'd do it. They thought it would be an asset to the city. But Falcone was afraid of that. He and some of the powerful men he gathers around him sent a block into my mind. When I try to use that power now . . . it hurts."

"Christ!"

"I can use it a little. I used it that first night when you were in the trap. I got you to change."

"Yes! I remember."

"If he did that to me, he could do other things. That was why I ran away, that and . . . the other." She raised her head. "I mean his taking me to his bed and . . . forcing me to serve him."

"Raping you!"

"A slave woman never uses that word."

He gritted his teeth, then spoke very slowly and distinctly. "Forget about the word 'slave.' It will never apply to you again. In this world, you are free to be anything you want."

She licked her lips. "It's hard to change a lifetime of thinking—so quickly."

"I think I can help you change your vision of who you are." He searched her eyes. "If you let me."

"I want to," she answered in a small voice. "But I don't know how."

"You can free yourself. Starting with what he did to you in bed. I know you've had a long time to think about it. But you and I can make the memory into something that doesn't rule your life."

She hardly believed him. Yet he looked at her with such hope that she knew she had to try—for him as much as for herself.

He must have seen agreement in her eyes, because he went on. "He made it so you're afraid to trust another man. But I'm nothing like him. And I'd like to prove it to you. Will you trust me enough to let me touch you and kiss you—just that? Just things that feel good to you—nothing more."

She licked suddenly dry lips. "I want to. The whole time you were sleeping, I was thinking how much I wanted to be with you again."

"Good. At the house, I asked you to be in charge of what we were doing."

She looked uncertain.

"I want to do things that will please you. But you'll

still be in charge, because if I do something you don't like, tell me, and I'll stop."

When she took her bottom lip between her teeth, he said, "All you have to do is tell me, and I'll follow your orders." He reached for her hand and pressed his fingers over hers. "Do you believe that?"

"I think so," she answered, because she wanted it to be true. So much.

He rolled to his side, looking down at her, stroking a lock of dark hair back from her face.

"You are so beautiful."

"I'm not!"

He laughed. "I think you're no judge of women's looks. So don't argue with me about it."

He leaned down to nuzzle his face against her cheek, her neck, turning his head so that he could nibble at her jaw, then her collarbone.

"I can feel your tension," he whispered. "I know you're afraid, and I know you're very brave to stay with me—in bed."

"I'm not brave."

"Of course you are! You're brave enough to let me change your tension to something good."

She hung on his words, mesmerized by his voice. "How do you know so much about this?"

He laughed. "Reading women's magazines in the doctor's office."

"What?"

"This world is full of books and magazines with advice for women. Love advice."

He kept stroking her lightly as he talked, sliding his hand through her hair and over her cheek, then tracing the shape of her lips.

"All the men in my family are married to strong,

sexy women. I envied them. And I wondered if I would ever find someone of my own. Someone to equal their wives. Now I know I have. And I know that we're going to be very, very good together."

He stroked his fingers down her arms, then drew them back to her shoulders, playing with her collarbone before letting his fingers drift to the tops of her breasts, watching her face.

She felt emotions warring inside her.

"What if it all goes wrong? What if I disappoint you?"

"You won't disappoint me. Right now, I just want to make you feel good."

His voice lulled her, calmed her, yet she couldn't quite believe what he was saying. "That's all?"

"Well . . . I want to touch you more intimately. If you'll let me, I can show you how much pleasure a woman can feel."

"It already feels wonderful," she whispered.

"How?"

She felt her cheeks heat. "It's hard to talk about it."

"I know. But I'd like to know if we're on the right track."

CHAPTER SIXTEEN

RINNA LICKED HER dry lips, watching Logan follow the small movement. "It feels . . . like a buzzing in my body."

"I'd like to show you where it leads."

She had never known she could feel words. But the way he said it was like a caress against her skin. Before she could stop herself, she added more. "And . . . and it feels like the skin is too tight across my breasts."

"Good." He angled his mouth so that he could kiss her. This time the kiss was so tender that she felt her heart melting.

"Rinna. I won't hurt you. Ever."

She still couldn't quite believe him, but her body craved more of what he offered, and she was helpless to turn away.

With tender care, he kissed the line of her jaw, the side of her neck, the small triangle of flesh at the opening of her collar.

Her heart was pounding, and her head was spinning—

from the sensations he created and from the knowledge that she was taking the biggest risk of her life.

Carefully, he unbuttoned the top button of the shirt she wore, then lightly kissed the skin he exposed. His lips sent a shiver through her.

"Don't be afraid of me."

"I'm not," she told him, willing it to be true.

"Some men take their pleasure from a woman and don't care about giving any of that pleasure back. Or they don't know how. I've always thought that was criminal."

He opened another button, then another. When she looked down, she could see the inner curve of her breasts where the front of the shirt no longer closed.

Slowly, giving her time to absorb what he was doing, stopping to talk to her and kiss her, he stroked those curves, first one side and then the other.

She closed her eyes and clenched her hands, ordering herself not to leap away.

He kept up the stroking, and she felt her nipples tighten until they became hard points of sensation.

He touched them through the shirt, rubbing back and forth across each crest.

"Oh!"

"You like that?"

"Yes," she breathed out.

"It feels even better skin to skin. Like when you brushed your breasts against me. Can I show you?"

She hesitated for a moment, then gave a small nod. He slipped his hand under the shirt, finding one tight point, rubbing it, then taking it between his thumb and finger and squeezing gently.

When he pushed the fabric aside and circled the other aching bud with his tongue, she began to tremble.

"Are you all right?"

"Yes. I didn't know anything could feel that good."

"There's a lot more. We're just getting started." He kissed her lightly, then drew back. "But it only works if you feel comfortable with me. Will it scare you if I take off my shirt?"

"I . . ." She honestly didn't know.

Reaching for the hem of his T-shirt, he pulled it off. The top part of him was naked. When she caught her breath, he took her hand and brought it to his lips, kissing the hollow of her palm, then nibbling at her knuckles.

She turned her hand, stroking his lips with her finger.

"That's nice."

She focused on his face, because she had to keep reminding herself that this was Logan—and he had said he would take care of her. And this wasn't so different from the night before when she had rolled up his shirt.

Still, her heart was hammering inside her chest as he pushed her shirt aside, then gathered her to him, moving her body so that he slid her nipples against the roughened hair of his chest.

Like last night, she reminded herself, only now he was the one doing it.

"That feels wonderful," he told her, his voice shaky, and she knew it was affecting him as much as it affected her. That helped steady her. Dropping her gaze, she looked down his body, seeing the bulge in his pants, and a dart of worry pierced her.

"Yeah, this is turning me on."

She gulped. "You want to do it to me."

"Of course. But, like I said, that part of my body doesn't rule me."

"I've heard women talking . . ."

He made a scoffing noise. "Don't believe all the crap

about uncontrolled lust. I'll keep my pants on," he said, like last night. "We're doing this for you, just so you can find out how much you like being with me." He gave her a long look. "Everything's still all right?"

She nodded, tensing a little as he shifted position again. But he only reached down to stroke her ankle, then massage her arch, before taking each of her toes in his fingers and twisting them. "Does that feel good?" he asked.

"Yes," she breathed.

He stroked her ankle again, then pressed his fingers over her pants leg and slid his hand upward, playing with her knee then drifting to her thigh, but never higher.

The technique was effective, because it made her want more.

One hand returned to her breasts, caressing one and then the other, making her nipples ache so that she arched into the caress, silently begging for more.

"You like that?"

She moved her legs restlessly. His hand on her thigh slid upward, pressing between her legs where sensation pulsed. "You feel it here, too?"

She could only answer with an inarticulate sound.

His slow, careful touches and the increasing intimacy were overwhelming her senses, turning her molten with pleasure she had never known before.

It was more than she could have imagined, yet she wanted more still. And when he pressed harder against the aching spot between her legs, she writhed under his touch.

"I want you to feel all the pleasure I can give you."

Slowly he slipped his fingers inside the waistband of her pants, pressing over her mound, combing his fingers through the crinkly hairs then dipping lower.

When she tensed, he waited, teasing one nipple with his tongue and teeth, until she cried out and twisted against him.

She had never imagined asking for this. She couldn't ask, not with words. But he seemed to understand what she wanted. The hand under her pants dipped lower. He stroked her with two fingers, reaching down to glide and press against her most intimate flesh while he lowered his mouth to her breast again, sucking her nipple into his mouth.

The sensations reinforced each other, building so that she teetered on the brink between pleasure and frustration, feeling her body questing urgently for something she didn't know how to name.

There was no thought of stopping him when he slipped his fingers inside her, then up to that throbbing spot that ached with need.

"Just let go. Fly with it. Just let yourself feel how good it can be," he whispered, holding her close as he guided her into a world where need wiped away fear.

He was right. She felt like she was flying away from the earth—as free as her white bird form, her hips rising and falling as she struggled to increase the wonderful sensations his fingers were drawing from her.

As if he sensed what she needed, he changed the angle of his hand, pressing harder and driving her pleasure up and up until he pushed her into a high air current where only heat and light existed.

Crying out his name, she clung to him as wave after wave of ecstasy radiated from the place where his fingers stroked between her legs. The sensations crashed over her, through her, leaving her limp and shaken.

She had arched off the sleeping bag. He lowered her down again gently, kissing her brow, smoothing her damp hair back from her face. And when her eyes blinked open, she found he was smiling at her.

"That was so beautiful," he whispered.

She could only stare at him, marveling at the explosion that had taken her away from the world.

"What happened?"

"You reached sexual climax."

"I didn't know there was . . . anything like that for a woman."

"I guessed that." He gathered her to him, kissed her gently, and she snuggled against him.

"Don't the women in your world have any fun in bed?"

"I think some do." She swallowed hard. "I think maybe . . . maybe in school they gave us something so we wouldn't."

"A nasty trick to play on you. Why would they do that?"

"This would have been distracting."

"Oh, yeah."

She sensed that his body was still humming with tension—the same tension she had felt before he'd brought her to that vivid peak of satisfaction.

She drew back, her gaze going to the slacks he still wore, seeing the rigid shaft of flesh straining behind his zipper. Raising her eyes, she searched his face. "You did that for me, and you didn't take anything for yourself."

"Yes. I wanted to love you, any way I could."

The next step was overwhelming, but she took it anyway. "I want you to feel what I felt."

He kissed her cheek, sifted his fingers through her hair. "We can save the rest for another time."

"I want to do it now. I want to give you as much pleasure as you gave me—if you'll let me." Pretending more boldness than she felt, she reached between them, pressing her hand over him, moving her palm and fingers, her eyes still on his face.

"Oh, Lord, Rinna," he gasped, his hips arching toward her, and she knew he had banked his own urgency to please her.

"Show me how . . . Show me what feels as good to you as what you did for me."

"You're sure?"

She wasn't, of course. But she wasn't going to let herself back away. Still she had to stifle a gasp as he pulled off his pants, and she saw his penis was hard and red.

Unconfined by his clothing, it sprang away from his body, and as she watched, it seemed to move on its own.

She clenched her fists as she stared at the part of his body that he could use as a weapon.

To her eyes, it was enormous, with the swollen head a good deal wider across than the shaft.

He pressed his palms against the sleeping bag. "You're still the one in control," he said, his voice gritty.

She nodded but some part of her mind was shocked and amazed that she was still lying in the tent beside him. Her throat had turned so dry that she could hardly swallow. But somehow she stayed where she was. And when she dared to look at more than that one part of him, she saw that he was still lying with his palms pressed against the sleeping bag.

"That frightens you," he said in a hoarse voice.

She moistened her lips. "Yes."

"Well, we can put it back in my pants."

"No."

"Okay, then. Anything you want to do to me will feel wonderful."

"You trust me that much?"

"Yes."

She had learned that a man could say one thing and mean another. But Logan lay staring up at her with a look of total confidence in his eyes. She knew he had made himself vulnerable to her as few men would dare to do, and that was enough to tighten her throat muscles.

"What should I do?" she whispered.

"That's up to you," he said, his fingers clenching the sleeping bag.

She pressed her hand to his flat stomach, feeling the muscles jump. Then she stroked his chest, playing with his nipples the way he had played with hers, gratified by his response.

It took a few moments before she could slide her hand lower again, over the flat plane of his belly, threading her fingers through the thatch of dark hair, working her way toward the base of his penis. Tentatively, she stroked one finger up the length of the hardened flesh, tracing the ridge of a vein.

He didn't speak again. He didn't move. Yet she sensed the tension radiating from him.

Before she could stop herself, she closed her hand around the hot shaft and heard him make a strangled exclamation.

She half expected him to rear up and push her backward so that he'd come down on top of her. But he stayed where he was, still giving her permission to do anything she wanted—or nothing.

It was that permission which emboldened her. Letting her own sensual needs guide her, she squeezed him—first gently, then with more force. He hardened even further under her touch, until his penis became a velvet-covered steel rod.

"That feels good," she whispered.

He laughed. "At this end, too."

She clasped him more tightly, playing with him, experimenting to see what he liked best. As she moved her hand up and down, she felt his whole body go rigid.

"Tell me how to give you the same pleasure you gave me."

"Harder. Can you do it harder? And faster," he gasped out.

She did as he asked. And if she had any doubt left that she was doing the right thing, it evaporated when his hips rose off the sleeping bag, straining upward.

She could hear his breathing, fast and heavy and full of groans cut short by the next gasp for breath.

She kept moving her hand, her gaze rising to his face, seeing the tightness, the focus, the pleasure that she was giving him.

Then she felt his body jerk as thick white liquid spurted from him.

He called her name between panting breaths. Then he lay still. And when he circled her shoulder and pulled her down to lie beside him, she felt a kind of pride that astonished her.

She had done something very simple and basic, and yet doing it had freed her in a way that she hadn't expected.

"Thank you," he whispered.

"I'm glad I did that."

"Oh, yeah." He clasped her close, and they rested there for a long moment.

"When I was little, I would be in my bedroom, and I would hear my momma with Jandor. I would hear them talking and laughing. Then I'd hear their breathing get fast, like panting. I didn't understand it, and I'd put the covers over my head. I thought he was hurting her because she was his slave and she had to do anything he wanted."

He made a rough sound. "I heard my parents, too. But I guess I knew they were having a good time."

"How?"

"From the way they were together when they weren't in bed. She'd be cooking dinner and he'd come up behind her and kiss her neck or do something else, and I knew that when they got in bed, they were going to enjoy each other. That's what I want for us."

"He didn't dominate her?"

He shifted next to her. "That's a problem in my family. The guys tend to be commanding, at least in my father's generation. But with my brothers and my cousins, the marriages are more of a partnership."

"A partnership," she murmured, trying to imagine it.

They lay warm and relaxed together for another few minutes, until he stirred. "We should go home."

"To your house?"

"Yes."

She nodded, knowing that another chapter in her life was about to unfold. Another chapter in this new world.

"I'll help you break camp," she said.

"Thanks."

They both pulled their clothes back on. Then he took a hat with a sun visor from his duffel bag and handed it to her.

"Put this on, and tuck your hair up under the cap."

"Why?"

"So you look a little different. Just a precaution in case anybody notices us driving around together."

"Okay."

Following his directions, she helped him break up

the camp, then watched as he stowed his gear and boxes of plants in the back of the vehicle.

It was big. Bigger than the car parked at the house where they'd gotten into trouble.

"This is a . . . car?"

"You can call it a car. Technically, it's an SUV."

"SUV," she repeated.

"A sports utility vehicle."

She nodded as if she knew what he was talking about. "It's . . . nice."

He laughed. "Macho guys like them."

When he opened the door, she leaned into the interior, struck by the rich leather and what looked like wood. But when she touched it, the feel was all wrong.

Uncertainly, she climbed into the seat, still intrigued by the interior.

While Logan went to the back to stow some more gear, she ran her hands along the surface in front of her. There was a seam in the leather, telling her there might be a compartment hidden from view. The assumption was confirmed as her fingers hit a latch.

When she applied pressure, a little horizontal door fell open toward her knees. And one of those weapons—a gun—was practically lying in her lap.

As she stared at it, her throat clenched. She'd seen the man at the convenience store use the weapon, and she'd been awestruck. Now here was one of the things right in front of her.

Mesmerized, she reached for the gun, then lifted it up. It felt cool to the touch. And when she took it in her hand, it was alien and strange and heavier than she expected. Yet she wanted to know how it worked.

She turned it in her hand, trying to remember how

the thug had held it: with the barrel part facing away from him. There was a metal ring at the bottom side, and a little lever in the middle of that. She slipped her finger into the ring just as Logan opened the door on the other side of the car.

When he saw the gun was pointed toward him, he froze. "Aim that away from me, then take your finger out of the trigger guard," he said in a low, quiet voice. "If you don't want me to end up with a hole in the middle of my stomach."

CHAPTER SEVENTEEN

RINNA STARED AT Logan, trying to take in what he'd just said.

"I'd rather not end up dead. So point that away from me, and get your finger out of the trigger guard."

Her finger went suddenly stiff.

"How?" she wheezed.

Carefully she did as he asked and laid the gun back in the compartment.

Then she began to shake.

Logan breathed out a little sigh. "Thank you."

"I . . . I . . . opened the . . ." she stammered.

"Glove compartment," he supplied as he came around to her side of the vehicle and picked up the gun. Turning it over in his hand, he walked back to the driver's side and slipped it into the compartment in the door.

"Most handguns have a safety catch," he said, as though he were one of her teachers back in school delivering a lesson. "You have to push a lever before you can fire it. But the Glock is different. The safety is inside the trigger guard. So with your finger where it was, you could have killed me."

She stared at him in shock. "I . . ."

"You need to learn about guns," he supplied. "After we get home, I'll give you some shooting lessons."

"I could have killed you," she repeated, the enormity of it grabbing her by the throat and making it almost impossible for her to breathe. "You should punish me," she whispered.

"Of course not!"

"I should cut a switch so you can whip me."

"Jesus! No." He pulled her toward him and wrapped his arms around her. As he folded her close, moisture stung the backs of her eyes.

"I'm so sorry." She struggled to hold her tears back, but they leaked out of her eyes and trickled down her cheeks.

When Logan felt her shoulders shaking, he rubbed his fingers across her back.

"First I almost killed myself with the electricity. Then I almost killed you with the gun."

"But you didn't. It's okay. Everything's okay."

She fought the tears. "No. I keep messing up."

"No, you don't. Or . . . not any more than I did in your world. When everything's totally unfamiliar, it's hard to know how to react. I'm the one at fault. I wasn't thinking. I shouldn't have left the gun where you could grab it."

He kept stroking her back and running his fingers through her hair, and finally she got control of herself. She felt him fumbling in the pocket of his door. When she lifted her head, he handed her a small rectangle that felt like flimsy cotton.

"What's that?"

"A tissue. To wipe your eyes and blow your nose."

She did, and he took the crumpled thing and put it in a small bag that was also in his door.

"I suppose a child here would know what that was," she murmured.

"Actually, sometimes they play with guns or show them off, and they kill another child by accident."

"You should get rid of the guns!"

"A lot of people want to. But there are more people who want to defend themselves. Or they argue that even if guns are against the law, criminals will still have them."

"Who's right?"

"It's hard to know."

"In my world a man would act sure of himself, even if . . ."

"Even if he were blowing smoke out his ass."

She gave a bark of a laugh. "I never heard that. But I know what it means."

"Yeah."

"Why do you have the gun?" she asked.

"Because we're out here in the woods. And I want to be prepared. I had it in the tent. Then I moved it to the car when I went out for a run."

"Oh."

"I'll give you shooting lessons after we get home."

"You'd trust me with that thing?"

"Of course. But we should leave. I want to get the plants back home before they dry out."

She leaned back in the seat.

"Fasten your seat belt."

"What is it, and how do I do it?"

"It's to . . ." He stopped and laughed. "I was about to

tell you it's to keep you safe in case I crash the car. But I guess that doesn't sound very reassuring."

"No."

"A crash is unlikely. But a seat belt is a good safety precaution."

He pulled out a strap from some hidden compartment and showed her how to make the two parts click together. Then he showed her how to open it again.

After she hooked the belt, he inserted a key in a metal slot. The car gave a roar that made her grab the handle next to her.

"It's okay," he soothed.

"I don't like it."

He turned toward her, his face serious. "I know it's all strange and new."

When she reached for the door handle, he lifted her hand away. "Don't pull that. It will open the door, and you don't want to do that while we're moving."

She swallowed. "Okay."

"You can put your hand here . . . or here." He showed her several places where it was okay to hold on.

He must have caught the worried expression on her face because he said, "You'll get used to it."

"You keep saying that," she answered, although she wondered if it was really true. He had grown up with these things. She was as lost as he would have been in the slave quarters of a great house.

Suddenly the car began to move, and she sucked in a breath.

"How are you doing that?"

"With my foot. I press on a pedal to give it fuel."

"Electricity?"

"In this case, liquid fuel called gasoline. Something like the oil you burn in a lamp. But different."

She had almost succeeded in relaxing when Logan drove from the narrow dirt lane into a wider road with a smooth surface like the one from last night. Immediately he speeded up, faster than any carriage could go.

She held on, being careful to touch where he'd showed her.

"It's fast."

"Some guys go faster."

She tried to imagine that. "When I was in school, some of the highborn children brought sleds to school for the winter months. A few times they let me slide down a hill in the snow."

"Did you like it?"

"Yes. It was fast. And the wind whipped past my head. This is like that, but the glass keeps the wind away."

"We can have a little wind effect." He reached to press a button, and the glass panel above her head slid back.

She dragged in a sharp breath, and he closed it again.

To distract herself, she asked, "Is your house like the place where we spent the night?"

"No. That was kitschy colonial. Mine is werewolf modern."

"What does that mean?"

"We tend to like the rustic look. One of my brothers is a builder, and he constructed it for me."

She wasn't sure what rustic meant, so she tried to relax in the seat as he talked.

Maybe because he saw she was nervous, he kept up a flow of words, telling her about the native plants that he was cultivating and about the work he did designing gardens for people who wanted the ground around their house to look natural but artful.

He had said he was in a hurry to get home, so when

he pulled to the gravel at the side of the blacktop road in the middle of nowhere, she looked up in alarm.

"Sorry. Just a second," he apologized as he climbed out and picked up several large rocks that had fallen from a cliff above them. After putting them on the floor behind them, he drove away again.

"What are you doing?"

"I'm always on the lookout for material I can use in a landscape design. These are perfect."

They passed other cars and big vehicles he called trucks.

"If one of them hit us, they would smash us flat," she murmured.

"It doesn't happen very often."

"But sometimes?"

"Unfortunately."

She winced. "I thought coming here would make me safe, but your world is dangerous."

"I guess life is dangerous."

Trees and buildings sped past. Some were impossibly large and ugly. Then they came to an area with more trees than houses. Finally, he slowed.

"Here we are."

She craned her neck, watching for the house, then gasped as they rounded a curve, and she saw a car and a man inside.

LOGAN'S hands tightened on the steering wheel. He wasn't expecting company. And this probably wasn't a Fuller Brush salesman.

So he spoke to Rinna in a low voice. "Let me do the talking."

"What's happening?"

"I don't know. Try not to look scared."

"Is it the police?"

"I don't know," he answered, but he thought that might be the case when a tough-looking guy in a tweed sports jacket and gray slacks got out.

"They know we broke into the house," she whispered.

"Not necessarily," he said, hoping he spoke the truth.

Before he could give Rinna any more advice, the guy walked up beside the SUV. He looked to be in his early thirties with neatly trimmed dark hair and eyes hidden behind sunglasses.

Logan rolled down his window.

"Detective Jake Cooper," the man said, opening his wallet and showing his ID.

"Logan Marshall."

"I want to ask you some questions."

"About what?" he asked, hoping his voice sounded steady.

Beside him, Rinna was sitting rigidly, and he was pretty sure she wished she had a knife in her hand.

"The Easy Shopper in Mount Airy."

Logan struggled to keep his expression neutral. He'd racked his brain to explain about the break-in last night. Now he realized that nobody was planning to arrest a wolf and a big white bird. Maybe they hadn't even seen the naked guy in the woods. And even if the cops found fingerprints in the house, his weren't on file anywhere. And Rinna's certainly weren't.

"What about it?" he asked, hoping he sounded completely puzzled.

"You were identified as being in the store during an incident."

"What incident?"

"An attempted robbery."

"I think you're mistaken. It wasn't me."

Cooper flipped open a notebook and consulted a page. Leaning in the window, he looked Rinna up and down before focusing on Logan again.

"You were in that store on Tuesday, the twenty-second, and you signed a credit card slip."

He thought back over the previous week, which seemed like a lifetime ago. "Yes. I bought some flash-light batteries, but I haven't been back since."

"The clerk identified you."

"Sorry. He must be mistaken," Logan said, deliberately getting the pronoun wrong.

"She," the cop corrected.

"What did you say happened?"

"A robbery."

Logan shrugged. "Well, I'm sorry that I can't help you."

Cooper looked at Rinna again. "Were you in the Easy Shopper in Mount Airy yesterday evening?"

"No."

The cop kept his gaze on Rinna. "Can I have your name, please?"

She opened her mouth, but Logan reached to clasp her hand. "Rinna Marshall," he said. "My wife."

Beside him, she made a strangled sound.

"Are you all right, ma'am?" the detective asked.

"Actually, she's sick. She could be expecting. That's why we cut our camping trip short. She needs to get inside and lie down."

"Do you mind if I ask you some questions about the convenience store?" Cooper said politely but still persistently.

"I told you, we don't know anything about it, besides

the fact that I bought those batteries. I didn't go back. And my wife was never there."

"Mind if I come in and talk to you?"

"This isn't a good time. Now if you'll excuse us." He climbed out of the car and came around to Rinna's door. "Come on honey, I'll get you inside so you can lie down."

When she fumbled with the seat belt, he opened it for her, and she stood on shaky legs. Leaving the luggage in the car, he took her arm and led her to the front door, which he unlocked before leading her inside.

Turning to cast a brief glance over his shoulder, he saw that the detective was still looking at them.

He wanted to tell the guy to get off his property. Instead, he pressed his lips together.

JAKE Cooper watched Mr. and Mrs. Marshall disappear into the house. Actually, he'd overstated the case a bit. The clerk had thought the man in the back of the store was the one who had come in a few days earlier. She wasn't sure. And unfortunately, the security camera had not been functioning.

The clerk, a Mrs. Dormaster, had told a pretty wild story. Not just about the robbery—but about men appearing out of nowhere in the back of the store. Nobody else had seen them, and Jake had put it down to a case of raw nerves, brought on by the robbery.

But she'd also kept insisting that the man and the woman in the back hadn't come in the front door. They'd appeared in the back, just the way the other guys had.

Mrs. Dormaster's story had sounded like the ravings of a woman with mental health issues. But the more the woman talked, the more convincing she sounded. Of course, there was no way to verify the story. Jake had gone back and examined the wall at the back of the store, and it had seemed perfectly solid.

Once he'd been the kind of cop who only believed in things that he could verify through his own senses, but then he'd worked with a psychic to find a kidnapped kid.

He'd started off thinking the whole psychic thing was a bunch of crap. Then the woman had found the kid, just minutes before the bastard would have slit his throat. And Jake had changed his attitude.

He was open to the possibility that not everything in the universe was exactly as it seemed. So maybe something had happened in that convenience store that couldn't be explained in conventional terms.

Too bad the video camera had been on the fritz. Or maybe that was part of the whole phenomenon.

At any rate, he did know one thing for sure. After their brief conversation, he was certain that Marshall and his wife had something to hide. Although it might not be connected with the store at all.

When they were out of sight, he walked around to the door handle of the SUV. Keeping his body between the car and the house, he pressed a piece of fingerprint tape to the handle. It was an excellent surface from which to get prints. As was the can of pork and beans someone had used to conk the would-be robber. When they'd run the prints, there had been no match in the FBI database.

The man who'd saved Mrs. Dormaster wasn't a criminal. And he had never served in the military or held a government job. But now it would be interesting to see if the prints from the door handle matched the ones on the can. If they did, Jake would come back and ask some more questions.

He stroked his chin. If something weird had happened in that store, the man and woman who had just given him the brush-off were witnesses. At the very least, they were witnesses to the attempted robbery.

So now he'd wait to see if the fingerprints matched. And meanwhile he was keeping an eye on the store to find out if anything else strange happened there.

CLOSING the door firmly behind them, Logan felt Rinna sag against him.

"You did fine," he murmured, turning her in his arms and folding her close. He felt her shaking.

"You said I was your wife," she breathed.

"That's the best cover for you."

"The policeman . . ."

"That was damn bad luck." His hand tightened on her shoulder. "I thought he was going to ask you for an ID. That's why I rushed you into the house."

"ID?"

He sighed. "In this society, you need identification. A driver's license. A credit card. A card with your name and picture."

"Like the tattoo on my arm?"

"No! Not like that." He gave her a searching look, then lowered his voice. "Not because people belong to other people. But because you need to prove who you are." Before she could ask for more details, he added, "I never asked . . . do you have a last name?"

"A what?"

He struggled not to let his feelings of frustration bleed into his voice. All he'd been thinking about was getting Rinna home and keeping her safe. He was starting to find out just how complicated that was going to be. Taking a step back so he could look at her, he said, "I'm Logan Marshall. Logan is my first name and Marshall is my last name. Do you have something similar?"

"Slaves have a name and a number," she said in a barely audible voice. "I'm Rinna thirty-eight. But that won't work here, right?"

"No. But we'll get you a last name."

"How?"

"I believe I can buy one." He stopped, thinking about the logistics. "Well, maybe we'll need to use some other name."

She looked down at her hands. "Jandor changed my mother's name from Hester to Lana because he liked it better."

"I would never do that! But I might have to get you an ID for someone who was born in this country."

"How?"

"There are ways to do it. Sometimes people who are switching their identities take a name off the gravestone of a child who died young. Someone around their age." He thought for a moment. "But I need to think about the social security number problem."

"You said you didn't use numbers," she answered.

"Well, not when you give your name. But everybody has a number, for tax purposes. And for a retirement account."

She looked like her head was spinning, and he tried to imagine how overwhelmed she must feel.

"I got into trouble in your world because I didn't know the right thing to do. It's natural," he said.

She remained silent, taking her lower lip between her teeth.

"We'll talk about it later."

He found her hand and led her down the hall to the

family room, where she stopped short and dragged in a shaky breath.

"What?"

"You live like this, like a . . . a . . . noble?"

"No. A lot of people live like this."

"Your house . . ."

"Is nice. But the real value is in the land I own. Ten acres is a lot for this part of the country."

She nodded, but he suspected she really wasn't following him.

Before he could elaborate, she asked another question. "You said to the policeman that I could be expecting. Expecting what?"

"A baby."

She gasped.

"It's okay." He laughed. "We can probably arrange for it to be true."

She let her head drop to his shoulder, and he stroked his hands up and down her arms, thinking of how he'd like to distract her now.

But apparently her mind wasn't exactly running along the same track.

"You said you'd show me how to use the gun. Maybe you'd better do it."

"If you promise not to shoot any cops."

"I promise," she whispered, her tone very serious.

CHAPTER EIGHTEEN

"YOU WANT A gun lesson right now?" Logan asked in a husky voice, since his thoughts had been moving in an entirely different direction.

"Yes," Rinna answered, and he caught the edge of desperation in her voice.

He knew she was feeling like her life was spinning out of control, and she wanted to know she had mastered a skill that seemed important in this universe.

So he swallowed a sigh. "There's a place down the hill where it's safe to practice," he said.

"Thank you."

"But first I want to talk to my cousin Ross."

"About what?" she said, the anxiety back in her voice.

"About getting an ID for you. Is that okay?"

"You said I need it."

"But I'll have to explain a little about you."

She kept her gaze fixed on his face. "You trust him?"

"Yes. But I can't say too much over the phone."

"That thing like the other night. When Terry called Bart and Helen about the game of . . . bridge?"

"Yes."

"Why can't you talk to him on it about me?"

"Because sometimes other people can be listening."

Rinna studied the lines of his face. "You're getting tired of explaining things, aren't you?"

"No." But it was true. It was a strain explaining the everyday details of modern life.

He pulled out his cell phone, cranked up the volume so Rinna could hear, then punched in the autodial number, wondering exactly how he was going to start the conversation.

"Ross Marshall," his cousin answered.

"This is Logan."

"I take it you're not just calling to say hello."

"No." He swallowed, then plunged ahead. "You remember when we had that problem with Boralas?"

He heard Ross's voice change. "Yes. Is there another problem in that area?"

"Not directly. But we had help from a . . . friend."

"Uh huh."

"She's here with me now. Unfortunately, she's lost her driver's license. I was hoping you'd know how to get her a replacement."

"I'd like to hear more about that. But probably we should sit down and talk about it."

Logan inclined his head toward Rinna. "When would it be convenient for us to come over?"

"Is tomorrow morning okay?"

"Yes."

"What's her name, by the way?"

Logan glanced toward Rinna. "Rinna. Rinna Marshall."

There was a long pause on the other end of the line. Then Ross said, "Congratulations."

"Yeah. We'll see you tomorrow."

"Megan and I will be looking forward to it."

When he hung up, he said, "We'll go over in the morning. But now we'll have that gun lesson."

"Thank you. I don't mean just about the gun part."

"I know."

He retrieved the Glock from the car, along with some of the targets he used when he was sharpening his own skills.

They walked past his greenhouses and down the hill into a secluded valley, then set up the targets against the hill, where there was no chance of hitting anything besides the paper and straw—or dirt.

"We should be doing this at a shooting range," he said.

"Why?"

"Because it's always best to learn from a professional. But we'd still have the problem of identifying you. So we'll have to do it here if we do it at all."

After unloading the weapon, he delivered a lecture on gun safety, starting with a warning about never pointing the weapon at anyone unless you intended to kill them.

Next he let her familiarize herself with the feel of the gun in her hand. After that, he gave them both ear protectors and loaded the weapon. First he fired off several rounds at the target. Then he let her have a try.

He knew she had been watching carefully when she imitated his stance and squeezed the trigger, obviously surprised by the recoil. But she gamely tried again. And by the time she'd emptied the clip, she was looking more confident.

After she'd put the weapon down, he retrieved the target and showed her the bullet holes.

She poked her finger into them. "This could go into someone's body."

"And do a lot of damage."

"I see that." She swallowed. "Thank you for the lesson."

"Do you feel more comfortable with the weapon?" he asked.

Her face was very serious. "Not comfortable. But I understand it better."

"We'll decide where to keep it in the house. And where to store the clips. It's dangerous to keep the gun loaded."

"Yes," she answered, her tone so serious that he felt his heart contract. He'd hoped he could make her feel more secure, but he wasn't sure he'd done it.

They walked back to the house and together decided to keep the gun in the top of the bedroom closet. He put the clip in the bottom of a bedroom drawer.

"You've made me see that having a gun is a big responsibility," she murmured.

"That's very perceptive of you. There are a lot of men running around who don't get it."

"You're a good teacher." She turned to face him. "The whole time we were down there, I kept my mind on business."

"Yes."

"But I was also thinking that the gun is very dangerous, and you must trust me very much to let me use it."

"Yes."

"If you can show me how much you trust me, I should do the same."

His throat felt suddenly tight. "There's no *should*."

"Well, maybe I said it wrong. I *want to* show you that I trust you." She took a step toward him and clasped her arms around him. Suddenly he couldn't move.

She held on to him for several seconds, then raised up so that she could press her lips against his.

She had taken him by surprise, but only for a moment. And when she began to move her lips against his, he responded by leaning forward and angling his head to give her better access.

Heat sparked between them—clean and strong and arousing.

She made a small sound as she drank him in and gave him back the passion she tasted on his lips. When he finally raised his head, they were both gasping for breath.

"It doesn't take so long," she whispered.

"What?"

"To get that hot, tingly feeling."

"You're getting used to it."

"I want you to tell me something," she asked shyly.

"Anything."

She took his hand and pressed it directly over her center. "What do I call this? I mean the part of me where the good feeling is the strongest."

"Your clitoris. That's the technical word. But people call it a clit for short."

"My clit," she said, pressing his hand more firmly against her.

She lowered her arms, so that they were slung around his hips. Moving his hand out of the way, he let her pull him toward her, bringing his erection against her abdomen.

She moved against him, driving him wild at the contact. But he heard her make a small sound of frustration.

"You're too tall," she murmured. "I want to feel that against my clit."

"God, yes."

"What should we do?"

"This." He backed up so that his hips were braced against the wall, then splayed his legs so that he could equalize their heights. When he pulled her against his cock, she made a sound of agreement.

"Do you think I'm acting too . . . forward?" she asked.

"Of course not. You're showing me you feel the same way I do."

She opened her mouth, pressing her teeth against his shoulder. "The hot, needy feeling never went away. I mean, it was there in the background, the whole time since the tent. Well, maybe not when the policeman was asking us question. But the rest of the time."

"Yeah."

He gathered her close, then lowered his head, kissing her with all the greedy urgency that he'd kept in check for the past few hours. While he kissed her, he found the buttons of her shirt, opening them with hands that he couldn't hold steady.

He grinned to himself. Some day, he'd have to tell her that most American women wore bras. But not yet, not when he had such ready access to her wonderful breasts.

He pushed the fabric aside, cupping her in his hands, sighing in pleasure as he felt her tight nipples press into his palms.

"That feels so good."

"Yes. But it will be better when all this clothing isn't in the way."

He pulled his own shirt over his head, then dragged hers off her shoulders so that he could slide her breasts against his chest.

When she made a small strangled sound, his gaze shot to her face, fearful that in his hunger he had pushed her too far, too fast. But he only saw his own pleasure mirrored there.

His movements almost out of control, he unhooked the snap at the front of her waistband, then lowered her zipper so he could shuck off her pants. When he had her naked, he slid his hands over her rounded bottom, caressing her there, before reaching lower to slide his fingers between her folds.

"What do you call that part of me?" she murmured.

"What do *you* call it?"

"Down there," she answered in a husky voice.

He laughed. "Not very romantic."

"Tell me something better."

He considered all the alternatives, some of them clinical, some of them straight from the gutter. "There are lots of words we could use. How do you like pussy?"

"Pussy? Like a cat?"

"Yeah. Because I want to stroke you there."

Her hand slid between them and closed around his erection. "And this is your cock."

"Yes," he managed. "And if you keep your hand there, you're going to make me come."

"That's another word for sexual climax . . . for when the good feelings explode through you?"

"Yeah. But I think the anatomy and physiology lesson is over for the moment." Picking her up in his arms, he carried her to the bed, bending to pull aside the spread and the top sheet before laying her down so that he could climb out of his pants.

Taking her to bed had been a natural impulse. But as he stood over her, naked and ready for sex, he could see the mixture of arousal and worry on her face, and he knew that the symbolism of the bed was quite different for her.

Slowly he eased to the side of the mattress, so that he was sitting beside her.

When he reached to stroke back her hair, he saw her eyes screw shut and her jaw tighten.

"Over by the door, you were aroused. But lying down here scares you."

She didn't answer, but the harsh sound of her breathing told him what he needed to know.

"I think this isn't such a good idea," he muttered.

Her eyes flew open. "I want . . ."

"So do I. But maybe not in bed."

"How?"

He picked up her hand, carrying it to his mouth so that he could worry the pad of her thumb with his teeth as he looked around the room, then spotted the dining room chair he'd set in the corner to use as a clothes rack.

Climbing off the bed, he turned the chair toward the bed, then came back to reach for her hand again.

"Come over here."

"What are we going to do?"

"You'll see."

She came off the bed, looking at him questioningly as he sat on the chair, the angle of his body thrusting his cock upward.

He saw her gaze flick to his erection, then away.

"Come stand in front of me where I can touch you," he said in a husky voice as he opened his legs.

She did as he asked, and he stroked her hip and across her stomach, then kissed her shoulder as he let his hands drift upward, caressing the under curve of her breasts.

"I'm going to stay in this chair. So anytime you want to stop what we're doing, all you have to do is step away from me."

She stared at him in surprise, then gave a little nod.

As he touched her, he slowly gathered her to him, giving her time to draw back. But she remained in his embrace, swaying a little on unsteady legs.

She leaned forward to clasp her arms around his shoulders, then dragged her hands upward into his hair.

"This is a very nice view I have here," he murmured.

She managed a laugh.

"Very nice," he repeated as he caressed her breasts with his face and mouth, then sucked on one nipple while he teased the other with his thumb and finger.

He felt a shiver go through her.

"Are you all right?"

"Yes," she answered, her voice breathy.

"Good."

His other hand drifted lower, caressing her bottom, then reaching inward to stroke high up between her legs.

"That's nice. So nice," he whispered. "God, I love the feel of you. And you're so hot and slick for me.

"If you want to feel my cock against you, all you have to do is straddle me and bend your knees a little."

He waited with his breath frozen in his lungs.

"Close your legs," she said.

He did and she straddled his lap, dipping down so that his erection barely touched her, then moved a little, stroking herself with his hard shaft.

He ached to plunge into her, but he stayed where he was, letting her get used to the intimate contact.

When she swayed on her feet, he steadied her with one hand, while he used the other hand to stroke his penis against her.

"I'm going to slip my finger inside you," he murmured. "Just my finger. Just a little."

He felt her tense, then relax as he caressed her at the sensitive opening and up to her clit.

"Okay?"

"Yes," she choked out. "But this is going to make me . . . come."

"That's the idea."

"Not with your hand . . ."

The broken sound of her voice tore at him.

"You want to feel my cock inside you?"

She answered with a tiny nod.

"If you push down, it will happen," he told her, somehow managing to keep his voice steady.

For a few heartbeats, she didn't move, and he held his breath, preparing himself for the pain of feeling her step away.

But she stayed where she was. Then, in a rush of movement, she came down onto his lap, burying him in her warmth and heat.

At the feel of his body joined to hers, they both cried out.

For a moment, she stared at him in shock. "You're inside me."

"Yeah." He grinned at her. "How is it?"

"It doesn't hurt," she breathed, her expression changing from surprise to triumph.

"I think we can do a little better than that."

He cupped the back of her head, bringing her mouth to his for a long, erotic kiss as he stroked her spine, then eased her away enough so that he could play with her breasts.

"What should I do?" she gasped out.

"Move a little. Back and forth. Up and down. See what feels good to you," he managed.

She began to move and he pressed his mouth to her neck. He was so hot he had to fight to keep from thrusting upward. But he stayed where he was, letting her explore the sensations she was creating.

Slipping one hand between them, he pressed it over her clit and felt her instant response. She began to move faster, her motions jerky. In seconds, he felt her inner muscles contract around him. She gripped his shoulders as she called his name, clinging to him as orgasm took her. As his own climax rocketed through him, he clasped her to him, then felt her body sag against his.

He held her for a long moment, kissing her face and her mouth as he stroked her back and shoulders.

When she raised her head, he saw that her eyes were damp.

"Are you all right?" he whispered.

She looked at him, wonder shining in her eyes. "I did it!"

"Oh, yeah."

She looked into his eyes. "And it was so good."

"Yes."

"Thank you. Not just for the pleasure. For the healing."

"I'm glad."

She laid her head on his shoulder, and he stroked the sweat-slick skin of her back as he nibbled at her neck. "We should lie down."

She raised her head and gave a shaky laugh. "Probably I'm crushing you."

"No. But I think we'd both be more comfortable horizontal, if you're willing to climb into bed with me now."

"I think the hard part's over."

He laughed. "Not for long."

When she flushed, he helped her up, breaking the intimate contact between them.

He reached for her hand. Together they crossed to the bed and climbed under the covers.

He'd thought he understood what the bond between a werewolf and his mate meant. But now a little zing of fear sizzled through him. He knew how it worked with his brothers and his cousins. Too bad none of them had found a woman who was also a shape-shifter.

Would that make a difference for him and Rinna? And what about their children? What would happen when they got shape-shifter genes from both their mother and father?

He didn't know. But he pushed the worry to the back of his mind and turned Rinna to him, clasping her close.

FALCONE managed to stay calm by thinking about his plans for the future. When he found Rinna, he would force her to bear him a son. A child with the combination of their powerful genes.

He would raise the child with great care and great wisdom, so that the boy would be completely loyal to his father. And together they would have the power to rule Sun Acres, with Falcone always as the guiding force. Some people already called him the Iron Man of Sun Acres. He would make it true. He would push rivals like Griffin aside.

But before he could put that plan into action, Haig must find the damn woman. And it wasn't just a matter of tramping through the badlands. She had escaped into that other universe.

Falcone clenched his hands into fists. He'd finally tortured the old man into compliance. Then Avery and Bellows had thrown him a curve.

They'd given him the bad news that it wasn't going to be so easy to get into that other world. After closing the portal farther west, they couldn't just open it again because the reversal would take a great deal of energy. The only portal left was at the commercial establishment.

Much too public a place to bring through fifteen or twenty men.

Now he was waiting for Avery to come up with an alternate plan.

When the old man returned, Falcone tried to read his face.

"You have something for me?" he demanded.

Avery shifted his weight from one foot to the other. "I think so."

"You don't sound too positive."

"I have a way to get your troops through without being seen."

"What?"

"An invisibility charm."

"That would work," Falcone mused, then focused on the other man's eyes.

"But something's wrong. What are you hiding?"

"Nobody has ever tried to make so many men invisible."

"Well, you'd better hope it works," Falcone growled. "Because if it doesn't, your head is on the chopping block."

CHAPTER NINETEEN

THE LAB WAS backed up. So while Jake Cooper waited to find out if the prints from the door handle matched the ones on the can of pork and beans, he ordered patrol cars to drive past the convenience store every few hours. None of the officers had reported any unusual activity.

But Jake couldn't rid himself of the conviction that there was something weird about the place. Starting with the clerk's strange story about men bursting from the back of the store and ending with the pile of clothing the patrol officers had found in the woods.

Too bad Tony Blanchard, the guy who'd tried to rob the place, was in no shape to talk about the experience. The small-time crook was in a coma in the hospital and hadn't spoken word one since the incident.

Because Jake couldn't deal with his curiosity any other way, he had gotten into the habit of having a look-see when he was in the area.

If he'd still been living with Annie, he would have

gone straight home and climbed into bed with her. But she'd cleared out months ago, and he hadn't known how to make things right between them—not when she couldn't deal with the reality that his job always had the potential to put him in danger. So he'd been drifting along on his own, looking for excuses to stay out of the house.

Tonight he made a detour from the citizen's association meeting where he'd given a safety lecture and swung by the Easy Shopper, which sat between a fast food restaurant and a stretch of woods that hadn't been developed yet.

When he reached the location, he slowed, staring at the large glass windows at the front of the low building, where posters advertised everything from lottery tickets to the featured monthly sandwich and drink combo.

A couple of lights burned inside, but it was obvious from the lack of activity that the place was empty. He started to drive on by, but instead he pulled into the far end of the empty parking lot and cut his engine.

He patted the pocket of his sports jacket, then remembered that he'd given up smoking over a year ago. Too bad. He could use some nicotine.

He was dead tired from putting in a full day of investigations, and as he sat in his unmarked, he leaned back against the headrest. Then he closed his eyes. Just for a moment, he told himself.

Instead, he drifted into sleep—until something snapped him abruptly awake.

His eyes came open and he stared at the darkened silhouette of the store, feeling a sudden tingling sensation at the back of his neck. The place looked as empty as when he'd arrived, yet he couldn't shake the conviction that somebody or something was inside—and up to no good.

Something?

Like a paranormal being?

That thought had been teasing the back of his mind for days. Even though he couldn't explain it to anyone else.

Which was maybe why he didn't call for backup. And what the hell was he going to say—that he'd seen a ghost at the Easy Shopper store, and he wanted guys at the ready with their guns?

Yeah, sure.

He could drive away. But he knew he wouldn't be doing his duty if he left. So he climbed out of the car and drew his service weapon but stayed twenty yards from the building, keeping to the shadows.

For a long moment he saw nothing. Then a sound inside made him rivet on the door.

It slid open, and he prepared to watch someone step out, someone up to no good. All he saw was empty air, but he heard more than one set of footsteps.

He ran back to his cruiser and turned on the headlights, aiming them directly at the entrance of the building, but still he saw nothing.

Again he approached, then stopped short as something came flying out of the air toward him.

Instinctively, he ducked, feeling a missile whizz past him. It landed with a clank against his right front fender.

He ducked behind the car, staring at the thing that lay on the ground. It could have been a spear from a costume drama.

Only the eight-inch point looked like the genuine article—forged steel that would go right through a man's body.

As he hefted the spear in his hands, the glass door of

the store slammed shut. From Jake's vantage point, it looked like it had glided closed on its own.

To his right, in the patch of woods beside the store, he heard someone shout what sounded like a military order. Again, there was no sign of who had spoken and who he was talking to.

Now Jake wished to hell he'd called for backup. Someone was out there, all right. Several someones. But he still couldn't see who they were.

It was like in those Harry Potter movies when the kid put on an invisibility cloak. Only this cloak was big enough to cover what sounded like at least a dozen men. Which didn't make sense.

After half a minute of silence, Jake ran from his position behind the car to the side of the building, keeping low, trying to figure out how he was going to fight an enemy he couldn't even see. Or maybe he wasn't going to have to fight at all, because it sounded like the men who had come out of the store were moving rapidly away from the building.

Leaning around the corner, he peered into the woods, trying to see something. In the trees, he thought he detected shapes flickering but there was nothing he could point to and identify.

The whole thing was too weird to describe. But he was going to figure out what the hell was going on.

Cautiously he stepped around the corner, then moved in a crouch toward the woods. Using a soft drink machine as a shield, he peered toward the trees, then went rigid when he heard someone sneaking up behind him. At the same time, he caught a whiff of strong body odor—from a guy who hadn't bathed in a week. Whirling to face the attacker, he saw nothing.

The gun was still in his hand, but he couldn't shoot because he didn't know where to aim.

Then a hand chopping down on his wrist made him drop the gun.

Cursing, he struck out with his left arm, hitting a solid wall of muscle and hearing his attacker grunt. For all the good that did.

Fighting an opponent you couldn't see meant you couldn't anticipate his moves.

Another blow came from the left, as the invisible man ducked under his defenses. This time Jake went down on his knees. Another blow connected with the back of his head. Then everything went black.

RINNA lay sleepless in the bed beside Logan, unable to stop her mind from circling back over the mistakes she'd made during the past few days.

Every time she turned around, she did something wrong. Or Logan had to explain something she didn't understand.

She felt the way she had when she'd first arrived at the school, and she'd had no idea how to do any of the psychic tasks presented to her.

Back then she'd wanted to run away and hide. Now she couldn't stop herself from feeling the same way.

She tried to tell herself that everything was all right. She had just made love with Logan, and it had been wonderful. More than she could have expected. But still, she couldn't stop the air from thickening in her lungs. Finally, when she couldn't stand the sensation any longer, she got up and tiptoed across the floor. From the doorway, she turned and looked back at Logan.

Until he had started kissing her and touching her, she had thought she could never freely give herself to a man. But he had proved her wrong.

If she woke him, she could tell him how she was feeling, and perhaps he could help her deal with the fear that she would never be comfortable in this place.

But it wasn't all that long since she had pulled him from the trap. He didn't have his full strength back, and he needed to sleep.

And she needed to be by herself for a while. So she walked from the bedroom into the front part of the house. She was wearing only the T-shirt she'd put on earlier. After pulling it off and leaving it on the floor, she stepped outside and headed for the woods at the side of the house. The form of the wolf called her. Yet she hesitated. It hadn't taken long to figure out that hazards she didn't understand lurked in this world. The wolf would be vulnerable. But the bird would be high above the ground—free from danger. Unless someone shot at her with one of those guns.

A shiver rippled over her naked skin. She should have asked Logan if men in this country shot at birds. Then she looked into the starry sky. It was still night. Even if men killed winged creatures for sport, they probably wouldn't do it in the dark.

Hoping she was right in her assessment, she let her mind slip into the pattern she had learned long ago. She imagined herself as a great white hawk soaring through the sky. The image took hold in her mind, and as her thoughts tuned themselves to the bird, her body flowed into that familiar shape. With a feeling of freedom, she beat the air with her wings, then leaped from the ground into the sky, gaining altitude quickly. Cautious at first, she circled the house, noting the way it looked from the air so that she would know where to land. Then she looked for other landmarks that would guide her back here—if she was coming back.

She still hadn't decided that for certain. Maybe Logan was better off without her. And she would be doing him a favor by simply disappearing.

There was no comfort in that thought. But it helped her breathe more freely.

She took off toward the east, toward the direction from which they'd come when they'd first stepped through the portal. They had left the convenience store in a terrible rush, and she hadn't gotten a chance to study it.

Why was it a portal? Had one of Falcone's adepts opened it? Or had the doorway just occurred by chance?

LOGAN woke. Still half asleep, he reached for his mate. But she wasn't in bed. His heart leaped into his throat as he sat up and looked around.

"Rinna?" he called softly.

When she didn't answer, he levered himself out of bed. He checked the bathroom first. With a tight feeling in his chest, he hurried toward the front of the house. When he saw her T-shirt lying on the floor, he stopped short.

She had taken off her clothes so she could change. He knew that much. Had she gone out into the woods as a wolf? Or had she taken her bird form?

He stepped outside, calling her name again, alarm expanding inside his chest.

He didn't know why she had gone out, except that she needed to get away from him. The question was—would she come back?

He had thought the two of them had worked out their problems. Now he knew that was just male arrogance.

He had satisfied her as a lover. But had that settled anything else?

Damn. What should he do now? He wanted to rush out and look for her. Maybe she was even in trouble out there.

It flashed through his mind that maybe he needed more wolves to help find her. Then he told himself he was overreacting.

And more importantly, if she had taken her bird form, a bunch of wolves would never catch up with her.

RINNA had learned to listen to her inner feelings when they guided her in one direction or the other.

Too bad that wasn't true about her relationship to Logan.

She flew due east, trying to pick out familiar landmarks. When she spotted the convenience store, the place Logan called the Easy Shopper, she slowed, her wings beating the air just enough so that she could hover over one spot. A man was sprawled on the hard surface in front of the building. He was lying on his back, and as she circled lower, she felt a shock wave roll through her. She knew him!

It was the police detective who had been waiting for them at Logan's house yesterday. And it looked like he was hurt.

In the sky above him, she hesitated. He had wanted information from her and Logan—information Logan hadn't been willing to give. And she should stay away from him.

But she couldn't just leave him like that. And as she hovered over him, she saw something lying on the ground that made her heart start to pound. A spear! From one of Falcone's warriors.

She came down beside the detective, landing lightly on the hard surface, then moving closer to peer into his pale face. He didn't move.

Her heart still pounding, she pressed her beak against his cheek.

To her relief, his eyes blinked open, and he stared at her as though he were contemplating a vision from a nightmare.

She wanted to tell him that she meant him no harm. But speech was beyond her. All she could do was make a kind of deep-throated chirping sound.

"What the hell?" He fumbled on the ground and grabbed the gun that was lying beside him.

Gasping, she dodged to the side. If she rose into the air, he could shoot her from behind, so she stayed where she was, her gaze moving from his hand to his face and back again.

"What are you, a trained bird?" he asked.

She didn't answer, but she summoned her old skill, using it as best she could to send him an urgent message, pushing past the pain that gathered in her head as she spoke to him.

You don't want to hurt me. When he lowered the gun, she added something else, something she didn't entirely understand herself. *You should keep people away from the Easy Shopper. It's a dangerous place.*

"What?" he croaked.

Again she sent him the thought.

"Jesus. Am I going nuts?" His eyes wary, he put his hand to the back of his head and winced. "Better call for help," he muttered.

She rose into the air, then saw something that made her throat close.

A troop of men was moving through the woods. They were dressed like people from this world. But she recognized some of them as Falcone's soldiers. And some of his adepts.

Her pulse pounding, she scanned the group and saw Falcone himself. From above, she fought a sick, dizzy feeling. But she felt even sicker when she saw who was in front of him—leading the line of men.

It was Haig.

The man who had been like a father to her since she had been taken away from her mother eighteen years ago.

Great Mother! Haig had argued with her for months that there were no portals to a world like their own. But here he was, on the other side.

As she watched, he stopped with a quick, jerky motion and pointed into the air—right at her, then he dropped his hand and stood with his head bowed. He looked like a man captured by utter defeat. Yet he had just told Falcone, her worst enemy, that she was right above them.

Every instinct urged her to fly as far away as she could get.

But she needed more information. Knowing she must understand the situation, she circled the men, her heart in her throat. One of them broke from the group and launched a spear, and it flew past her.

She heard Falcone shout, "No! Hold your fire, you Carfolian idiot." And she wondered if he knew the soldiers by the river had fired at her.

As he leaped toward the back of the line, the men moved swiftly out of his way. Falcone brushed past them as he raised a hand, pointing it at the man who had thrown the spear.

The soldier fell to the ground, writhing in pain, clamping his hands to his ears as though that could block the psychic bolt that had just crashed into his brain.

Falcone stood over him, coolly administering more pain. Then he raised his head and looked at two of the soldiers. "Con, Rugar, get him on his feet!"

The warriors obeyed their leader's command, pulling their companion up and supporting him as he swayed on unsteady legs.

"If he can't go on with us, kill him."

The whole incident told Rinna something important. Falcone wanted to capture her alive—if he could. Maybe she was even the reason he had come through the portal with this squad of soldiers.

He knew where she had gone, he wanted her back, and he was willing to go to great lengths to get her.

As though he were reading her mind, he looked up and stared directly at her. For a moment their eyes met.

"Don't bother to try and escape. Wherever you go, I'll hunt you down."

She beat the air with her wings, thinking that if she could take him by surprise now, she could claw his eyes out.

But he had too many men. They would come to his rescue. And that would be the end of her.

He gave her one more defiant look, as though he had read her mind. Then he went straight to Haig's side where he bent toward the old man's ear, speaking in a tone that she couldn't hear.

Haig's head jerked.

When he looked up at her, she felt the old pull that had existed between them. Long ago, when the monitors had taken her to the school, she had been scared and confused. During the day, she had held her head high and pretended that her insides weren't raw and bleeding. She'd listened to the teachers tell her that she had escaped from a life of slavery.

But she knew it wasn't really true. She might live in a better house, eat better food, and be excused from manual labor, but she would still be expected to do someone else's work.

Not for a conventional master. But the council. Or someone powerful on the council.

At night when she was alone in her tiny room, she cried for what she had lost. And tried to imagine her future.

Then one night, the old man who worked in the kitchen came into her room and asked her what was wrong.

She had tried to hide her thoughts from him. But even then he had gotten past her defenses, and she had ended up pouring out her heart to him.

He was alone, too. His wife and little girl had died in a raid on the school when adepts from White Flint tried to wipe out the next generation of gifted psychics.

Sensing that he was as wounded as she, she had reached out to him, trying to give him peace. And the two of them had comforted each other. Like a father and daughter might.

In their sadness, they had forged an indelible bond. If one of them was hurt or in trouble, the other would always know it and find them.

As he reached out to find her now, she recoiled. He was calling her out of the sky, calling her to the man she hated and feared most in this world or any other.

She faltered in the air. For a moment her wings were paralyzed and she felt herself falling toward the ground.

But she wasn't going to give up so easily. With a mighty effort, she wrenched herself away from Haig's pull.

Dizzy, hardly able to see, she flapped away, landing in a tree about fifty yards from the men on the ground, her talons digging into the rough bark as she struggled to keep herself from tumbling off the safe perch.

Haig raised his head and began to move again, walking steadily toward her.

She watched him, trying to read the expression on his face. Finally, she rose into the air, moving a hundred yards away, hiding herself in a thatch of leafy branches.

From her refuge, she peered out, sure that none of the men on the ground could see her.

But Haig didn't need to find her through his sense of sight. He stood very still, like a man listening to something. Then his body jerked as though a string were attached to his chest, and he started off in her direction again. As she watched his awkward movements, she knew Haig was using the tie between them to find her.

Why? Because Falcone had subverted him? Promised him freedom or great wealth? Or because Falcone had put a compulsion on Haig? Earlier, she had been sure it was a compulsion.

Now she honestly didn't know. But she was sure that her oldest and best friend would find her again, no matter how long it took. There was no way to hide from him, because the two of them were tied together.

He could find her. And if she got too far out of his range, he would go to the places where she had been recently.

Their bond would lead him to her—or her haunts.

She heard a sound of horror and frustration rise in her own throat. There was no way she could stop him, short of killing him. And she knew she would never be able to do that, no matter what he did to her. As a child she had loved him fiercely because he was the only person in the whole frightening school compound who had been totally on her side. Then they'd been on their own in the badlands, and the bond between them had only grown stronger.

So he could find her. And if he couldn't locate her, he would lead Falcone to Logan's house. Falcone would torture him, then kill Logan when he couldn't say where she was.

She knew that as well as she knew anything about the Iron Man of Sun Acres.

Which meant that she had to protect Logan.

But how?

A desperate plan formed in her mind, and she took off from the tree branch, heading back to Logan's house.

FALCONE gave the old man a hearty slap on the back, then watched him struggle to keep his footing. "You found her, even in her bird shape. That's good news. Very good news."

The old man licked his lips. "She got away."

"But you can lead me to her again."

"I . . ."

Ruthlessly, Falcone cut him off. "Take me to her." He paused and looked around, dragging in a breath of the morning air. It was cool and fresh. Cleaner than at home.

The old man gave a curt nod, then started off at a deliberate pace. Falcone followed, gesturing for the soldiers to do the same.

Haig came to a wide ribbon of blacktop, remarkable for its smooth surface and uniform texture.

The old man looked back for instructions.

"Go ahead and cross," Falcone told him.

A vehicle was rushing toward them. As Haig hesitated on the gravel beside the road, a loud blast sounded from a horn as the carriage hurtled past, leaving wind blowing in its wake.

Behind Falcone some of the soldiers gasped, and he turned to give them a stern look.

"What was that?" one of them was brave enough to ask.

"An automobile," he answered promptly.

He knew that much. He had taken pains in the past to learn about this world by sending men through the two existing portals. Some of them had never been seen again. He didn't know if they had met some horrible fate or if they had decided to take their chances over here without the guidance of their master. If so, when he came here permanently, he would hunt them down and make them sorry they had dared to defy them.

But most of them were loyal to him, and they had come back with reports of wonders that he never would have imagined. Still, it would be better if he had more information now.

Two more automobiles rushed past. When no more appeared, he stepped onto the blacktop, boldly striding across the road, then motioned for his adepts and the rest of the troops to follow.

They sprinted across, quickly assembling on the other side.

Haig was almost out of sight, but Falcone didn't call out to slow the old man down. He wanted Rinna, and the sooner they took her into custody, the better.

So he hurried to catch up with his tracker, the rest of his party following in his wake.

He turned and looked back, feeling his throat tighten. They were far from the portal, and he didn't like that. One portal had closed. This other one was his lifeline back to his own world. He had come through and set up a base of operations fairly close to the gateway, in case it was necessary to retreat back to his own side.

But now Rinna was flying away from him, and the only way he could be sure of getting her back was to capture her himself—and kill the man with her.

CHAPTER TWENTY

RINNA HAD NEVER flown so fast, but panic set her wings beating the air.

Then she almost fell out of the sky when something large roared past her. Something shaped like a bird, but as she craned her neck upward, she saw it was man-made. And very high above her.

Perhaps it was that airplane thing they had talked about on the television set. But even far away, she could see it was much larger than a car.

Orienting herself, she found her own course again.

As she approached Logan's home, her arm muscles ached and the breath burned in her lungs. The wind stung her eyes, but when she looked down, she spotted a figure standing in front of the house.

Her heart contracted when she saw it was Logan. He was naked and staring toward the edge of the woods, and she knew he was about to change to wolf form so that he could look for her.

From above, she gave a great cry, trying to catch his

attention and stop him before he could make the change. To her vast relief he went still, then looked up and shaded his eyes. When he spotted her, he waved his arm in a wide arc.

She came down swiftly, landing on the grass a few feet away, and he reached for her. But she squawked again and shook her head. She needed to be able to talk to him and quickly.

Taking a step back, she pictured herself in human form, and her body followed her thoughts.

Even as she made the change, she saw Logan closing the distance between them.

"Rinna!" He caught her in his arms, pulling her naked body against his, and for that moment she was lost in the gladness of being with him once more.

"I thought you had left."

"No," she answered, knowing in that moment of sweet contact that she would have come back to him if she were free to do it.

When he brought his lips down to hers for a fierce, hungry kiss, she returned it with equal passion, devouring his mouth as though she had been months without him.

He stroked his hands over her body, his fingers gliding across her shoulders and down her back so that he could cup her bottom.

The sensations were exquisite. She came alive in his arms, tasting him, breathing in his scent, touching him. Maybe for the last time. That knowledge brought a hard knot to the inside of her chest, and she swallowed a cry of loss.

But he must have sensed that something was wrong. Lifting his head, he looked down at her.

"Where did you go?"

She had put off the moment of reckoning as long as she could. "Logan, Falcone is coming."

His hold tightened on her. "Where? How?"

"He brought a squad of warriors through the portal. They're coming here. Haig is leading them."

"Haig! I knew I couldn't trust that bastard."

Without even thinking, she leaped to her friend's defense. "He's under a compulsion. He can't help himself."

The moment the words were out of her mouth, she knew that she was only wasting valuable time. When Logan started to argue with her, she pressed her fingers to his lips. "There isn't time to talk about Haig. You have to listen to me."

As he pressed his lips together, she once again summoned the special power she had developed as a child—the power that Falcone had so cruelly locked inside her mind. She had used it with the detective. Now the need was more urgent, when the task was harder to accomplish because she had done it so recently.

This time the pain was searing, but she forced her way into that injured part of her brain, fighting not to gasp.

Logan's face contorted and his hands tightened on her shoulders. "Rinna, what is it? What's wrong?"

She didn't spare the energy for an answer, only kept her thoughts focused on the message she must convey to the man who held her in his arms.

"You have to go for help."

He shook his head. "I can't leave you here. Falcone could find you. I'm not going to let him hurt you again."

The pain threatened to rob her of breath. But she knew she had to keep her focus on the man and the message. "You must leave here. You must find help."

"What about . . . ?" He stopped, looking confused, as

though he'd lost his train of thought. "Falcone," he finally said, dredging up the name.

She understood what had happened. He had been trying to string a set of steps together in his mind, and she had prevented him from following his own logic.

It felt like hot needles were digging into her brain cells. To steady herself and also strengthen the contact with him, she found his hand and knit her fingers with his. There was more to do if she was going to succeed. And she could feel time slipping through her fingers.

"Rinna? What are you doing? What's wrong?"

The pain in her head had almost blinded her, but she raised her face toward his.

"Everything's going to work out," she managed to say, praying that she was right as she kept up the pressure inside herself, directing her thoughts toward Logan, forcing him to follow a different logic path from the one he had chosen on his own.

"Is there someone who can help us?" she asked, managing to keep the question from coming out as a moan.

To her relief, he answered immediately. "My brothers. And my cousin."

"Good. Which one is closer?"

"My brother, Lance."

"Then go to him. Quickly. Get help." She could barely speak around the knives stabbing inside her skull, but she forced herself to keep talking. "Tell Lance what happened."

He took a step back, then stopped, looking uncertain. "What about you?"

Somehow she managed to say the biggest lie of all. "I'll be fine until you get back. Get dressed. Go. Before it's too late."

When he hesitated, she closed the space between

them and clasped her arms around him, drawing him to her, pressing her body to his even as she summoned up one final burst of energy directed at his mind.

"I have to hurry," he said, pushing away from her.

"Yes. Hurry."

She sent him one more jolt of mental energy, reinforcing the message, making sure that if he tried to turn aside from his mission, his mind would go back to her and the instructions she had given him.

"Go now."

He turned and rushed into the house, and she swayed on unsteady legs. They lost the ability to hold her up, and she collapsed into a pile of leaves, lying there panting, trying to regain her strength.

She allowed herself a few moments to lie with her eyes closed. But she knew she couldn't stay there for long. Logan would come out of the house. And if he thought she was in trouble, he would go to her. Then she'd have to start implanting the message all over again, and she didn't think she had the strength.

So she forced herself up, forced one foot in front of the other as she crossed the lawn toward the house.

Logan burst through the front door, his eyes wild. He was dressed in a T-shirt and jeans, but he had forgotten to put on his shoes.

She hoped that didn't matter.

"Rinna! What the hell am I thinking? You have to come with me."

"I'll be here, turning the house into a fortress," she said.

"How can you do that?"

"You'll see when you come back. Now hurry."

He looked torn, and she summoned all the mental energy she had left to give him one final push.

To her vast relief, he ran to his car, started the engine and roared out of the driveway.

Praying that the suggestion would last long enough to keep him out of danger, she watched him disappear.

Logan. Her love. Her mate.

And maybe the only way she could save him was to sacrifice herself.

She sat down on the edge of the porch and rested for a few more moments, gathering her remaining strength the way she might gather spools of thread that had fallen out of a sewing basket and scattered across the floor.

Her head still throbbed, and she struggled to clear it because she had to be sharp when she met Falcone. If she was going to get away from him, she would have to do and say the right things.

When she felt a little better, she stood, then took a moment to steady herself on her feet before making the change from woman to bird again.

LOGAN drove south, toward Lance's house. Like his own, it was in a wooded area, next to a state park where a werewolf could roam when the need to hunt took him.

His brain felt foggy. He was going to Lance's house. To ask for help. But he should be back with Rinna protecting his mate.

He pulled to the side of the road, cut the engine, and rested his head on the steering wheel, trying to clear the muzzy feeling from his mind. Why was he leaving Rinna?

He tried to puzzle it out. But he couldn't force the act of leaving to make sense in his mind.

He should turn around and go home. That thought tried to worm its way to the front of his mind.

He reached to start the engine. But the touch of soft fingers on his hand stopped him.

"Rinna?"

"Yes."

He had thought he was alone. But Rinna was beside him in the passenger seat, whispering softly to him, telling him that he must go to Lance's house.

He turned his head toward her, puzzled, trying to see where she sat.

"Where are you?"

"Right here."

"Didn't I leave you home?" he asked, hearing the confusion in his own voice.

"Yes. I'm protecting the house."

How could she be at home and with him, too? It didn't make sense. He couldn't see her. But he could hear her voice in his mind. And he thought that maybe he was only remembering what she had told him.

He said her name again, then imagined her smiling at him, reaching for him, pulling him down to a soft bed of leaves in the forest.

Wait! That was wrong. He couldn't make love to her now. He had to go to Lance's.

No. He had to go home. Quickly.

"Go to Lance's. Go to Lance's and get help."

He started the engine again and began to drive. And after a few minutes, he began thinking again that he might be doing the wrong thing. But every time he thought about stopping and turning around, Rinna's voice echoed in his mind. She had told him to go to Lance. She had told him to get help. And he knew that was what he must do.

So his hands gripped the wheel as he drove south, speeding through the early morning. At first there were hardly any cars on the road. But as dawn approached, commuters began clogging the road.

He was on an urgent mission, and he wanted to pound on his horn and get the bastards to move out of the way. But he knew it wouldn't do any good, so he suffered through the traffic, feeling a great swell of relief when he turned onto the road that led to the house where his brother lived with his wife, Savannah Carpenter.

They had been married only a few months. She was an artist, so she had kept her own name. And she had been at the thick of it when they had defeated the monster from another universe. It had been lurking in the basement of a D.C. S & M club called the Castle, feeding off the emotions of the patrons.

Savannah and Lance had gone there to find out who had pushed her sister off a cliff in Rock Creek Park. She and the other women had fought the monster. And the wolves had protected them.

Savannah and Lance knew about the parallel universe, and they would understand when he explained why Rinna needed their help.

He pulled into the driveway and jumped out of the car—in time to meet a gray wolf coming out of the woods.

It was Lance, and the wolf stopped short, his face questioning his brother's unexpected visit.

Logan bounced on the balls of his feet. "Hurry up and change. I need your help."

Lance disappeared back into the woods.

He seemed to take forever, and Logan pawed the ground with his bare feet.

Bare feet? He'd driven over here with no shoes on? He hadn't thought about that until this instant.

Finally, Lance was back, bare-chested but wearing a pair of sweatpants.

Lance looked him up and down—from the bare feet to the hair he hadn't bothered to comb that morning.

"You look like the devil is chasing you. What's wrong?"

The pressure of getting the message out made Logan shout out the first thing that came to his mind. "It's Rinna. Falcone is coming for her."

But Logan had been much too busy to tell his brother what had been going on in his life, so Lance didn't know any of those names or anything about what had been happening over the past week and a half.

"Rinna?"

Logan flapped his arm in exasperation. "You saw her at the castle. She's the woman from the other side of the portal."

Lance tipped his head to one side. "Maybe you'd better slow down and fill in some of the blanks."

Logan wanted to hurl a string of curses at his brother. But he ordered himself to hold on to his temper. Dragging in a deep breath, he let it out slowly, then said, "Remember when we fought Boralas?"

"Of course. The thing was after me and Savannah."

"Remember that we could see a woman helping us from the other side?"

Lance nodded, watching him with an intent expression.

Logan didn't like that look. "What?" he growled.

"Nothing. Go on."

"Well, Rinna saved my life."

"Did something happen at the Castle that I don't know about?"

Logan's exasperation had reached boiling point. "Jesus! You're not listening. I'm talking about last week. I was on an expedition gathering native plants that are going to be bulldozed. And I was running in the woods. In wolf form. Falcone had set a trap for her, but I walked into it—because it was tuned to catch a shape-shifter."

"And Falcone is?" Lance asked, his voice maddeningly reasonable.

"He's one of the bigwigs on the council at Sun Acres. He went to school with Rinna, and he knew her psychic potential. He wants to control her. And he wants her to give him children who will run the city."

Lance shook his head. "Sorry, but you're losing me. Am I supposed to know about Sun Acres?"

Frustrated by his brother's lack of understanding, Logan could no longer hold his anger in check. He'd come here because Rinna had sent him to get help, and all Lance was doing was asking stupid questions. "You son of a bitch. I'm trying to explain, but you're not listening."

Lance raised his hand.

Even if the gesture was innocent, ingrained werewolf behavior took over. Through the generations, the men of the Marshall clan had fought for dominance among themselves. It was like a conditioned reflex, until their cousin Ross had proved to them that they could work together if they curbed their more aggressive impulses.

But Ross wasn't here now to act as a mediator between these two particular werewolves. And Logan saw the upraised hand as a threatening gesture. Raising his own hand, he hauled off and socked his brother on the jaw.

Lance snarled and struck out at him.

Logan reached out and pulled his brother off his feet, landing on the ground on top of him.

Neither one of them was crazed enough to go for the other's throat. But they rolled across the grassy area between the woods and the house, trading punches and howling at each other.

"Stop it!"

A sharp voice cut through the fog of battle, but neither one of them paid any attention—until a stream of icy cold water struck Logan in the face. Sputtering, he jerked his head up, searching for the source of the new enemy, ready to redirect his attack.

Lance got in one more punch before the water landed solidly in his face.

"Hey!"

They both looked toward the house, and saw Savannah, wearing a bathrobe and standing on the lawn, the garden hose in her hand.

"What in the name of God are you doing?" she shouted.

They both stared at her as she pointed the hose away from them and adjusted the stream of water to a trickle.

"I came to get Lance's help," Logan sputtered as he pulled away from his brother.

"Well, you sure have a funny way of going about it," Savannah observed.

He scrubbed his hand over his face, wiping off the water, then shot Lance an embarrassed look. He was relieved to see that his brother looked just as abashed.

"Sorry," he muttered.

"Yeah," Lance responded.

"You were going to tell us why you're here," Savannah suggested.

"Yeah. Right. I . . ." He started to explain what had happened and suddenly became aware that he didn't know what he wanted to say. Rinna had told him . . . told him . . .

He blinked, and in that terrible moment, he understood that Rinna had tricked him.

CHAPTER TWENTY-ONE

RINNA'S HEART POUNDED in her chest as she circled high in the sky, high above the patch of woods. Off to the left and the right she could see houses among the greenery. Houses sitting out in the open, unprotected. There might be guns in this world, but the people felt safe enough to live outside a high fence. That simply wasn't true back home. Only the desperate lived without protection.

Finally she could also see a tent in the distance. Falcone must have set up camp.

It was so tempting to take her chances here and just keep flying—away from Falcone. Away from danger. But that would leave Logan in serious trouble. She had to follow through on the plan she had devised. But now that she was back near Falcone, the thought of landing made her insides churn.

Still, she had no choice. She had known that in the back of her mind as soon as she had seen Haig and Falcone and the soldiers marching through the woods.

Maybe she had even known what was going to happen when she'd landed beside the detective. Maybe a premonition had prompted her words to him.

She knew she was stalling.

But the thought of facing Falcone as a naked woman made her stomach roil. So she widened her circle, flying over the houses, her sharp eyes searching for one of those lines where people hung clothes to dry—right out in the open where anyone passing by could take them.

She was beginning to think she would have to find an empty house and break in when she finally spotted what she needed. Of course, the line was near the windows, and now it was broad daylight. Well, too bad!

She flew down, landing directly on the clothesline, assessing her choices. She saw men's shirts. And pants that probably belonged to a woman. They were wider than the men's slacks. But the legs were short.

Praying that her luck would hold, she pulled the pins from a long-sleeved shirt, then went after a pair of pants.

But before she was finished, the back door opened, and a blond-haired woman wearing a shapeless dress came out of the house, brandishing a broom and waving it angrily at the bird on the clothesline.

At least it was a broom, not a gun, so Rinna kept working frantically to free the pants.

"Get away, you damn thief. Get away," the woman shouted as she advanced with the broom.

Rinna plucked at the clothespin and finally managed to pull it loose, then dodged as the broom came down next to her, thwacking the line and making her almost lose her balance.

"Go on. Git."

Rinna hated to add violence to thievery. But it looked like that was her only option if she wanted to be dressed when she met Falcone. Turning, she spread her wings to their impressive width, then came at the woman, squawking and flapping.

AFTER getting coldcocked, Jake Cooper knew he should be in bed. After a few hours of restless sleep, he checked his pupils in the mirror and saw that they were contracting normally. Then he washed and dressed and climbed back into his unmarked.

He'd had a bad night, starting with a trip to the emergency room after he'd come to in front of the convenience store. He'd kept telling the doctors and nurses that he was okay. But because he'd been unconscious, he hadn't gotten out of the place until they'd x-rayed his head and done a CAT scan to make sure there was no internal bleeding.

Now he was supposed to be taking it easy. Instead he called Lieutenant Donaldson and said he had information that there could be some kind of attack on the convenience store.

The Lieu had been skeptical. But Jake had spun out a story about an informant claiming that a group of terrorists were planning to go after the place.

An informant? He gave a harsh laugh. Would that be the big white bird who had found him lying on the concrete in front of the store? The idea had come to him while she'd been there.

But she couldn't have anything to do with it, could she? And why did he think of the damn bird as she?

Getting Donaldson to agree to close the place and send in a bomb squad should have satisfied Jake. But he'd made the mistake of stopping by the office and found the information he'd been waiting for sitting on his desk. Logan

Marshall's fingerprints were on the can of pork and beans that someone had used to brain the guy trying to rob the store.

Marshall was a hero. He should be taking his bows on the evening news. And maybe getting a reward from the company that owned the store. Instead he didn't want to get involved. But Jake was going to use all the leverage he had to get some information out of the guy.

He'd done a background check on Marshall. He was a landscape architect with a good reputation in his field. He took frequent trips to collect plant specimens, which he used in his work. If he were moving illegal goods, he could have used the trips for that purpose. But he had no criminal record and nothing about his background or his lifestyle seemed "off." He paid his bills on time. His credit was excellent. And he minded his own business, except the night he'd happened into the Easy Shopper during a robbery.

One interesting fact, however, was that he didn't appear to be married. So why had he claimed that the woman named Rinna was his wife? Had he smuggled an illegal alien into the country?

It seemed unlikely, although Jake remembered that her speech did have a slightly exotic tinge. But whatever was going on with Marshall and his "wife," Jake was going to find out.

AS the large white bird went on the attack, the woman with the broom screamed. Dropping her weapon, she covered her blond head with her hands as she ran back into the house.

With the frightened homeowner in retreat, Rinna gathered up the pants and shirt, dragging them behind her as she flew a little way into the woods. After a short rest, she put another hundred yards between herself and the house.

When she had stopped panting, she changed to human form, then hastily pulled on the shirt, which came down almost to her knees. After dragging on the strangely short pants, she looked down at her feet. She was shoeless, but her body was covered.

Now that she was dressed, she had no more excuses. Still, it took all her resolve to dredge up the courage to find Falcone.

Grimly she started back through the woods, heading for the location where she had spotted the tent. Haig had been leading a troop of soldiers toward Logan's house.

She moved in a circle around the soldiers, approaching the old man from the side. But he had already stopped and was staring expectantly in her direction.

She was pretty sure he couldn't see her in the thick patch of brush where she hid, but he came right toward her, making her heart pound and leap into her windpipe.

He looked sick and shaken. But she saw no physical marks on him.

Gathering her resolve, she stepped out from behind the tangle of brush, then waved her arm.

He went stock-still.

As they stared at each other across twenty yards of charged space, she managed to say, "Were you looking for me?"

His face crumpled. And his message was the same one she had heard when the woman with the broom had attacked her. "Get out of here. Go. Run."

"Did he force you to find me?"

The old man opened his mouth and tried to answer the question, but no words came out of his mouth.

* * *

"OH my God," Logan gasped, sudden panic choking off his breath. "Rinna. Oh God, Rinna. I have to go back and stop her before it's too late."

He staggered to his feet and started back toward his car. But Savannah dropped the hose and came running toward him, grabbing his arm. "You must have come here for a good reason. You need to tell us what's happened."

"No. I have to go home," he insisted, watching his brother get to his feet. He tensed, wondering if Lance was going to attack.

Savannah turned and gave her husband a sharp look, then focused on Logan again. "Tell us why you came."

While he tried to collect his thoughts, he dragged in a breath and let it out in a rush. "I met my life mate."

Savannah's face took on a sudden glow. "That's wonderful," she breathed.

"No. It's complicated," he answered, struggling to keep his voice even. "She's from the other universe. Remember at the Castle? The woman on the other side of . . . the portal. The one helping us fight the monster."

"Yes."

"That was Rinna. I met her again. She saved my life and took me back to the world where she lives. It's not like our universe. A lot of the people have psychic abilities, and they use them to run things instead of our power sources. I mean they use mental energy instead of electricity and gasoline. They find children who have psychic potential and put them into training programs."

"Okay."

"They don't have countries. They have city-states that fight each other all the time—like in ancient Greece.

And one of the powerful guys in her city wants to . . . to take advantage of her powers. She's a shape-shifter. But she has other talents, too. She sent me to get help so she could leave my house and go back to him."

There was a lot more to it than that, but he'd spit out the important parts, and the idea of wasting any more time in explanations made his insides churn.

Pleadingly, he stared at Savannah, then saw his brother advancing from the side.

He stiffened, but Lance stopped a few feet away. "She's left you for him?" he asked in a harsh voice.

"It's not what you think! She's trying to keep him away from me." He had no hard evidence of that, yet he knew it deep in his gut. "I have to find her before she gets to him. But I can't do it alone."

"We can track her," Lance said.

Logan wanted to cry out in frustration. "If she'd changed into a wolf, we could."

"The two of you and Ross can track her," Savannah said.

He gave her a grateful look. "Maybe. But Rinna has two different animal shapes. I'm betting that she changed to a hawk and went flying back."

"A hawk?" Lance asked. "That's a neat trick, if you can do it."

"She can."

"So now what?" his brother asked.

Logan shifted his weight from one foot to the other. "If you're willing to help, we go back to my house, so you can pick up her scent. Then we . . ." He stopped short because he wasn't sure what to say. "Maybe if we keep tracking in widening circles, we can find her."

Lance raised one shoulder. "Sorry about the fight."

"Yeah. I'm sorry, too. And I appreciate the help."

"You two go on," Savannah said. "I'll call Ross and explain. Well, I'll say as much as I can on the phone."

"Thanks. He already knows a little. I called him last night about getting an ID for Rinna." Logan ran back to the car. Lance started to follow him, until his wife called him back.

"Maybe you'd better go separately. Lance needs shoes and a shirt."

His brother looked down, taking in his state of partial undress. "Yeah. I'll be five minutes behind you."

Logan wasn't wearing shoes, either. But he jumped into his SUV and roared back down the access road to the highway.

When he reached the blacktop, he forced himself not to speed, since getting stopped by a traffic cop wasn't going to increase his chances of finding Rinna.

He made good time, then raced inside the front door to his home. Inside, he picked up the shirt that Rinna had worn. Standing in the open doorway, he caressed the soft fabric with his fingers, then held it to his face, breathing in Rinna's scent.

"Damn you," he muttered. "We could have worked this out together, if you'd just trusted me."

Was that it? A matter of trust? He didn't want to think that was the problem. He wanted to *find* her, and he didn't even know where to start.

He heard tires crunching on the driveway and stepped outside, the hand with the shirt extended, expecting to see Lance pulling up the driveway.

But it wasn't his brother, and he froze, then hastily dropped his hand.

* * *

IT was too late to run. Rinna stood frozen in place as soldiers came racing out of the bushes and surrounded her. Two of them grabbed her arms to stop her from getting away.

They held her in place, and she stiffened her shoulders as she saw a man emerge from between the trees.

It was Falcone. He had the same dark hair, the same confident walk, the same smirk on his handsome face that she remembered.

As he strolled straight toward her, she felt like she was going to throw up, but somehow she controlled the sickness churning in her stomach.

He was dressed like a man from this world with a blue shirt that buttoned down the front, jeans and what Logan called running shoes on his feet. But he still looked like the noble who was going to be ruler of Sun Acres.

"It's good to see you again," he said.

She didn't bother to answer.

"You could have made this a lot harder for me."

She raised one shoulder. "I'm tired of running."

When he stepped forward and stroked his finger against her cheek, she felt her insides turn to ice. Everything that had happened between them in those terrible hours in his bed came racing back to her. He hadn't wanted to make love to her. He had wanted to punish her for being better in school than he had been.

"I don't like it when a woman leaves me without permission," he said in a low voice.

She was about to speak when he waved her to silence, and she fell back on old habits, instantly closing her mouth and cutting off what she was going to say.

She had lived free in the badlands and with Logan. Once again she was a slave, just as she had been in Sun Acres.

And she was standing in front of the man who had raped her. She had never used that word in her own mind. But Logan had made her understand that it was true. And now she was back in Falcone's clutches. A slave who had no rights.

He turned to one of the guards. "The old man has served his purpose. Get rid of him," he ordered.

Despite everything, Rinna gasped out, "No. Please. You don't have to . . . kill him."

"I'm afraid I do." Falcone studied her with a smug expression on his face. "He followed orders and led me to you."

"Because you made him do it."

He shrugged. "If you say so." He turned and spoke over his shoulder. "Let's go to my tent and have a chat," he said.

She knew her face must have given away how sick she felt, because he smiled at her.

She tried to reach out to Haig, to find his mind with hers. But he had closed himself off from her, and she knew it was because of his shame.

Guards flanked her sides, back and front, as they marched toward the tent, toward her doom.

JAKE pulled in at the Marshall driveway and came to a stop in front of the house. As he cut the engine, Marshall came charging out the door.

Jake stared at him appraisingly. Actually, he looked like he could have spent the night in a flophouse. His hair was uncombed, his shirt was stained and sticking to his skin, and a day's growth of beard darkened his cheeks.

He was clutching a T-shirt in his hand, holding it out

like he was offering it over as evidence. But as soon as he saw Jake, he dropped his arm.

Jake got out of the car and walked toward him, keeping his arms casually at his sides.

But Marshall's eyes were instantly wary. "What do you want?" he asked.

"To talk about the Easy Shopper."

"I told you, I wasn't there, except to buy some batteries the day before the robbery."

"So you say."

"What's that supposed to mean?"

"When I was here last time, I got your prints from the door handle of your SUV."

Marshall's stance turned aggressive. "That's an invasion of privacy."

"You could say that. You could also say they match the prints on the can of pork and beans you brought down on Tony Blanchard's head."

"I guess I picked up the can when I was in there last week," Marshall said coolly. "When I bought the flashlight batteries. I was going to buy the beans, but they were too expensive."

"Is there some reason why you don't want to get involved in the investigation?"

Marshall hesitated. It looked like he was about to answer when another SUV pulled up the driveway.

It was Jake's turn to curse, but under his breath. It had seemed like he would get something out of Marshall. Now the guy had a chance to reconsider.

The SUV pulled into the parking area in front of the house. Probably it was the car Marshall had been waiting for when he'd come charging out of the house.

Another man got out and ambled toward them. His

gaze flicked from Jake to Marshall. "You call the cops?" the newcomer asked.

"No."

Interesting, Jake thought. Apparently one or both of them had a problem that might require police assistance.

"Then what's the law doing here?" the other man asked, his voice still casual.

Marshall sighed. "This is detective Jake Cooper. He's looking for information about witnesses to a convenience store robbery."

Beyond the spoken conversation, the tall, lean men exchanged silent messages that raised Jake's curiosity. Maybe Marshall hadn't shared any robbery details with his friend, no . . . relative, Jake decided. These guys looked like they came from the same gene pool.

Finally Marshall cleared his throat and gestured toward the other man. "This is my brother, Lance Marshall. He's come to help me find my wife. She's . . . missing."

Instantly, Jake saw the situation in a new light. No wonder the man looked strung out.

And then there was the other guy. The brother. He was supposed to be here to help. But he'd reacted to what Marshall had said. Why? Could it be that this was the first time he'd heard that Marshall was married? Or was Marshall really married? The answer to that question was still pending.

Fishing for answers, Jake asked, "Marital problem?"

"No!" The answer was too quick and too decisive, making Jake wonder if it was the truth.

"Did somebody snatch her?"

Marshall balled his hands into fists. "I'm not playing twenty questions with you."

Jake held his ground. "Take it easy. I'm the police. I can help."

"I doubt it. And I can't help you on the convenience store, because we have to look for Rinna."

Making a quick mental connection, Jake tried another question. "Is her disappearance related to what happened the other day?"

Marshall's eyes narrowed. "I have to go."

"Yeah, I understand where you're coming from. But give me a few minutes of your time. I may have some information you can use."

When he saw hope flash in the other man's eyes, he figured he was on the right track.

CHAPTER TWENTY-TWO

"WHAT INFORMATION?" LOGAN demanded.

"There's something funny going on at that store, right? Is your wife involved in something there? Are you trying to protect her?"

Logan wanted to punch out the cop's lights. He'd thought this guy could give him a clue about where to find Rinna. But Cooper was only on a fishing expedition.

"I don't have time for this," he muttered, starting to turn away.

"Wait a minute," Cooper said quickly. "Let's exchange information."

Logan stared at him, stony faced.

The detective continued, talking fast. "I've had patrols going past the store every couple of hours. They didn't see anything, so I went there last night. I didn't see a damn thing."

"Then stop wasting my time!" Logan growled.

"I said I didn't *see* anything. That was part of what

was so strange. I thought I heard men coming out of the store. When I tried to pursue them, somebody threw a spear at me. Then somebody else came up behind me and started a fight. I couldn't see the spear carrier. And I couldn't see the one who attacked me, but I smelled his sweaty body. It was like somebody made him invisible. Him and his friends."

Logan stared at him, hardly daring to hope. He'd seen enough cop shows to know that they could say anything they wanted to you and it didn't have to be true. But why would Cooper have come up with such a bizarre story?

"You're saying you think there were a bunch of guys there last night. But they were invisible?" he asked, keeping his voice low and even.

"If I told that story to someone else, they'd haul me off to the loony bin," the cop remarked. "But you're taking it in like I was telling you about a cool play during Monday night football."

"Yeah," Logan admitted, looking from Cooper to his brother, then back again. "I have an idea about what's going on at the Easy Shopper. But you probably won't believe me."

"Try me."

"If you're willing to keep an open mind."

The detective nodded.

"You watch science fiction shows on televison? *Star Trek*? Stuff like that?"

"Some."

"You remember they landed on a different planet every week, with inhabitants who were different from us?"

"Where are you going with this?"

Logan swallowed. "One more thing. Have you heard

of the string theory? It's a concept developed by physicists that says there are universes parallel to this one."

The detective cocked his head to one side, studying him. "You've got me on that one."

Logan knew he could be making a big mistake. But he figured he didn't have anything to lose.

Looking the detective squarely in the eye, he said, "What's happening at that damn store proves the theory. There's a door to another universe in the back. The guys you couldn't see came through it. They come from a universe where a lot of the people have psychic powers. I'm guessing one of them made them invisible."

Cooper heaved a sigh. "I thought you were going to come clean with me."

"I am."

"I don't think so. What are you covering up?"

"Nothing!" Logan made an effort not to grab the guy by the collar and shake him. One fight in an hour was enough. "I'm not going to stand around talking about it. Not when Rinna is missing."

He pushed past the detective, walking rapidly toward his car. "Come on," he said to Lance.

His brother followed.

"I don't have a record of your being married," the cop called after him. "What is she, an illegal alien?"

WHEN Rinna saw Falcone disappear inside the campaign tent and close the flap behind him, her footsteps faltered. But two of the soldiers grabbed her. They must know what Falcone had done to her. They were in his household, and gossip traveled quickly around a closed little world like Falcone's estate.

She wanted to scream, "No," but the protest stayed locked in her throat.

They were afraid to help her, and she understood why.

She wanted to tell them that they could run away. She and Logan would help them get adjusted to this world. And together they could deal with Falcone.

But she knew they wouldn't believe her. They were too conditioned to the reality of Sun Acres.

So they followed orders, pushing her relentlessly toward the tent. It took every bit of resolve she possessed to keep from turning and clawing at them, then running as fast as she could into the woods, praying that somebody heaved a spear into her back before Falcone could get his cold, cruel hands on her again. Better death than another session in his bed.

But somewhere in her frantic mind she remembered why she had come here. If she was strong enough, she might change her own fate.

LOGAN turned back toward the detective, determined to make him explain that crack about Rinna being an illegal alien. But before he could challenge the cop, Lance put his hand on his arm and squeezed.

Logan went rigid, hardly able to control his need to strike out—at someone. Anyone. The detective. His brother. Anybody convenient.

But Lance's voice cut through the red fog in his brain. "Come on," he ordered. "Getting slapped into jail isn't going to do you any good."

Logan gritted his teeth and struggled for control.

The detective gave him an assessing look. Logan thought the guy was going to make a comment about his state of mind. But he switched to something completely different.

"One more thing. You have any insights about a big white bird hanging around the Easy Shopper?"

Logan felt his heart stop and start up again in double time. "You saw a large white bird?" he asked carefully.

"It came flapping down to the pad in front of the store after I got coldcocked, while I was lying there, trying to get up the energy to move."

"And when was that?"

"Last night."

Logan stared at him. The bird sounded like it was Rinna, unless someone else who took that form had come through the portal. That was always a possibility.

So why had Cooper mentioned it? Was he just doing more fishing for information? Or did he think the bird was part of the strange events coalescing around the convenience store?

Logan chose to believe it was Rinna. But he'd know soon enough. Because if she'd been at the store, her scent would be fresh there, and closer to where Falcone and his men had come through the portal.

"You've seen that bird?" Cooper asked.

Logan managed to answer with a small negative shake of his head, then allowed Lance to escort him to his SUV.

"Want me to drive?" his brother asked.

"No!" He climbed behind the wheel. The moment his brother was in his seat, he gunned the engine and sped down the drive.

Beside him, Lance fumbled with his seat belt. "You trying to get us killed?"

"I'm trying to make sure he doesn't follow us."

Behind him, he heard Cooper's car start. Before the detective could turn his car around and head down the driveway, Logan took a detour into a nearby development, making several turns, then going out the back way so that they were on a different road from where they'd entered.

"Let's hope we lost him."

"But you and the cop are both going to the convenience store, right?"

"Yeah. Only he's just going to see a couple of big shaggy dogs in the woods." He changed subjects abruptly. "You got your cell phone?"

"Um hmm."

"Call Ross and tell him we're meeting at the recreational area just west of the Easy Shopper in Mount Airy." He gave Lance the address of the store and also directions to a parking area on the other side of the woods.

THE soldiers pushed Rinna into the campaign tent, then stood behind her, blocking any means of escape. She struggled not to tremble as she waited for her eyes to adjust to the dim light.

When she finally looked up, she felt a wave of relief. Falcone was not alone. Two of his adepts were also there—Avery and Brusco.

"Here she is at last," he said in a conversational tone.

The two men were looking at her in a way that made her stomach knot. They knew something she didn't.

"What are you planning?" she asked.

"Another little psychic operation for you. You're too

dangerous as you are. But I believe the three of us can fix it so you won't be threatening the stability of Sun Acres again."

She looked from one man to the other. "Is that what he told you? That I'm threatening the stability of his little kingdom? Who says he has the right to rule Sun Acres?"

Avery looked abashed. Brusco gave her a stony stare. He was younger than Avery. Perhaps he hoped for a good place in the new government.

Falcone pushed Rinna into a camp chair, then bound her arms to the chair arms with rope. More rope secured her legs and feet.

When she was secured in place, her captor stepped back and looked at her. She made a subtle try at sending him a suggestion that he wanted to leave her alone. The effort made her head throb, but it had the opposite effect than she'd intended.

"I was ready for that," Falcone muttered as he reinforced the block he'd put up, then punished her with a wave of pain that he sent directly into her skull.

As the blast hit her, she gasped, going limp in the chair, then tried to collect her scattered thoughts over the ringing in her ears, in her brain.

Making a terrible effort, she stared up at Falcone.

But it was Avery who spoke. "I felt that jab from her. I thought you made it impossible for her to use that power."

"Apparently she still can."

"She's dangerous."

"That's what I've been trying to tell you," Falcone snapped. "And you've been putting up all kinds of arguments. Do you believe me now?"

"I believe you. But I have been on the council for a long time. Years ago we agreed that destroying the brain of a human being is counter to . . . morality. Death is more humane."

"It may be humane. But that's not what we're going to do. I want her alive so she can bear me children. If we leave her the way she is, there's no telling what she can do."

The old man nodded, looking regretful.

Falcone turned to Brusco. "And you agree that she can't be allowed to influence other people's behavior?"

The younger man gave his agreement quickly.

Rinna turned toward Avery. "You could just let me go," she gasped out. "That's all you have to do. Let me live out my life in this world where I won't be a threat to Sun Acres."

"She has a point," Avery murmured. "That would solve any problems concerning her for Sun Acres.

"You're forgetting that I want her children," Falcone snapped. He gave her a smile that didn't reach her eyes. "Women tell me I'm a skillful lover. You might have already discovered that, if you hadn't been so intent on hating me. But after we operate on your mind, you won't be thinking about who is giving you pleasure."

The boastful words made her stomach curdle.

Falcone turned from her and addressed the two men. "Let's get it over with. I want her neutralized so that we can bring her back safely."

As she watched in horror, the three men gathered in a circle around her. When they joined hands, a wave of cold swept over her. They were all strong psychics, and she knew they had the power to damage her mind beyond repair, especially if Falcone was directing the proceedings.

With a silent prayer to the Great Mother, she struggled for calm, even as she braced for the pain.

CHAPTER
TWENTY-THREE

LOGAN PULLED INTO a parking spot beside a picnic table in the recreational area directly west of the Easy Shopper.

He tried to lean back in the seat and relax. But he found it was impossible to simply sit in the car and wait for Ross. He got out and looked up at the afternoon sky, amazed at how much time had slipped through his fingers.

He wanted to find Rinna immediately, but it didn't seem to be happening. After pacing to the far end of the parking lot, he stepped into the woods, thinking that he'd have a look at the convenience store, then come back. Just then another car pulled into the parking lot.

He tensed, then saw it was Ross. He got out and trotted over to him.

"What can I do to help?" his cousin asked, and Logan felt a surge of gratitude. He'd gone straight to Lance because he lived closer. But he saw now that if he'd found Ross first, they wouldn't have ended up fighting. His cousin was determined to make relationships work in the

Marshall family, and he was good at keeping tempers at a manageable level.

Logan struggled to keep his voice steady. "My life mate has disappeared. I think she's been kidnapped by a guy named Falcone, the same one who already raped her."

Ross winced.

They'd spoken a little on the way over. But Logan knew that cell phone transmissions were far from secure, and he hadn't wanted to give any paranormal details that someone else could pick up.

"The executive summary is that she's the woman we saw through the doorway when we were fighting that monster in the basement of the Castle. She helped us kill the damn thing."

"I was upstairs getting Kevin and Erica free. But Megan told me all about it."

"Rinna is a shape-shifter—from a parallel universe. She can change into either a white wolf or a white hawk. And she has other powers as well. But this guy has already crippled her abilities to some extent, and I think he'll do more if he has her for any length of time."

"Okay," Ross answered in a perfectly deadpan voice, and Logan appreciated that he wasn't having any trouble dealing with the strange facts. Not like the cop.

As they talked, Lance climbed out of the car and joined them. Logan clasped his shoulder. A few hours ago they had been fighting. But now he knew that his brother and his cousin were there for him.

"We need to track her," Logan continued. "And I know she was at the convenience store recently. The portal to her world is at the back of the store. From what a confused cop told me, I'm betting that the bad guy and some soldiers came through last night, and that they were using some kind of invisibility shield."

"It's kind of inconvenient if they're still using it," Ross muttered.

"Let's assume that they can't hide a large group of soldiers like that for long."

Ross nodded.

"We can leave that problem for now. We have to find Rinna. I think the bad guy started tracking her as soon as he came through."

"And he caught up with her?"

Logan clenched his hands into fists. "I think she went back to him—to keep him away from me. She used her power to plant the idea in my head that I should go for help. When I got to Lance's house I realized that she sent me away, leaving herself totally unprotected. If he's got her, they're going to be between here and my house."

"Okay."

"I was thinking that we could go as wolves to the convenience store and start in the direction of my place."

Ross nodded, then asked in a perfectly conversational voice, "And when we find the bastard who's got her, do we attack as wolves? Or as men?"

"Wolves. We'll change here, and I'll show you where to find the store." He started toward the woods, then stopped as he thought about the kind of danger he was getting his brother and his cousin into. "He's not alone. He's got soldiers from his private army with him. Maybe we'd better not attack until we see what we're up against."

"We'll play it by ear," Ross said. "So maybe we need to be prepared with clothing."

"I've started carrying stuff in my car," Logan said, "but I don't have any way to take clothing with me."

"I have a couple of backpacks," Ross said. "We'll put as much as we can in there. And we can wear whistles so we can communicate."

"Good idea."

"They each have a different call," Ross explained. "I'll be a dove. Lance can be a cardinal and Logan can be a blue jay."

They all spent a lot of time in the woods, so they all knew the calls.

They got the packs ready, then moved into a tangle of brambles, where they changed to wolf form.

When they were ready, they started toward the convenience store.

Logan stopped at the edge of the woods, when he saw Jake Cooper standing in front of the Easy Shopper. Lance had been right; the bastard hadn't wasted any time getting back there.

And apparently searching the place. The area in front of the building was roped off with familiar yellow tape. As Logan watched, two men emerged and shook their heads.

Cooper's features hardened as he stepped toward them. He turned his back on the crowd, and talked to the men, exchanging information in low voices. The men walked back to a police car. Cooper stayed where he was.

So what was he doing, looking for the portal that he'd said flat out he didn't believe existed?

Or did he think this convenience store had a tunnel in the back where drug smugglers were coming in from the next county?

Yeah, that was probably it! Logan gave a bark of a laugh. And the drug smugglers had sprayed the area with a hallucinogen, so Cooper thought they were invisible. That would work as a rationalization. Logan was sorry he hadn't suggested it to the detective instead of that wild story about alternate universes.

A crowd of people, including the clerk who had ratted

him out, were standing in back of the yellow tape, staring at the store.

Cooper folded his arms across his chest and stared at the building.

As Logan watched the scene, he knew something was wrong. Something he wouldn't have been able to articulate even if he'd been in human form. He felt a thickening in the air, a building pressure that he didn't understand. But on a subliminal level, he knew something bad was about to happen.

Beside him Ross growled. Lance pawed the ground, and he knew that they felt it, too.

He looked from one of them to the other, then dashed out of the woods. Skirting the crowd, he ran toward the detective, who glanced up in astonishment as he saw a wolf—or maybe a German shepherd heading straight toward him. A wolf wearing a backpack.

Logan made a yipping sound.

As Cooper stared at him, he grabbed the man's sleeve, tugging at him, tugging him away from the building.

Come on. Come on, he silently shouted. But the words stayed locked in his throat.

Someone in the crowd gasped. Then more gasps and screams erupted as two other wolves joined the scene. One of them got behind Cooper and pushed. The other one grabbed his free arm and tried to move him away from the building.

Logan felt as though time had slowed down. Each second was like the frame of a movie held in suspended animation on the screen.

Somewhere in the neighborhood, he heard a dog howl, then another.

"Get the dogs off him," someone shouted.

"Those are goddamned wolves," another voice called out.

Some people backed away. Others moved in closer for a better look.

"Turn me loose. What the hell are you doing?" Cooper shouted, trying to wrench himself free.

Luckily Ross had his right arm, because that kept him from going for the sidearm in his shoulder holster.

A man left the scene and ran toward his truck, and Logan hoped to hell he wasn't coming back with a gun. Would he be stupid enough to shoot into the middle of a crowd if he got to his weapon?

Every self-protective instinct urged Logan to turn and run. From Cooper. From the crowd. But he knew he couldn't abandon the detective, even if he didn't understand exactly what was wrong.

He found out in the next second as an enormous clap of thunder split the air.

Screams erupted from the onlookers, as the building exploded, sending a shower of debris into the sky, which rained down around the crater where the store had been.

People scattered in all directions, some of them calling out in pain as chunks of the building hit them on the head and shoulders.

IN the tent, the three men around Rinna staggered back, gasping as the psychic shock wave hit them. Avery fell onto the ground, his body curling into a fetal position. Brusco sat down heavily on a chair, missed the seat, and plopped to the floor. Falcone stayed on his feet, but he had to grab a tent pole, shaking the makeshift structure and almost bringing the whole thing down around them.

The pain that filled Rinna's head was almost too great to bear, but she stared at the men with satisfaction.

Working together, these three had been going to destroy her brain, and she had come up with a desperate plan to defeat them. It was like nothing she had ever done before. But she had learned the theory at school. And understood that it was her only chance to leave with her mind intact.

Falcone recovered first. With a savage cry, he lunged forward, grabbed her by the shoulders and shook her so hard her bones rattled. "What the hell did you do?"

Her head felt like demons were inside banging on the walls of her skull with pickaxes. Taking a breath, she struggled not to scream.

"What happened?" he bellowed. "What in Carfolian Hell did you do?"

By gathering all her resolve, she managed to keep her own voice low and steady. "I grabbed hold of the energy you three beamed at me and sent it into the portal. It's gone. You're trapped here. And if you destroy my brain, you'll never get back."

"I have men who can open portals," he bellowed. "How do you think I got the one we just used?"

She tipped her head to one side, looking at him as though he'd just claimed he could speak to the dead—his worst subject in school. "But they're back in Sun Acres, aren't they?"

He gave her one more shake, then took a step back, his eyes narrowing as he focused on her.

Pushing himself to a sitting position, Avery made a gagging sound, and Rinna directed her next remark to him.

"I'm sorry the psychic transfer was painful to you. Now

you have some idea of what it feels like to have someone inside your head throwing energy bolts around."

Avery swallowed but said nothing. Brusco looked at Falcone. "You didn't warn us that she could do something like that."

"Do you think I would have proceeded with the operation if I'd known?" he bellowed.

"What are we going to do?" Avery asked.

Falcone turned back to Rinna, and she saw he was struggling to keep his features from twisting into a mask of anger. Or maybe it was fear. She liked that better. "I order you to open another portal."

Even through her pain, she managed a harsh laugh. "You order me? I don't think so. This isn't Sun Acres. I have choices here. So what's the advantage to me in following your orders?"

His voice turned into a growl, and he reached under her chin, tipping her head up. "Because if you defy me, I can make your life very painful."

Still tied to the chair, she was forced to look into his fierce eyes. "That would give you pleasure," she answered. "But it won't get you back to Sun Acres."

Either she had temporarily disabled his psychic abilities or he was so angry that only physical violence would satisfy his needs. He raised his hand to strike her, but Brusco swayed forward and caught his arm.

Falcone whirled to face him. "How dare you?"

"Think about what you're doing before you act," the other man advised.

Almost totally out of control, Falcone looked at the faces staring at him. "I don't need her. I was planning to invade this world, anyway," he bellowed.

The other two men looked away. But Rinna kept her gaze on him—and her voice even. "But your supply lines have been cut off. And you don't know enough about this place, do you? The longer you stay here without knowing how things work, the more likely that you'll get into serious trouble. Take this tent," she said, gesturing toward the canvas walls. "It's nothing like the tents they use here. It will be conspicuous. People will come nosing around. You could kill them, of course. But that's going to call even more attention to you. And probably you're on private property, so somebody will show up trying to find out what you and a squad of men are doing on their land. Unless you can make them invisible," she added.

"We did that when we came through," Brusco said. "We can't do it again so soon."

Falcone turned and glared at the man, and he closed his mouth abruptly, undoubtedly sorry that he'd given anything away.

She watched Falcone press his fingers to his forehead, massaging his skin, and she knew that his head hurt. *Good.*

"If you want me to open a portal, you're going to have to help me do it," she murmured.

WHEN Logan reached the woods, he turned back to the detective. Cooper was staring at him with a confused expression on his face.

"How did you know what was going down?" the detective called out.

Did he expect a wolf to come up with an answer? Obviously that was out of the question. And even if Logan could have gotten words out of his mouth, he didn't know what to say. He'd felt a dangerous vibration in the air, and he'd known something bad was going to happen.

Something connected with the building. But he hadn't known exactly what.

Cooper reached out a hand toward the wolf.

Logan shook his head, then turned and ran deeper into the woods, where the other Marshalls were waiting for him.

They raced back to the spot where they'd previously changed and all reversed the process. Once they'd returned to human form, they dragged on the clothing that Ross had stuffed in the backpacks.

Logan was the first to speak. "Did you feel it?" he asked his brother and his cousin.

"You mean feel a vibration in the air before the building exploded?" Ross answered.

"Yeah, that."

"I felt it, too," Lance said. "And I heard some dogs in the neighborhood. There must have been a sound wave that was below human awareness."

"Which doesn't answer the question: What the hell happened?" Lance said as he pulled on his sweatpants. "I mean, why did the place blow up?"

Logan's chest was so tight he could barely speak. "My best guess? I think Rinna somehow destroyed the portal so that bastard Falcone couldn't take her back to her world."

"Good for her."

"I hope nobody was inside," Logan muttered.

"It looks like the cops cleared the place out for her."

"Yeah," Logan agreed. "Maybe she even planted that suggestion in the detective's mind."

"So now what?" Lance asked.

"Same as before. We look for her. Maybe that's what she was thinking when she told me to go for help. Maybe she was planning to stall Falcone until I could bring reinforcements."

"Maybe," Ross murmured, although he looked doubtful.

"You don't think so?" Logan demanded.

"If that was her plan, it was pretty risky."

"But what else could she do?"

"Stick with you while you made a couple of phone calls?" Ross suggested.

Logan clenched his hands into fists, once again struggling to keep his temper. "They don't have phones in her world. She wouldn't think of a phone call."

"Let's not argue about it," Ross answered, his voice smooth and even. "The point is she bought us time to find her."

"Right."

FALCONE looked like a small boy who had been told that he had to come inside for dinner when he still wanted to play kickball with his friends. He actually started to stamp his foot, then glanced at her and stopped himself.

"I will not stay in this world now. Not when . . ." His voice trailed off.

"Now when you're unprepared?" she asked

When he glared at her, she shrugged. "It's not that easy to open a portal. It takes a lot of energy. I don't have the strength now. And when I try it, you and the others are going to have to lend me your power."

"All right."

Knowing that she was taking a big risk, she told him what she really wanted. "And you're going to have to agree to let me stay here."

"All right," he said at once.

Of course, she didn't trust his answer. She knew he

would say anything right now to get her cooperation. But she would let him think that he'd fooled her.

Brusco looked at their surroundings. "What about the tent? She says we can't stay here."

"She could be lying," Falcone snapped.

"Believe that if you want to. But I was in the tent that Logan uses when he was camping. It's nothing like this."

"What's my alternative?" he demanded, watching her carefully.

"We can stay in a house. In this world, people leave their houses unoccupied and go away on trips."

Falcone made a snorting noise. "You expect me to believe that?"

She struggled to keep a satisfied expression off her face. She had come here with Logan, and she had felt like she knew nothing about his environment. However, the little she did know gave her a tremendous advantage over Falcone and his men.

Looking him in the eye, she said, "After Logan and I came through the portal, we found a house where the owners were away. We stayed there overnight."

"How did you know they were not at home?" Avery asked.

"In this world, a newspaper is delivered to houses every day. If there are a lot of them at the end of the driveway, it means the people are away. Also, a . . . a government service delivers letters and junk mail into a metal box. It fills up if nobody empties it."

"I've heard of newspapers," Falcone answered. "Explain junk mail."

"Advertising circulars," she answered promptly, glad she had remembered the term Logan used.

"It sounds like she knows a lot about this world," Avery said.

She gave him a grateful look.

Falcone scowled at him.

"I can help you look for a suitable place," she said.

Falcone's gaze bore into her. "Why would you help me?"

"So I can get back to Logan as soon as possible."

Falcone continued to stare at her. "Who is this Logan person?" he asked.

"A shape-shifter. He got caught in that trap you left for me. That's how I met him."

"We're wasting time talking about this shape-shifter," Avery interjected. "We should find a place to hide."

Falcone glared at him, but he went outside and gave orders for the men to pack up camp.

When he came back, she raised her head. "Untie me," she said.

JAKE Cooper leaned against his unmarked. It had a few dents in it where chunks of the building had landed, but other than that, it was unharmed.

He was supposed to be on sick leave. But he'd gotten the lieutenant to reassign him back to active duty.

He still had the mother of all headaches from the incident last night. But the good news was that he hadn't been inside the building when it exploded. And neither had anyone else, thanks to his stroke of intuition, or whatever it was.

Earlier in the day, the owner had screamed bloody murder about having his place shut down. Now he was going after his insurance company.

So had he blown the place up himself to collect on the insurance? That was always a possibility.

A team from the Maryland State Police were on their

way to determine what had caused the explosion. Someone had suggested a gas leak, and that was one possibility.

Or maybe someone had set a bomb. He repressed a laugh. *Yeah, terrorists,* like he'd told the Lieu.

Or maybe it was someone who wanted to destroy evidence.

And who would have done that?

Marshall? It didn't seem likely, since he was busy searching for his wife. Unless he was lying about that.

Jake had sent a patrol car back to the residence, and the guy wasn't there.

He switched his thoughts from Marshall to his own lucky escape. He would have been pretty close to the explosion, if a large dog hadn't dashed out of the woods and pulled him toward safety.

A large dog wearing a backpack of all things. Make that three large dogs and two backpacks.

It was like the dogs knew something was going to happen moments before the building went up.

Well, he'd heard about animals getting vibrations that people couldn't hear. But that didn't explain why they had wanted to pull a police detective out of harm's way.

Jake made a muffled sound. Last night when he'd come to the Easy Shopper, he'd gotten tangled up with a big white bird who seemed pretty intelligent. This morning it was trained dogs. Or maybe not. Some people who had seen the incident thought the dogs looked more like wolves.

His restless mind kept making leaps from one possibility to the next. He'd wondered if psychic phenomena might be involved. But he hadn't been willing to believe Marshall's nut-ball theory. So where did that leave him?

When a team from the Maryland State Police arrived,

he pushed himself away from the unmarked and trotted toward them.

"Let's find out what happened here," he said.

"WHY should I untie you?" Falcone asked Rinna.

"Because I'm not your slave anymore—not here."

"How do I know you won't try to escape?"

"I came to you in the first place."

"But that doesn't make me trust you. Not after you blew up the portal."

"To protect myself," she said.

He looked like he wanted to slap her. Instead, he stepped through the tent door. When he came back, two of his soldiers were with him.

"If she gets away, you will be responsible," he said.

Both men stiffened their posture. She felt sorry for them, although she wasn't going to make a run for it. She was too weak to outrun Falcone at the moment, although she wouldn't share that information with him.

"Let me out of this chair," she said again.

He glared at her, waiting several heartbeats, letting her wonder what he had decided. Finally, he bent and began untying the knots.

When he had freed her, she flexed her arms and legs, restoring circulation to limbs that had been held in one position for too long.

"I'll help you find a house where we can hide," she said.

"I don't want your help."

"Suit yourself."

"I will," he snapped, but she smiled inwardly when she heard the worry below the surface of his bravado.

"If you find a house with newspapers, be sure it doesn't have a security system," she said.

Falcone didn't ask what a security system was. He'd figure that out when he came to it.

Turning away from Rinna, he stepped out of the tent and took a breath of air to calm himself.

It was a struggle not to go back inside and beat the woman. She was a slave, and she had forgotten her place.

But in the end, she would be sorry for what she had done. She had gotten the better of him, but he knew more about this world than she thought. And she had given him an idea—about neutralizing the man who had been with her.

Swiftly he walked toward his supply officer and gave terse orders.

CHAPTER TWENTY-FOUR

TO SHOW THAT he wasn't afraid to venture out into this unfamiliar world, Falcone took two of his best men—Kenner and Shafter—and started through the woods.

He came to a road within five minutes and followed it, looking for the signs that Rinna had mentioned. He marveled at how far apart the houses were. They had no protections, and they were open to invasion from anyone who took a fancy to the contents.

But he didn't just rely on Rinna's judgment that this world was safer than his own. The men who'd reconnoitered here had given him similar reports.

The houses in this area had trees around them. But instead of natural woods, the ground under the trees had been tended by gardeners.

He had strong legs. And he was used to walking. Several automobiles passed by, but he was sure he and his men were not conspicuous since they were dressed just like the inhabitants of this world. They all wore jeans, dress shirts, and what were called running shoes. They also had on baseball caps which they had turned around with the bill facing the back. The idea of wearing them that way seemed peculiar, since he would have expected the bill to serve as a sunshade. But his spies had assured him that was the way it was done.

He'd ordered the men to leave their usual weapons back at the camp. Now they were all carrying handguns, which several of his spies had secretly brought back and showed him. The guns were concealed under their shirts.

At home, they'd taken the weapons outside the city to practice. He knew how to fire the gun. And so did Kenner and Shafter.

Every minute or so, a car passed them as they walked along the road. But he stayed out of the way of the vehicles, and he even got used to the wind they generated in their wake.

They had walked about a mile from the campground and passed more than a dozen houses when he saw a pile of newspapers lying on the ground.

According to Rinna, that meant that the owners of the house were away. But he didn't take her word for it, in case she was leading him into a trap. He and the men stepped off the blacktop and into the woods, approaching the house from two different angles. When he looked inside, he saw furnishings that made his eyes pop.

His spies had told him that the people of this world lived well. Through the windows he could see rich fabrics and gleaming wood. And what he took to be a cooking area with shiny appliances that he didn't know how to use. Maybe Rinna understood how they worked. If not, they'd cook over a fire in back of the house, since there was plenty of fuel around.

They broke in through a side door. Immediately, a loud bell began to ring.

The security system.

Rushing to the bell, he used his powers to shut it off.

A minute later, he heard a jangling noise. Before he could figure out where it was, the thing stopped, and he breathed out a sigh. Quickly he and the men searched the premises. No one was home.

He walked through the rooms, picking up objects and carefully setting them down again. His heart was pounding, and he felt a kind of glee gathering inside himself as he swiveled a smooth ball of shimmering glass in his hand. In his world, it would be priceless.

He turned to see Kenner and Shafter looking around with dazed expressions on their faces. This place was probably richer than anything they could imagine.

"No stealing," he ordered.

"Yes, sir."

"You will be searched before you return to our world."

"Yes, sir."

He could have ordered one of them to stay here and guard him, but he felt very secure in this solidly built structure. So he addressed them both.

"Kenner, Shafter, go get the rest of the group—on the double," he ordered. "Have them strike camp and come here as quickly as possible. And I want a chain on Rinna when you lead her through the open."

The two men snapped to attention. "Yes, sir."

When they had left, he did some more exploring. There were comfortable couches in several rooms, one of them facing a box with what looked like a place for a picture in the middle. He ran his hand over the smooth glass, trying to find what made the picture work. Then he saw a button that said Power.

Could he work it? Or did it take a certain kind of psychic ability?

No. That wasn't it. They didn't run things by psychic power here.

He pressed. There was a kind of pinging sound.

Then a talking bear appeared in the picture frame.

"Carfolian Hell!" He jumped back, then looked quickly around to make sure nobody had seen him.

When his heart stopped hammering, he caught some of the words. The bear was talking about a certain kind of toilet tissue, saying it would feel good against his bottom.

He gaped at the moving picture. It changed. The bear went away and a very attractive blond woman came on. She was wearing a tailored blue jacket and her hair was carefully fixed. She was sitting in front of a city landscape. A big city. Although as Falcone studied the scene carefully, he thought it was only a picture.

The woman was also talking directly to Falcone in an authoritative voice.

"This afternoon, a bomb or other explosive device destroyed the Easy Shopper on Huntington Road in Mount Airy. The convenience store was robbed earlier in the week, and police were investigating a tip that terrorists had threatened an attack on the store. Because of the tip, the premises had been cleared of employees and patrons before the explosion occurred. Our reporter, Paul Cummings, is standing by with more details."

Falcone gawked. The woman's face went away, and Falcone found himself staring at a man. He was standing in front of a ruined building holding up a stick in front of his mouth.

He had to assume it was the building where he had come through the portal the night before.

The woman's voice asked, "Paul, do the police have any leads?"

"They aren't giving out any information."

The woman and man talked back and forth for several minutes, but it was clear that they had no new information and were just rehashing old reports. And another thing was clear. The woman was the one in charge. And the man was subservient to her.

That would never have happened in his world. Men ran things, and the women stayed home and took care of the house and the children. Unless they had unusual talents. And then they were put to work—but always at the direction of some man.

He sat down on a couch that faced the moving picture, watching and listening. This thing was a good source of information. He could learn what they knew about the Easy Shopper. And he could learn more about this world by watching.

He had come here only half believing what his spies told him. Now he believed. There were wonders in this world that he could never have imagined. And he could use them to his advantage.

He had psychic power. Combined with the new powers he found here, the effect would be enormous. He leaned back, picturing himself in this world. He would bring a few hundred people with him through the portal, people who were loyal to him. They had city-states here, too. They were called gated communities.

The woman on the television went away and a man replaced her, talking about things that didn't interest Falcone. Sporting events in this world. He didn't know the teams and he didn't know the games, so he let his mind drift back to his own plans.

He would have a gated community here and name it

after Sun Acres. And he would be the ruler. He would find another woman with powers to bear his children. Not Rinna. It was clear that she was much too dangerous. He'd find a younger one, perhaps from another city-state. Someone who hadn't gone through the excellent school for psychics in Sun Acres. He wanted a woman with potential, but one who hadn't been taught as well as Rinna. Yes, that was the right approach. A woman he could control more easily. A woman who would be thrilled that he'd picked her for his concubine. Or maybe his wife, depending on the status of her family.

He got up and wandered into the cooking area. His men had told him about such places. He ran his hands over the equipment, then looked up and saw circles in the ceiling with curved glass covering the center. He thought they were lights. He could turn them on with a toggle at the wall. He looked for such a device and found one near the sink.

Reaching over, he flipped the switch, and something inside the sink drain began making a horrible, dangerous-sounding racket.

"Shit!"

Flipping the switch the other way, he turned it off quickly.

When Rinna came, he'd make her show him how to turn on the lights. But he'd pretend he hadn't encountered the noisemaker in the sink.

THE wolves spread out, fanning through the woods, looking for Falcone and his men.

They were all carrying the whistles Ross had given them—the ones with fake bird calls. No ordinary wolf could have blown the whistles. But they knew how to shape their muzzles to do it.

If any of them came on anything interesting or urgent, he could sound an alarm. Of course there were real birds in the woods, but they could use a different pattern for the fake calls. Hopefully, the guys they were tracking wouldn't know the local birdsongs.

They stayed within a couple of hundred yards of each other, but in the thick underbrush, they weren't always able to see each other.

Logan's frustration grew as he tried to pick up Rinna's scent. He'd thought he just had to head toward home. But so far he hadn't located her.

He was starting to think his theory was wrong when he heard the metallic cheep of a cardinal.

Lance had found something! Finally.

Or had he? The call had sounded strange, like his brother wasn't fully focused on what he was doing.

Hearing the underbrush to his right stir, he stiffened. A gray shape emerged from around a blackberry thicket, and he saw that it was Ross.

His cousin stopped beside him and gave him a questioning look, then fumbled his whistle into his mouth and gave a short toot.

Logan nodded.

Lance's signal came again, more muffled than before. Logan stopped short, trying to fix the direction. The sound had come from his left.

He trotted forward, then saw Lance through the underbrush.

Whistle in his mouth, he blew a short note, expecting to get Lance's attention. But his brother stood stock-still, and he didn't turn.

Ross tipped his head to one side, then pawed the ground—their sign for danger.

Logan nodded, and they both started slowly forward. But when he saw Lance waver on his feet, he sprinted toward his brother, then felt a terrible pull tugging him toward a pile of leaves.

A familiar pull. Instantly he knew it was from one of the traps that had almost killed him before Rinna had gotten him out of the damn thing. But the range was less than last time, as if someone had changed the calibration.

Not bothering with the whistle, he lifted his head and howled. But the wolf call didn't even get his brother's attention.

Rushing forward, he bounded to Lance's side and knocked him to the ground before he could take another step toward the trap.

Now that Logan was so close, the terrible pull tugged at him. But the previous experience gave him some idea how to resist. He set his will against the trap even as he fell on Lance, holding him back when he would have stumbled forward toward his destruction.

His brother turned and snarled at him, his teeth bared. All Logan could do was try to hold him in place. But Lance pawed at the ground, pulling them both toward the deadly device hidden in the leaves.

Then Ross was beside them.

Logan jerked his head toward the trap and snarled, then jerked back hoping he was conveying the message that they had to stay away from the thing.

Ross shivered, but he kept his distance from the pile of leaves where the trap lurked.

Instead, he came up beside Logan, and together they pushed and shoved Lance back.

As soon as they had moved a few yards away, Logan

could feel a difference. The mental pull was still there, but as long as he stayed this far away, he thought he could avoid getting ensnared.

Lance lay on the ground panting, and Ross rubbed his nuzzle against him.

Lance lifted his head and looked around, a dazed expression on his face. They had kept him from rushing toward the snare, but he wasn't out of danger yet.

Farther back, Logan thought. *We have to get farther back before it pulls us in.*

He pushed at Lance again, trying to maneuver him out of harm's way, just as he heard a cry of, "Get them."

Raising his head, he saw two fierce-looking men erupt from the woods and charge at them.

CHAPTER TWENTY-FIVE

WITH HIS CHOICES suddenly limited, Logan let go of his brother and turned toward the attackers. Probably they'd been sent here to wait for a shape-shifter. But maybe they hadn't actually fought any before. And they certainly hadn't been expecting more than one wolf.

Praying that Lance wouldn't head for the trap, Logan backed up, hoping that one of the men would follow him.

He did, moving in a crouch, his knife at the ready.

Silently, Logan continued his retreat, drawing the soldier away from Lance. From the corner of his eye, he could see that Ross was doing the same with the other man.

When they were ten feet from Lance, Ross howled—the signal for an attack. He and Logan both leaped at the soldiers who had come after them, ducking under their weapons and going for the legs, then the hands, snapping and snarling to make the attack seem more vicious.

The men tried to fight. But they were no match for two angry wolves. Or maybe they had nothing invested in the conflict. They were just hired help, and the wolves were defending one of their own.

They gave up after a few minutes, limping back into the trees, but Logan didn't take anything for granted. They could be going for reinforcements.

He looked around, then growled. While he and Ross had been busy, Lance had started crawling toward the trap again.

He was stretching out a paw toward the snare when Logan reached him.

Logan was so close to the damn thing that his vison turned instantly blurry, and a thousand hornets set up a buzzing in his brain. In some part of his mind he was reliving the horrible feeling of the iron-jawed trap closing around his leg and digging into his flesh.

Fear made him want to jump back. But he pushed the terror to the side and kept his focus on one objective—rescuing Lance from the same fate. Rinna had saved him by joining her mind with his and getting him to change. But he couldn't do the same thing for Lance because he didn't possess that ability.

There was no way he could have gotten Lance out of danger by himself.

He spared a glance at Ross. His cousin didn't look too good either. But he didn't head for the lure, and Logan figured he must be exercising his famous iron control.

Instinctively, they knew they had to cooperate to free Lance. Working as a team, they pushed him away, but they couldn't move him far—not as wolves because they simply didn't have a good way of holding him.

Which left them no alternative. Making a decision he didn't much like, Logan mentally began chanting the ancient words that would transform him from wolf to man.

As he made the transformation, he felt a searing pain

in his shoulder. Once he had morphed, he turned his head and saw a bloody slash that he hadn't noticed through his fur. The soldier had cut him with the knife, but the wound wasn't deep. Just long and painful.

He saw Ross also making the transformation. They were both naked and vulnerable. And if the soldiers caught them like this, they were dog meat.

"Let's get the hell out of here," Ross muttered.

They turned toward Lance and grabbed his legs. He snapped at them, but he was weak, and Ross was able to wrap one hand around his muzzle as they dragged him away from the snare that had captured his mind. It was probably a rough ride through the woods, but there was nothing they could do about that.

When they were a hundred yards from the trap, Ross bent to Lance. "If I let go of your muzzle, will you promise not to bite me?"

To Logan's relief, his brother's eyes seemed to have cleared. He nodded.

Ross unclamped his fingers and stepped back. "Can you change?"

They waited for a long moment before they saw any results. Then Lance's body shape began to flow. But as Logan focused on his brother, he heard shouts in the woods.

"Son of a bitch," Ross growled. "They're coming back—with reinforcements."

Lance had barely transformed from wolf to man when they grabbed his shoulders and pulled him to his feet.

As best they could, they hustled him through the woods. Now they were three naked men on the run. They pounded across the stretch of trees and into the park.

With every yard they ran, the soldiers gained on them. And Logan only gave them fifty-fifty odds of making it to the car.

When they reached the parking lot, they dashed past a man and a woman just spreading out a meal at a picnic table.

The woman screamed.

"Damn queers," the man muttered, standing up and rounding the table, just as the soldiers burst from the woods in hot pursuit.

Logan had left the keys under a rock near the curb. For a terrible moment, he didn't see them. Then he realized he was a few feet from the right spot.

He snatched up the keys and pressed the remote as the soldiers pounded out of the woods. The three Marshalls leaped toward the car and jumped in as the soldiers dashed past the startled couple.

Logan gunned the engine and roared away, and the pursuers were left standing at the edge of the parking lot staring after the car.

"Thank God," he breathed.

"You need to get that cut disinfected."

"Yeah." He glanced over his shoulder and saw his brother sprawled across the back seat.

"How do you feel?" he asked.

"Logy, but better." Lance sat up and pulled on a shirt, then looked toward the front seat. "Thanks for saving my ass."

"Anytime," Ross answered.

THE soldiers marched Rinna along the gravel strip at the edge of the smooth road. It was hard to walk because she had an iron cuff on one leg and another on her wrist, both of which were attached to one of the soldiers, so she couldn't escape.

Men in back of them carried the tent and the other

supplies from the camp. Avery and Brusco were at the back of the column, since the old man was having trouble keeping up.

As they walked, she watched the drivers of cars slow to gawk. So much for Falcone's fitting into this environment. He didn't have a clue how much she and the warriors stood out.

They passed several driveways, and finally the soldier named Kenner stopped. "This is it."

The one named Shafter, who had also gone with Falcone, started up the narrow lane. The man who was chained to her gave a tug, and she followed him.

Behind her tires squealed, and she jerked around to see that a car had stopped in the middle of the road. And another one had almost smashed into the back of it.

"You stupid dickhead," somebody shouted.

"Fuck you!"

The wheels on the car in front spun on the road, and the vehicle shot forward. The other driver stayed where he was for a moment, staring at her and the men. Then he also sped away.

They proceeded up the driveway and rounded a curve, where she saw a house even bigger than the one she and Logan had borrowed a few nights earlier.

The front door opened, and Falcone stepped onto the porch. It looked like he'd gone upstairs in the house and found clothing that belonged to the owner. He was wearing a leather jacket over a white T-shirt and a pair of very tight pants.

He walked down a couple of steps to a bricked-in area in front of the structure and gave Rinna a satisfied look.

"I'm settling in here nicely."

She met his eye squarely. "On the contrary, I think you've made a mistake," she said.

"How?" he challenged. "You weren't even here."

"Not at the house. On the road. There are no slaves here. They don't walk women around in chains. A lot of people who were passing by stopped to look at us."

Falcone's gaze shot to Kenner. "Is that true?"

"Yes, sir."

"Did anybody see you come up this lane?"

"Yes, sir."

"Then perhaps we'd better move to a new location."

In the distance, Rinna heard a siren. "I think it's too late," she murmured.

"Too late for what?"

"The police are already on the way."

"Carfolian Hell." Falcone looked around at the group. "Everybody in the house. Hurry."

LANCE tossed a shirt and pants to Ross, who wiggled into them.

Logan turned onto a side road so he could climb into his clothing.

"What the hell was that thing that grabbed my mind?" Lance asked.

"A trap for a shape-shifter. I guess Falcone figured I'd come after Rinna. Like I told you, I stepped into a trap meant for her, and she came along and got me out of it. She could have run in the other direction," he added. "But she didn't."

"It clamped hold of my mind, and it was reeling me in," Lance muttered. "I still feel like my head is full of steel wool."

"Yeah. I know the sensation. Only, believe me, it's worse if the damn thing actually catches you. I gather from what Rinna said that if it grabs you, you can't get out by yourself. And she couldn't touch it."

"Then how did she get you out?"

"She got me to change, and while my cells were . . . were in flux, she pulled my leg away."

"A brave and resourceful woman," Ross said.

"Yeah. After that, it took me a couple of days to put coherent thoughts together."

"Is there anything we can use as a shield? In case we run into another one?"

"Maybe Rinna knows."

"And they have her in their damn camp. The only good news is that the trap is probably close to where they're holding her. But we'll have to be careful when we go back."

They were debating what to do, when a police siren interrupted the conversation.

One patrol car sped by on the highway. Then another.

The three men exchanged glances.

"It sounds like something big is going down."

"Yeah," Logan muttered as he turned on the radio to an all-news station.

"Breaking news," an announcer said. "A militia group has taken over a house in the Huntington Woods section of Mount Airy. Eyewitness reports say they've taken a woman hostage."

Logan felt an electric shock travel along his nerve endings. "Rinna," he breathed.

"You don't know that for sure," Ross cautioned.

"Who else could it be?"

Another patrol car sped by and he turned on the engine, then lurched away from the curb. He was on the road and heading for the highway before anyone else could speak. Whipping onto the blacktop, he followed the red and blue flashing lights.

Ross and Lance sat back, apparently smart enough not to question his judgment.

In about a mile, he came to a roadblock. Cops were turning motorists back.

Craning his neck, Logan could see the driveway to one of the houses was blocked by a police cruiser.

"It's up there," Ross murmured.

"Yeah. Time for some big dogs to go prowling through the woods.

"Let's hope the cops aren't shooting at anything that moves," Ross said.

"I'll take my chances that they're focused on the house," Logan answered. He turned the car around and headed in the direction from which they'd come. But at the first opportunity, he turned off the road again and into a rural area with custom homes on large wooded lots. He kept going to the end of the road, which ended in a circle, where he saw prep work for new construction. But no building had taken place yet, so he was able to pull past a cleared area and into the woods.

"This should do," he said, then looked back at Lance. "Maybe you'd better stay here if you're still feeling sick."

"I'm well enough," Lance snapped.

JAKE Cooper pulled into the driveway at 1235 Picket Road. He'd asked to be informed if anything unusual was going on in the neighborhood, and this certainly qualified.

Motorists had seen a troop of men and one woman tramping along the shoulder, and the group had turned in here.

The woman was chained up.

He'd asked for her description, and it pretty well matched Mrs. Rinna Marshall.

So what the hell was going on now?

Logan Marshall had said his wife had disappeared. So had these guys captured her? And if they had, what damn fool would march her up a public road in chains?

What was this—an S & M club gone berserk? Or was this some kind of performance art? Checking with the station, he found that a burglar alarm had also gone off at the location. Only the monitoring station had pegged it as a false alarm, since the homeowners were notorious for screwing up the system.

He drove toward the house, then stopped in back of the three patrol cars that already had entered the driveway.

The officers conferred, then one of them stepped from cover.

Not a good move, Jake thought. "Get back here," he shouted.

In the next second, shots erupted from one of the front windows, and the officer fell to the ground.

CHAPTER TWENTY-SIX

THE THREE WOLVES were already heading through the woods when Logan heard gunfire.

His heart leaped into his throat, and he sped up, tearing through the trees in the direction from which the shots had come. Lance and Ross were right behind him.

All of them screeched to a halt when he saw three police cars. An officer was lying on the ground, dead or wounded.

Other officers were using the cruisers for cover as they faced the house, guns drawn.

And behind the cars, Jake Cooper was yelling into a cell phone, calling for an ambulance. He must have caught a flash of movement from the corner of his eye because he looked up and spotted the three wolves.

The detective's mouth dropped open as he stared at them.

"You," he said.

Logan was too far away to hear the words, but he saw the man's lips form the syllable.

Then the person on the other end of the line must have asked something because he returned his attention to the phone.

The three wolves moved back into the trees, hidden by the lengthening shadows, but they were still able to see what was going on.

Logan saw two officers bring out a large metal shield. Holding it between themselves and the house, they rushed forward and crouched over the man on the ground.

Lance saw him moving. He was wounded.

The others pulled him to safety in back of the cars, as another siren sounded in the distance.

The medics were on their way.

INSIDE the house, Falcone turned in fury on the soldier who had fired the shot. "You idiot," he cried out, then sent a wave of psychic energy into the man's brain. He went down on his knees, cradling his head in his hands.

"I told you to hold your fire," Falcone bellowed, then turned to Avery. "You have to get us out of here."

"I can't."

"Make us invisible."

"I need preparation for that."

Falcone's face contorted in rage. "We'll have to negotiate with them," he muttered.

"What do we have to offer?" Brusco asked.

"The idiot who injured one of their men."

COOPER grabbed a bullhorn and turned toward the house.

"Come out with your hands up," he boomed.

"We can negotiate," a voice inside called out.

Then another shot sounded, and Logan felt his guts wrench.

Rinna. Oh God, Rinna.

He would have dashed forward, but the two other wolves blocked him, one in front of him and one in back.

Ross growled low in his throat.

Logan prepared to lunge at him, but in the next second, the door opened again. Logan stopped in his tracks as something came flying out. It was a limp human figure.

Not Rinna. One of Falcone's soldiers, and he landed in a heap in the circular drive. It was immediately apparent that he'd been shot in the head.

The cops stood in stunned silence. Then one of them spoke.

"Jesus Christ!"

"What the hell was that for?" Cooper boomed over the bullhorn.

"That's the man who fired the weapon," the voice from inside called. "I've given him to you. Now we can negotiate."

"I don't think so," Cooper answered. "Come out with your hands up."

INSIDE, Falcone turned to Rinna. "Why won't he talk terms?"

She tried not to look smug. "Because you just broke one of their laws. They have laws."

"Laws!" he snarled. "I don't give a rat's ass for their laws."

"But they do," she answered. "In this society, you don't just kill people."

"Not even to appease the authorities?"

"No. Tell your men to put down their guns, so nobody else gets shot. And close the blinds so they can't see in."

"Close the blinds," Falcone ordered, and men snapped to obey. "We have to get home."

She took a deep breath. "Maybe I can help you get out of here."

"How?"

She thought about getting him to stick a fork in an electric socket. Too bad that would only hurt him. She needed something more permanent.

"I can open a portal."

"You said you couldn't," he growled.

"I said I was too weak. I'm still weak for something like that. But I'm willing to try."

"You'll get us out of here?"

"If you let me stay behind."

He nodded tightly, and she knew that he was only agreeing because he thought he had no choice.

"You have to buy us some time," she said.

"How?"

"With a story they'll believe. Tell them that you are from the Middle East and you are holding a woman hostage. Tell them that you will kill me unless they guarantee an airplane for you and your men."

"An airplane? A thing that flies in the sky?"

"You don't have to really do it. You'll be leaving through the portal. But you'll stall them with that story."

"But . . . how can they get me an airplane?"

"They'll tell you they're trying. And while they are negotiating—talking to you and trying to get you to free me—I can work on the portal. But I can't do it alone. When the time comes, I will need your power." She looked from Falcone to Avery and Brusco.

"All right," Falcone muttered.

"Tell your men to put down their guns."

He gave the order, and weapons clanked to tables or onto the floor.

Just then a jangling noise made the men jump. Frantically they looked around.

"I heard that before. What the hell is it?" Falcone growled.

Rinna answered with confidence. "The telephone."

"Which is?"

"A talking device. Maybe the man outside wants to talk to you." Confidently she picked up the receiver and looked at the readout. It said, "Frederick County Police."

"Hello? Hello?" a voice said.

"Put it to your ear," Rinna whispered. "And talk into this part."

"Hello?" Falcone said.

"This is Jake Cooper of the Frederick County Police."

Falcone glanced at Rinna, then said, "I am from the Middle East, and I am holding a woman hostage. I want an airplane to the Middle East."

"Let's talk about it," Jake Cooper said.

"We can talk," Falcone answered. "But stay away from the house, or I will shoot her. Like the policeman."

"Just stay cool," the man on the other end of the line said. "We can work this out."

"Yes. But I need some time." Falcone turned to Rinna. "How do I make the voice go away?"

She took the receiver from him and set it back in the cradle. Then she pointed to the television set where a woman was breathlessly describing the hostage situation.

* * *

THE wolves withdrew into the woods. Not being able to speak was too much of a disadvantage. So they ran back to where they'd left their clothes, then changed.

"Did you hear that?" Logan growled as they moved toward the house again where they could get a better view.

"Yeah. Lucky wolves have good hearing. It has to be Falcone. He says he wants a plane to the Middle East." Logan stopped short. "A plane to the Middle East. Jesus!"

"What?"

"He got that from Rinna. She was watching a cop show on TV the other night. And a guy was holding people hostage. That was the demand the guy made, and Rinna fed the line to Falcone. And she probably told him how to work the phone."

"So she's got some kind of plan."

"Yeah, but what?"

"Stalling. It's got to involve stalling."

"Why?"

"Because we know that bastard Falcone isn't going to the Middle East. That's her idea."

Logan looked toward the back of the house. It was dark, and there was a fair amount of cover. Maybe enough for a wolf to get close without getting shot by the guys inside or the cops.

He turned back to Ross. "I have an idea, but it's risky."

"Let's hear it," his cousin said without hesitation.

"WE should sit down where we can talk." Rinna led the way into another room. As she passed one of the tables, she picked up a gun and shoved it into her waistband, under her shirt. She knew one of the soldiers had seen her.

Hoping he wouldn't tell Falcone, she sat down on the couch.

Falcone looked at one of his men. "Go back to the television thing. Tell me if they say anything that we don't know."

"Yes sir." The man hurried back to the kitchen, and Falcone leaned casually against the wall. He was acting like he was perfectly comfortable here. Fine with her. The more he pretended, the more he was likely to mess up.

"Sit," she said to Avery and Brusco.

They sat.

"Have you ever opened a portal?" she asked.

"I was part of a group that did it," Avery answered. "And we closed the other one."

"I saw you."

Avery nodded.

Rinna asked, "But you couldn't open another one before Falcone came to this world, that was why you used the one in the Easy Shopper?"

"Yes," Brusco snapped.

"Have *you* opened a portal?" Avery asked her.

"Yes," she lied. Of course she had never done it. But she'd been secretly studying the process since she'd first discovered that Boralas had broken through to this world. Haig had scoffed at her attempts. But he had been wrong to discourage her.

Haig. Her heart squeezed when she thought of him. He had been like a father to her. And she had lost him to Falcone's cruelty. She knew he was dead because she felt his total absence from the world. Now she must punish his killer.

She dragged in a deep breath and let it out slowly before looking at Avery and Brusco. "I have to meditate.

I have to look for the . . . plates between the world. They can slip and slide. And I have to find a way to push one aside."

The older man nodded. "That's the way Tinus described it to us. And that's the way we snapped the other one shut."

She gave him a grateful look. Then she swung her gaze toward Falcone and the soldiers. "I must have quiet. And I must be alone."

"Not alone!"

"Avery can watch me. But he has to give me . . . space. He can call you when I have found something."

"How do I know you won't slip through the portal when you have it open?"

"Because I can't open it by myself." She looked toward Avery. "Tell him how difficult it is. If I can do it at all, I need additional power."

"She's telling the truth," Avery said.

Her gaze shot to Falcone. "Figure out how to hold off the police, while I work on the portal."

Falcone glared at her, then turned away.

RINNA found a quiet room where heavy drapes were drawn across the windows. She sat down in a chair that was covered with soft leather and closed her eyes.

She had said she was trying to open a portal, but it was hard to get the right focus. Her mind drifted toward Logan. She wanted to reach out to him, to feel his comforting presence near her. But she ruthlessly stayed away from that. She would come back to him, if she could. And the only way she could do that was to get rid of Falcone.

So she closed Logan out of her thoughts and let her

mind drift, first in a kind of free-floating state so that she could calm herself and focus on the difficult job she had to do.

When she had centered herself, she began searching for the plates that walled off this world from the ones that rested beside it. She couldn't have described the process to anyone. She only knew that she could sense the barriers between the timelines. She let her mind stroke over them, feel their shape, look for chinks that she could open wider and use to her advantage.

She wasn't sure how long she searched and evaluated. But finally she knew that she was as ready as she would ever be.

When she looked up, she saw Avery's tense face.

"I have it," she whispered.

"What should I do?"

"Get Falcone. And Brusco. Have all the men standing by."

The old man hurried off and was back moments later with Falcone and the others.

Rinna stayed in the chair, feeling all the men watching her.

"Link hands," she murmured. "All of you. I need as much energy as I can get."

OUTSIDE, Jake Cooper studied the house. He'd seen shadows moving behind the blinds. More than one man and one woman. So how many people were in there, and how were they armed?

He didn't want to make any mistakes. The guy inside had already killed a man. He could kill the woman, too.

But what was the best way to get her out of there in one piece?

The SWAT team wasn't going to work, because now the drapes were drawn.

The man on the phone had said he wanted an airplane to the Middle East. Did he really think he was going to get it? Or was he completely out of his mind? He didn't sound like he came from the Middle East. He had the same vaguely Scandinavian accent as Rinna Marshall. So was that a coincidence? What if the woman in there really was Mrs. Marshall?

Jake picked up the phone and dialed the number of the house again.

THE communications thing rang, and Falcone looked at Rinna.

"Don't answer it," she whispered. "I need your focus on me."

The phone continued to ring, and she wanted to throw it out the window.

Avery sent it a mental jolt, and the distracting noise stopped.

"Thank you," she said.

He nodded.

"We have to hurry now," Rinna told him. "The policeman outside is going to wonder what you did." She looked around at the faces turned toward her. "All of you, open your minds so I can use your power."

"Even the men who aren't adepts?" Falcone challenged.

"Yes."

She waited with her heart pounding while he brought all the men into the room. Finding a chink in the plates hadn't been easy. But the hard part was still ahead of her.

"Just open yourself up. Let me draw your energy."

"Where will the portal be?" Falcone asked in a strained voice, and she knew he was as tense as she was herself.

She had picked a spot where she would try to bring the opening into this reality. As though she knew her scheme was going to work, she pointed toward a wall with bookshelves. "There."

Falcone looked like he was preparing to spring through the opening as soon as it materialized.

"Relax," she told him. "Give me your energy."

He swallowed. "Will you be in my mind?"

"No. Just let me use your power." She looked from him to Brusco and Avery. "Let the power flow."

She watched them mentally preparing themselves. She was pretty sure the two adepts would help her. They wanted to get home, and they knew she was their best chance.

But she didn't know about Falcone. He didn't trust her. And if he couldn't cooperate, her plan was doomed to failure.

CHAPTER TWENTY-SEVEN

"**FOCUS ON THE** wall with the bookshelves," Rinna murmured. "Picture the plate behind it shifting so a doorway can open."

As she gave the direction, she prayed that she could make it happen.

All the men except Falcone did as she asked. And she could feel them sending energy her way, feel them pulling for her to get them out of this place. The contribution from the soldiers was minimal, since most of them had little psychic ability. But the two adepts added considerably to her power. Still, it wasn't enough because Falcone only stood back, watching.

She took what power she had and directed it toward the wall, imagining the plates between the worlds, imagining that she could focus a beam on them and carve out a hole in the barrier—opening a doorway between this world and another one.

As she directed the energy she had gathered, her head began to throb. And she knew that she couldn't keep up the attempt for long. She was too spent from the effort she had put out defeating the adepts when they had tried to zap her brain.

If she didn't break through the plates quickly, she wouldn't be able to do it at all.

Sweat dripped down her neck, and her body went rigid as she threw everything she had at the barrier, straining to open a door in the wall.

It didn't work.

"What's going on?" Falcone growled.

She shook her head, unwilling to spare any part of her resources for an answer.

"She's lying to us. She's stalling so the police can come in," Falcone muttered.

"No," Avery answered. "She's trying to open a doorway. I can feel her trying. But it's not going to work unless you help."

"For God's sake, do it!" Brusco shouted.

Falcone gave him a murderous look.

"Do it," Rinna whispered. "Please," she added, hardly able to choke out the word.

She waited, feeling her fate hanging in the balance. Finally, Falcone gave her a threatening look, then joined the others, sending a mental boost to her efforts. But she knew he was holding something back.

Still, she accepted his help with a tip of her head as she focused on the wall, willing the plates to slip and the portal to open, but still nothing happened.

Falcone turned to her, anger contorting his features. "This is a trick."

"No," she gasped out, then struggled to make her voice more normal. "Give me all of your energy. If you do, you'll see the doorway opening."

"You'll make me weak," he bellowed.

"Do it!" Avery commanded.

Through her own pain, she sensed more power coming from Falcone. "Give me all of it," she demanded.

He grimaced, and she felt a barrier tumble down. As he lent her the psychic energy she needed, the bookshelves across from her began to blur.

Some of the soldiers shouted their approval, breaking her concentration, and the image wavered.

"Quiet," she whispered, redoubling her focus, desperate to open the doorway before she lost her ability to function on any meaningful level.

Putting everything she had into the effort, she focused one last monumental blast. The bookcases seemed to dissolve before her. And then she could see a forest on the other side.

"Hurry," she gasped. "Hurry through."

The soldiers were more than ready. Like a panicked horde, most of them made a mad scramble to leave this world and go back where they belonged. She watched them fighting each other in their haste to get through the doorway before it closed. A few held back, and she knew some would rather take their chances here than with the Iron Man of Sun Acres. Some rushed for the basement, and she silently wished them good luck.

As she watched, the majority ran headlong into the trees. When the doorway was clear, Avery and Brusco followed.

Brusco disappeared quickly. But when Avery had gained the other side of the doorway, he turned and stared at her, his face suddenly contorting.

"No!" he shouted. He tried to run back to her side of the barrier. But his body jerked, and he grabbed his throat as he sank to his knees.

Falcone stared through the doorway. "What in Carfolian Hell have you done?" he screamed at her

"Nothing. It must have been too much for him. Go. Get out of here."

"Not without you," he growled. "You're coming with me where I can deal with you the way I should have in the first place."

When he reached for her, she pulled out the gun that she had concealed in the cushion beside her. "Get away from me. Or I'll shoot you with this thing."

He stopped short, staring at the weapon. "You wouldn't dare!"

"Yes, I would. Get back."

He must have decided she didn't have the guts, because he kept advancing on her, and she squeezed the trigger the way Logan had showed her. But nothing happened.

GREAT Mother, something was wrong. Logan had told her all the things she needed to know to make the gun shoot, but the weapon wasn't firing. Then she remembered—only the Glock worked with the safety inside the trigger guard.

As she frantically looked down at the weapon, Falcone pulled out his own gun.

Before he could fire, a tremendous booming sound shook the house. It took a moment to realize it was outside the building.

"What the hell?"

As Falcone focused on her again, a gray form leaped from the darkness and collided with him.

A wolf! Logan.

The gun went off, sending a bullet into the wall.

Falcone screamed and tried to point the gun at the wolf, but two more animals leaped from the shadows. One grabbed his hand, biting down until he dropped the weapon. The other knocked him to his knees.

Falcone screamed again, kicking and clawing at the wolves, fighting them with what looked like more than human strength.

The air on the other side of the portal stirred, and something drifted toward Rinna, tugging at her. She got up and tried to stumble toward the opening, compelled by a terrible force that clawed at her mind.

It wasn't pulling her into her own world. She had lied to Falcone. She had never intended to open a portal to safety. Instead she had found the world of the Suckers. And the mind vampires were trying to drag her and Falcone through. To join the others who had rushed to their destruction

She'd thought she could get out of the room before they attacked her. But Falcone had kept her close to the portal.

She stared at the doorway. It couldn't stay open for long because she only had enough power to gain a temporary opening. Now the Suckers were making a desperate attempt to grab the remainder of their prey before the doorway closed.

Hurry. Come to us. Before it's too late.

She forgot any plans she'd made about getting away. The seductive call of the Suckers offered her everything she had ever wanted in her life. But as she took a shaky step forward, the wolf she recognized as Logan leaped up and blocked her way. Snapping and snarling at her, he caught her attention, pulling it away from the creatures beyond the portal.

"No!" *Didn't he understand?* No, maybe he didn't, because she dimly remembered that the Suckers hadn't affected the werewolves' minds the way they affected someone in human form.

Falcone obviously felt the same tug she did. He picked himself up and staggered toward the portal. He was halfway through the opening when one of the wolves grabbed him by his jacket and pulled him back into the room, throwing him onto the floor.

Lance kept her from reaching the opening, moving her steadily back as he snapped and snarled. He pushed her across the room, holding her down as the portal began to close.

"Nooooo," Falcone shrieked. While she watched in horrible fascination he threw off the wolf and lunged for the disappearing doorway. But it was too late. The opening had shrunk to the size of a porthole.

As it snapped closed, Falcone grabbed his head, crying in agony. He sank to the floor, shrieking as though someone had stabbed him in the heart, and she knew a Sucker had sunk its claws into his mind. The abrupt snapping off of the connection had zapped his brain. Lance had kept her from suffering the same fate.

The door between the worlds had disappeared, leaving the five of them still in the room—the three wolves, her, and Falcone.

Lance let her up, and she sprawled on the rug, panting, relieved that the terrible pull on her mind had vanished. Now if only the blinding headache would go away.

The wolves looked at each other. Logan gave some sort of signal, and the other animals ran for the hall. She heard them on the stairs going down to the basement, and she realized they must have come in the back way under cover of darkness and the explosion outside.

Unable to move, she lay against the soft carpet, her head feeling like it might split open. Logan nudged her with his muzzle and licked her cheek.

She raised her hand, stroking his fur. "Thank you," she murmured.

He made a sound low in his throat, then began to tug at the pants she wore as though he were trying to tug them off.

He couldn't talk. Yet he must be sending her an urgent message because an idea formed in her mind. She must change from woman to wolf or bird. Change and get out of there before the police came in.

She brought the room into focus, then looked at Falcone lying on the floor, curled up like a child on his side. His thumb was in his mouth and he was sucking it.

The wolf nudged at her again, and she started pulling her clothes off.

When she was naked, Logan snatched up her shirt and pants in his muzzle.

Somehow, around the throbbing in her head, she imagined herself in wolf form. At first nothing happened, and panic grabbed her by the throat. But she struggled to keep her concentration, and her body flowed into the familiar pattern.

She came down on all fours, then followed Logan into the hall, downstairs, and out the back door—into the darkness of the woods.

The wolves streaked through the overgrown backyard and through the woods to a place where land had been cleared but no houses built.

Rinna ran to the other side of Logan's car, changing form where the men couldn't see her.

Then Logan was beside her, taking her in his arms,

holding her tight. And she clung to him with a gladness that threatened to burst her heart.

"You did it," he whispered. "Thank God, you did it."

"I . . . I sent them to the world of the Suckers. Then the creatures tried to drag me through."

"Yeah. I figured all that out."

She lifted her head. "Thank you for saving me. But why did you hold Falcone back?"

"So the cops would find someone in the house."

A throat-clearing noise made her look around. From the other side of the car, a voice said, "Maybe you'd better get some clothes on, so we can get the hell out of here. Before the cops figure out that explosion was just a diversion."

She felt her face heat.

One of the men tossed a pair of pants and a shirt to their side of the car. Logan pulled them on and Rinna dressed in the clothing he'd brought from the house. When they were dressed, they climbed into the car—she and Logan in front and the others in back.

As Logan started the engine, he said, "My brother Lance. And my cousin Ross."

"Thank you," she breathed.

"Logan went crazy when he knew you were gone," Lance said.

She looked from him to Logan. "I'm so sorry. I knew Falcone would hunt you and kill you. I had to get him away from you."

"I figured you were going to do it your way."

"You used the explosion to get past the police?" she asked.

"Yes," Ross answered. "Lucky your mate carries equipment for blasting rock."

She winced. "I'm sorry I caused so much trouble."

"We've had worse. And we owed you—from when you helped us get Boralas," Lance answered.

She nodded, then asked, "What will the police do?"

"They'll try to figure out what happened, but they won't get too far," Logan answered, "unless they round up some of those soldiers who dashed out the back door." He reached for her hand. "I know it's a lot to ask, but I'm hoping you can do one more thing."

"What?"

"That cop, Jake Cooper, probably thinks we're involved in some way. Can you send him a suggestion that he doesn't have time to check up on us for a couple of days? That will give Ross time to get you an ID."

She leaned back against the seat and closed her eyes. "I can try," she murmured.

CHAPTER TWENTY-EIGHT

JAKE COOPER KEPT thinking he should go have a chat with the Marshalls. But he had a lot of details to take care of after the hostage situation—and the explosion in the woods that had drawn a lot of his men away from the house. Had some guys from inside gotten out and set off the explosives? Or had it been someone else?

The only man they'd taken into custody had been lying on the floor, unable to speak. Maybe he'd rotted out his mind with some designer drug, because toxicology couldn't figure out what he'd taken.

Jake had tried to get an ID on him, but he hadn't had any luck with that either. With one thing or another needing his attention, he didn't show up at the Marshall house until two days after the hostage crisis was over.

As he stepped onto the front porch, he eyed two pairs of dirty tennis shoes—a man's and a woman's—tossed onto the wooden boards, like the couple had been gardening and taken off their shoes before they came in.

He rang the doorbell. After a few moments, Marshall

answered. He was casually dressed in sweatpants and a T-shirt. But his eyes were wary, and his shoulders were tense. He looked like a man with something to hide. What exactly?

"Is your wife at home?" Jake asked.

"Yes."

"So you found her okay?"

"Yes." The man didn't elaborate.

"What happened?"

"Just a misunderstanding," Marshall replied.

Jake was sure there was more to it than that. "Do you mind if I come in?" he asked.

Marshall shrugged and stepped aside.

"Did you hear about the hostage situation in Mount Airy?" Jake asked, watching the man's face.

Marshall kept his gaze steady. "Yes."

"You know anything about that?" Jake asked.

Marshall shrugged again. "Just what I saw on television."

"When I was here the other day, I didn't check your wife's ID," Jake said.

"Is that routine?"

"No. But I'd be remiss if I didn't see some identification."

Marshall turned toward the back of the house. "Honey, the detective we met the other day is here. Can you come out here and bring your purse?"

Moments later, Rinna Marshall stepped into the room, a worn leather purse slung over her shoulder.

"He'd like to see your ID," Marshall said.

The slender dark-haired woman reached into her bag and pulled out a leather wallet that had obviously seen a lot of use. From the card case, she extracted a Maryland driver's license.

Jake looked it over, noting the vital statistics.

Rinna Marshall was twenty-two, five feet six inches tall with green eyes and brown hair. The picture matched her pefectly.

Still, he should take the license out to the car and check it through the motor vehicle administration's computer. But something kept him standing there.

He should . . .

He forgot what he had been thinking about. He didn't want to hassle these people.

The woman held out her hand, and he gave back the plastic card.

"So . . . everything's okay here . . ." he managed to say.

"Yes. Just a misunderstanding," Mrs. Marshall said, using the same words as her husband.

Jake nodded. He should ask more questions. But somehow the things he'd wanted to know had evaporated from his brain.

Marshall shifted his weight from one foot to the other.

"What?"

"I've been thinking about what you told me about the Easy Shopper, about the invisible men."

"You still think they're from another . . . universe?"

Marshall winced. "I guess I've been watching too many science fiction shows, and my imagination started running away with me. But what if a bunch of druggies were burning some kind of hallucinogen in the woods, and, you know, you breathed some of it in."

Jake had thought of something like that himself.

"My cousin, Adam, is a forest ranger in Georgia, and he encountered something similar," Marshall continued. "A bunch of retro hippies were having parties in the park.

That would explain what happened to you. Maybe that big white bird you saw was a figment of the smoke."

"Uh huh," Jake muttered. He still wasn't sure what had happened, but he'd lost the urgency to find out. And he was still feeling a little confused.

"Thanks for your time," he said, then turned and left the Marshall house, thinking what a nice couple they were.

AS they stood at the window watching the detective climb into his car and drive away, Logan slung his arm around Rinna.

"You did good. Does your head hurt?" he asked.

"A little. But not much. That wasn't . . . a big job. I just had to push him in the right direction. And your drug story was good."

She leaned her head against his shoulder.

He stroked her arm. "It helped that you bought us a couple of extra days to get the ID. And a birth certificate to match." He swallowed, "And a marriage certificate."

She nodded against his shoulder. "He was suspicious. And my fingerprints must be in that house."

"But they're not on file anywhere. And I guess we took care of the prints at the house where we broke in."

"Yes."

"We'll just have to stay out of trouble in the future."

He cleared his throat. "About the marriage certificate. It looks legal. But I want to have a ceremony. Where we stand up in front of a minister and tell the world we belong to each other."

She swallowed. "It's still hard to believe . . . that I'm here living with you."

"Believe it. We can fly to Las Vegas with Ross and

Megan and Lance and Savannah and some of the others . . . when you feel comfortable enough to fly in an airplane."

"Give me a little time." She rushed ahead. "I mean . . . about the flying. I'm sure about the marriage part."

"That's progress."

She gave him a serious look. "Megan and Savannah helped me a lot."

"Good"

"Not just about being married to you. They got me to the point where I felt like I could face that detective and not fall apart."

"You could have done it without them."

"Maybe not."

"You did a wonderful job with him. You looked like you've lived here for years."

She turned to him, and raised her face to his, and he saw the moisture shimmering in her eyes.

He touched her cheek with a finger. "Don't cry."

"It's hard not to. I feel so . . . blessed by the Great Mother. In a thousand years, I never could have imagined finding you, living with you."

His own vision blurred. "You'll get used to it. We both will."

She swallowed. "I wish Haig could have lived to see this."

"He betrayed you."

"Falcone forced him. And . . ."

"What?"

"The badlands changed him. He couldn't live that way. I wish you had known him years ago. When he was himself. He was a good man. He kept me going when I was in school."

"Keep the good memories of him. And share them with me."

"I will. I'll share everything with you."

"Everything."

He kissed her cheek and held her close. When her arms crept around his neck, he smiled, then slid his own arms around her back and down to her hips.

"I think we should celebrate," he murmured. "I mean, celebrate getting that cop off our backs."

"He knows we were involved with Falcone . . . somehow."

"But he can't prove it. And he'll leave us alone."

"Yes."

She captured the back of his head and brought his mouth down to hers for a long, hungry kiss. When he broke the contact, he was as hard as one of the soldiers' spears.

"I talked to Megan and Savannah about . . . sex."

He tipped his head, waiting for her to elaborate.

"They told me how good it is between a werewolf and his mate."

"Oh, yeah! But they don't know how good it is when the woman is also a werewolf."

She flushed. "I don't have anything to compare that to."

"Well, we can compare it to how we were a few days ago." He slid his hand up her ribs, along the outside of her breast, and then inward, stroking her hardened nipple.

"It keeps getting better," she whispered.

"I guess we'll have to keep practicing. Maybe we can make the Olympic Sex Team." He grinned. "The events are . . . bed, chair, outdoors, against a wall, in the shower, in the bathtub, in the kitchen, the gym, and . . . anywhere else you want to try."

"They have a team for that?"

He laughed. "That was a joke." Then, because she had turned him on beyond endurance, he dipped his head and captured her mouth again.

"Come out. I want to show you something," he said, knitting his fingers with hers.

He hadn't taken her to his secret garden yet, the one he'd designed when Grant had built the house.

It was along the back wall, a twelve-foot area that looked out over rolling Maryland woodland. The garden was bordered by large rocks that he'd brought in with trucks and cranes. Among the rocks he'd planted dwarf pines and beds of wildflowers, so that it looked completely natural.

They stepped out the back door into the garden, and Rinna caught her breath as she gazed around.

"This is so beautiful." She turned toward him. "And you designed it."

"Yes. For you."

"But you didn't know me."

"No. But I was thinking my life mate and I would come out here and enjoy the beauty—and the solitude."

He watched her brush her fingers against the branch of a small spruce, then walk to a flower bed and stop to cup a purple cosmos. "I still can't believe I'm living in a place like this."

"You'll get used to it."

While she had her back to him, he kicked off his shoes, then took off his shirt and sweatpants and tossed them away. Naked, he stepped up behind her and kissed her neck, then slipped his hands under her shirt and gently slid it up and over her head, muffling her surprised exclamation.

"What!"

"I want to hold you—out here."

Turning her in his arms, he pressed her body against his as he worked his fingers into the elastic waistband of her pants and pushed them away.

She gave him a breathy laugh. "Hold me? Or make love?"

"Make love. But get rid of your shoes first." He led her barefoot across the soft grass to a tiled area beside a large rock formation, then reached out and turned on the rain shower he'd had installed in the wall of the house.

"A shower? Out in the open?" she asked.

"Well, it's got a practical purpose. I come in this way when I've been working in the mud, and I don't want to get the house dirty," he said, as he adjusted the temperature.

When it was hot, he stepped under the cascading water and pulled her in with him, holding her, rocking her in his arms.

"Oh!" she exclaimed.

"You should turn around and look at the view," he said, working to keep the grin out of his voice. "It's pretty good for a shower stall."

When she did, he reached to the shelf in back of him and picked up a cake of soap. Not his usual brand, but he'd asked Megan, Ross's wife, to bring him something a woman would like.

Still grinning, he lathered his hands.

Rinna smelled the flower fragrance immediately. "What's that?"

"Just soap."

He pulled her back against his front, then ran his soapy hands down her sides, over her hips and slowly up again, his slippery fingers caressing her breasts and gliding over her nipples.

"Logan! What are you doing?"

"Washing you. Relax and enjoy it."

The soap had made his hands slick as he made a slow, sensual journey over her silky flesh.

Reaching for more lather, he slipped his hand between their bodies, gliding his fingers over the curve of her ass and into the crack between the cheeks.

She stiffened. "You shouldn't do that."

"Why not? Does it feel good?"

"Yes," she breathed.

"I told you, we can do anything together that feels good."

She stood there for several moments, her breath accelerating, and he slid his hand farther down, into the sensitive folds of her pussy. Her hands clenched and unclenched. Then she turned in his arms, and reached for the soap in back of him. "Do you have the words 'what's good for the goose is good for the gander'?"

He laughed. "Yeah, we do."

Her hand was soapy when she clasped her fist around his erection, then slid up and down, the slickness making him exquisitely sensitive to her touch.

"Oh Lord!"

"You like that?"

"You know I do."

She explored him with her soapy hand, running her finger around the head, then sliding her fist all the way up again to the root. After two trips of her hand, he felt like he was going to explode.

"Enough." He gasped.

She let her hand drop, and he washed off the soap under the hot water.

"When you planned this garden, did you figure out where we could make love?" she asked in a breathy voice.

He clasped her in his arms, and stepped toward the bench at the side of the shower, bringing her down to his lap as he sat.

She slid back and turned to face him, then brought him inside her.

"Like the first time," she murmured. "But now I know what I'm doing."

"Oh yeah," he agreed as she raised up, then slowly, slowly brought him fully inside her again.

The water cascaded over them as she kept up the slow pace of long in-and-out strokes, driving them both to a high peak that didn't quite bring them to climax. When he couldn't stand it anymore, he reached to press his fingers against her clit, and she gasped, then picked up the pace.

They both cried out as orgasm washed over them, along with the sluicing water.

She went boneless in his arms, dropping her head to his shoulder, breathing hard. Then she turned to kiss his cheek.

"Thank you . . . for this. Thank you for bringing me here," she whispered.

"Thank you for trusting me," he said, his voice rough with emotion.

She raised her head and looked at him. "I never thought I could."

"But here you are. In my arms—in my world."

"I'm still nervous . . . about the world part."

"But you'll get used to it. You're smart and you're very adaptable."

"And I have you to tell me what I need to know," she whispered.

He stroked her shoulders, kissed her damp cheek, wet from the shower and wet with tears.

His own eyes were misty as he said, "And we have plenty of time to explore the world together."

Hugging her to him, he let his happiness soar, knowing he had found the perfect woman—the perfect mate.